CADES
HOME
FARM

ALSO BY
SHANI STRUTHERS

REACH FOR THE DEAD
BOOK TWO

CADES
HOME
FARM

SHANI STRUTHERS

Reach for the Dead: Book Two: Cades Home Farm
Copyright © Shani Struthers 2020

Authors Reach
www.authorsreach.co.uk

ISBN: 978-1-8382204-0-2

DEDICATION

To the country I miss the most right now – America.
When the world returns to normal, I'll be back.

ACKNOWLEDGEMENTS

Thank you once again to my core team of beta readers, Rob Struthers, Kate Jane Jones, Amanda Nash, Lesley Hughes, Louisa Taylor, and Sarah Savery – your input is invaluable. A big thanks also to my editor, Rumer Haven, who always makes the process so much fun – I love those Buffy references! Gina Dickerson of RoseWolf Design is responsible for the cover and the formatting and, as always, does an incredible job. I'm so lucky to be able to work with you all. Last but not least, thanks to you the reader, for all the feedback I get from you too, post publishing. You make my author's heart sing!

Please note, as with book one, Mandy, this book has been written in American English, due to its Idaho Falls setting. All those words spelt with a 'z', for example, are not mistakes!

PROLOGUE

All of it…so ugly.

Hate.

Hate you. Me. Hate that I'm here. That there's nowhere else to go.

"HATE! HATE! HATE!"

The child yelled the words out loud this time, screamed them at herself. Her reflection in the mirror was barely recognizable as her face contorted, as it twisted, her mouth wide open, her eyes black orbs that held no depth, no humanity…not in that moment.

She was energy, dark and fizzing. It leaked from her, kicking and sparking like static. She was in her bedroom, in the house of the people she hated most in the world, her stupid, lazy, good-for-nothin' parents, one sprawled in front of the TV downstairs, only half conscious, his gut exposed and his breath reeking as it always did of cigarettes and beer. As for her mother—who knew where she'd be? Downtown, most likely, leaning against a bar somewhere, chatting to a fella, any fella. It wasn't like she was fussy.

"Hate *this!*" the child screamed again. "*All* of it."

With the mirror still in her hand, her fingers tight around its long, pale stem, she fell back onto the bed and closed her eyes. That didn't mean she couldn't see. Her own reflection was still clear in her mind, and how full of loathing it was. She could also see every inch of the four walls surrounding her, grease, nicotine and damp their only adornment. There were no drapes at the window, not even a tattered sheet, and in the corners, dust bunnies collected. The rest of the house was just as bad. It was a mess of a house, in a mess of a neighborhood, one laying on the edge of town, that nice people tried to pretend didn't exist. She hated them too for their willful blindness.

A door slammed.

She was back, then. Momma.

"Joanie? Joanie, where are ya?"

Shit! She was back, and she was drunk, her words even more slurred than usual.

Would he stir, call her momma out for coming home so late, for having disappeared in the first place? Of course not. He'd barely be able to open his mouth to form words, that shit he smoked not just dulling the edges but destroying them. She envied him that, at least. It was what she wanted too, more than anything—a way out.

"Joanie!" her mom was still calling. "You in your room? I'm coming to find ya."

Joanie's eyes snapped open, her gaze fixing on the door, wondering for a second if she could barricade it, push her bed up against it or something, prevent her momma from barging in, from grabbing her by the shoulders and telling her about her night, every single detail.

Finally discarding the mirror, she jumped up from the bed and braced herself for a mother who, although she spent much of her day in a stupor, at night became like a hurricane.

Within seconds the door opened, and in she came—Sal Parker, in her late twenties but looking much older, her blonde hair straggly, blue eyes unnaturally wide, and lips smeared with a cheap pink lipstick bought from the local drugstore. She wore a red patterned dress that clashed with the lipstick, her long slim legs in laddered stockings, and her feet stuffed into patent leather shoes that were peeling. So many emotions ran riot on her mom's face, some similar to those Joanie had seen in herself in the mirror.

Mother and daughter stood there, staring at each other, the only sound the distant TV blaring from the living room. And then Sal stepped forward and slammed the door behind her, drowning out *The Tonight Show Starring Johnny Carson*, and it was only her voice that reached Joanie's ears, high and breathy.

"Oh, Joanie, I've met him, the one, and I mean *the one*, the guy who's gonna take me away from all this…all this"— the sweep of her arm as she gestured took in Joanie as well—"*shit*. He said…oh, he's promised me so many things. Told me I was beautiful." Violently, she thumbed toward the door. "He's never said I'm beautiful, you know that? Not once."

And perhaps because he hadn't, Sal had never complimented her daughter either. What goes around comes around, shit included. *Especially* that.

Joanie took a step back as her mother lurched forwards, and then another, her back colliding with the edge of the windowsill.

"Momma," Joanie began, seeking to calm her mother and her crazy notions. This wasn't the first time she'd come home saying such things—not about this guy, perhaps, but a variety of others—dreams, hopes, and plans amounting to nothing, always.

Sal, however, wasn't done.

"Baby girl," she said, so close now that Joanie could smell the sourness of beer on her breath, saw too how dilated her pupils were, so different from normal—*she* was different, something about her. Was she…telling the truth this time? "I'm leaving. I'm getting out." Again, she thumbed at the door behind her. "That useless son of a bitch probably wouldn't even notice anyway, and I'm sick of it. Sick of him doing jack shit all day, and me working shifts at the store for a pittance. I'm worth more than that."

Joanie managed to find her voice at last. "What about me?"

"You?"

"Are you taking me too?"

A burst of laughter escaped Sal, so much force behind it that she staggered back a step or two. "I can't take you. He wouldn't have it."

"Dad?"

"No! My guy. He won't want hangers-on."

"Have you asked him?"

"No point."

"But, Momma, you can't leave me here—"

"I have to, and I will. This is no pipe dream; it's an opportunity. Don't that mean a thing to you? I'm not like you. I'm not so young anymore. I gotta take all the chances I can get. And you—" she faltered, her hand, for a moment, resting lightly on her stomach "—you'll be all right. The world's changing, you know. It's exciting out there. There's so much going on. People are changing, and I want to be a

4

part of it. Hell, I want to be in the *thick* of it. I'm leaving. Tonight. I'm outta here. My guy's waiting in the car, just a coupla blocks away. I'm gonna grab a few things, and then I'm gone. Now, don't do that. Don't cry. I coulda gone right away, not bothered to come home at all, but I did, just for you. Now ain't that sweet of me? So's I could say goodbye."

"Goodbye?" Joanie whispered, her heart heavier than it had ever been, but also a part of her marveling that a situation already terrible enough could worsen. She hated her folks, had been busy telling herself that not so long ago, but now that her mom was leaving—*actually leaving*—she couldn't bear it. As unmotherly as Sal was, as useless in that respect, she provided at least some spark of life in this household. If she went, if she made good on her threat, then it would just be Joanie and him. Not her real dad—he'd long gone, pulled up stakes and left as soon as Joanie was born—but a stepfather who was truly worthless, who might as well be dead for all the good he did. "Momma, I'm thirteen!"

But her age was of no consequence. Sal was backing away, her heels clacking against bare floorboards, kicking aside any stray clothes as she retreated.

"You'll be all right," Sal Parker reiterated, a woman concerned with no one but herself, who'd gotten pregnant as a teenager and been forced to marry, if not the baby's father, then someone—anyone—for the sake of appearances. A woman who hadn't kept up appearances at all, who loathed the situation she'd found herself in, loathed her husband too, and perhaps even Joanie—the baby that had trapped her.

Sal had opened the bedroom door again, and clapping and laughter from the TV resumed, as if cheering her mother on. *Yeah, Sal! Way to go! Go! Go! Go!*

Desperation urged Joanie forward, panic and terror too. She didn't want to be left alone with her stepfather, because…because worse than his vegetative state were his more lucid moments, when he looked at Joanie and something in his eyes lit up, something also in the way he'd utter, "You know, you look just your momma used to, when I first met her." Words that didn't warm her but made her feel so cold instead.

"Momma!" she said, she yelled. "Don't leave me with him."

Her hands outstretched, she grabbed Sal, her mother immediately trying to shake her off, not halting in her retreat. "No, honey, stop it, just stop it."

"I promise I'll be good. You won't know you've got me. He…your guy…he won't either, I promise. Take me away from here. Please, Momma, I want to be a part of the changing world too, not left behind. There's nothing here for me. Nothing."

They were in the living room, almost at the front door. Whatever her momma had come back to grab, she'd decided against it.

"Get off me!" she continued saying. "Leave me be now. You're all grown up, not a kid anymore. I've done my bit. I've done enough. It's my time now. I'm starting again."

"Momma!"

"Wassat? What's going on?" The man masquerading as her father was stirring at last, Joanie only briefly glancing at him, his naked belly quivering as his eyes half opened.

Joanie turned back to her mother, more concerned with other matters.

"Momma, take me too!" Her eyes were pumping tears, her hands grabbing still, but Sal threw her off easily enough as she made her way out of the house, opening the front door and kicking off her heels, reaching down to hold them in her hands instead. She turned and ran down that cracked, weed-ridden pathway, two patches of grass on either side of it, the semblance of a sidewalk ahead, more of a dirt track, really. A trashy place for trashy people. And she, Sal Parker, was the trashiest of them all. She was leaving, and as Joanie watched her continue to flee, past other houses as run-down as theirs, a few drapes twitching as Joanie cried, pleaded, and stamped her feet, she knew one thing: she'd never see her again. Her mother. A woman who'd wanted none of this, the results of yet another night cruising.

She was escaping, the crowd on the TV still clapping, still cheering her on. *Go! Go! Go!* Eventually, Joanie's sobbing quieted, and she turned her head toward another mirror that hung on the wall. Her stepfather hadn't moved; he'd fallen back asleep, was snoring, the sound finally drowning out the crowd, akin to a convoy of trucks passing through, shaking the very foundations of the ground. Inside, she shook just as hard.

Like before, as she stared into the mirror, her expression was so contorted that she failed to recognize herself. What she recognized well enough, though, was the hate.

CHAPTER ONE

"Hey, Shady, want another?"

"What are you trying to do, get a girl drunk here?"

Ray grinned as, immediately, he held his hands up. "Just being polite, that's all. Tending to your needs. Great party, huh? Oh, and look, guess who's just walked in! Brett Easton. Hey, Brett, how you doing? Got plenty of cold beers if you want one!"

The night was beginning to buzz. Shady Groves, Ray Bartlett and several of their respective friends had started off at The Golden Crown in downtown Idaho Falls. A dive bar it might've been, but one with atmosphere, all of them kicking back and downing ice-cold bottles of Bud. Because alcohol didn't always agree with her, Shady had stuck to one of the low-proof versions, trying not to wince at the taste.

She wasn't sure what time it had been when Sam—trendy Sam Hope, who was rocking a seventies tie-dye hippie-chick dress, which Shady had to admit looked astounding—suggested the crowd retire back at her place so that the party could really begin.

The cause of celebration wasn't for any particular reason, just a bunch of old friends gathering who hadn't seen each other for a while due to work or educational commitments.

It was also a Friday night in February, and the snow, which had been relentless, making sultry summer days seem like pure imagining, had finally eased.

Earlier, while still in The Golden Crown, listening to what people had been up to in past months, Shady had exchanged a wry smile with Ray. What *they'd* been up to— meeting Annie Hawkins, starting work at the Mason Town Museum that Annie owned, a museum thirty miles outside of Idaho Falls that housed the extraordinary, a doll like Mandy, for one—well, that would take some explaining. And so, when both took their turns to answer, they'd kept it simple. The truth, though? It was as far from simple as simple could be, Shady's fey side, her sixth sense, her psychic ability, now developing rapidly as she handled objects at the museum. Ray's sixth sense too, although he continued to deny it. And Annie, their friend as well as an employer and mentor, guiding them every step of the way.

Again, Shady smiled, but it was largely to herself. These friends were all similar in age and at various stages of discovering themselves, some intent on becoming doctors or accountants or realtors, others just drifting, like Brett, who'd just turned up at Sam Hope's house—a real stoner, but with a kind enough heart. Sam Hope herself was in retail but with aspirations to become a fashion designer. As for Shady, she'd harbored dreams of being a teacher once, before life had taken her down a different route altogether.

Paranormal—a word, a concept that caused people's eyes to widen; perhaps they might even take a sharp intake of breath. Some were frightened of it, some fascinated, while others refused to believe in it at all, thought it blasphemous. But Shady knew different, perhaps had *always* known, the fey streak in her—as her parents had referred to it for so long—not something random but inherited from a woman she'd never met. Kanti was Shady's maternal grandmother, a Native American woman from whom she'd also inherited dark hair, dark eyes and olive skin. A woman who'd led a tragic life and met a tragic end, whose identity had been concealed from Shady by her mother exactly because of the tragedy surrounding her. But now that Shady *did* know about her, she felt Kanti beside her on this new and exciting journey.

"Come on, Shady, let's dance!"

It was Carrie, a shy girl, except when she had a drink or two inside her. She was grabbing hold of Shady's wrists and pulling her into the center of Sam's living room, her hips beginning to gyrate.

Normal. That's what this was. And Shady would be normal too tonight, soaking up the lively vibe that had been created, dancing along with the rest of them. She spared a thought for Sam's poor neighbors, although, to be fair, she'd spotted a couple of them here anyway; perhaps they all were. She also noticed someone join Ray and Brett where they'd been chatting in a corner, a girl Shady didn't know—and she noticed as well the smile lighting Ray's face on sight of this girl, one hand swooping upward to smooth his crazy red hair.

She closed her eyes and swigged from the bottle she held in her hand, singing along in her head to the tune that was playing: *Let Me Love You* by Mario. It wasn't as up-tempo as previous songs, but pleasingly dreamy instead. She opened her eyes briefly to see lots of other people swaying too, eyes either closed or at half-mast, cigarettes or a drink in hand, some coming together and beginning to kiss. Sam Hope herself was kissing a young man, one Shady'd have to ask her about in the cold light of day. It was just a shame Josie Lea wasn't here, one of Shady's closest friends, who'd recently moved to Baker City in Oregon to work in a general store her parents had bought there. Together she and Shady would have had such a giggle about so many smooching couples. Shady missed her so much but resolved to visit her soon; there was a lot to catch up on...

Bringing the bottle back up to her mouth, she was disappointed to find it empty. *Damn!* She should have accepted Ray's offer—Ray, who was now speaking to the mystery girl alone, Brett having disappeared.

She needn't have worried about the beer anyway, though, as Teddy Cardenas was passing, deftly taking the empty from her hand and replacing it with a full, icy bottle. If Sam Hope was the Queen of Parties, Teddy was the King, having just proven himself to perfection. He'd given her a regular Bud, but hey, she figured, it was still a cool move. She thanked him, noticing the grin that lit up his face, that widened as he then moved closer to Carrie, handing her a Bud too, arms reaching out to hold each other.

As Shady drank from the new bottle, she couldn't deny it: the taste was so much better. In between she hugged it to her. She wasn't looking for love, so she was perfectly content with the partner she had, felt lucky, even. Aged twenty-two, she had good friends, a great family, choices in life, and no one putting restrictions in her way. Sure, her parents, Ellen and Bill, hadn't been particularly thrilled when she'd told them she was working on improving her psychic abilities while also working at Mason Town

Museum, but seeing Shady stick to her guns, they'd relented, agreeing to let her "see where it will take" her.

"But we're here for you," Ellen had said, had insisted. "And if it becomes too much, you know…" She'd faltered. "It's perfectly fine to take a step back, honey, to say no. Your talent, what you've inherited, is a gift. Don't let it become something other than that."

A curse, that's what she meant, like it had been for Kanti. Given what had happened to her, who could blame Ellen for worrying? But it was a path Shady had to tread. In many ways she had no choice. Ellen didn't have the gift, at least not to the extent that Shady did; either it had skipped a generation or Ellen favored her paternal heritage. Certainly in looks she had, being so fair. Bill was too, and such a contrast to Shady.

"Shit!"

Having fallen back into a dreamy haze, Shady returned to the moment. Sam had been the one to curse, no longer in the arms of someone but on her cell phone instead.

"Shit," she said again, her face a perfect mask of horror. "It's my folks. They're supposed to be away for the entire weekend, but Mom's lost a tooth, and she's on her way back, says she's got an emergency appointment with the dentist in the morning. Shit! Shit! Shit! Everyone's gonna have to leave. Come on, people, grab your stuff! Get out of here."

Her eyes met Shady's, and the plea in them spurred Shady into action.

"Come on, everyone," Shady said, echoing Sam, touching the shoulders or elbows of whatever couples were still smooching, and reiterating the message. "Time to go."

As she drew closer to Ray, he stopped chatting with the mysterious girl and eyed Shady curiously. "Whassup, Shady?"

"Did you just hear what Sam said?"

"Sam?"

"Yeah, about her folks. They're on their way back."

Still he looked confused, leaving Shady to conclude he'd been too engrossed in whatever his companion had been talking about.

"Um…Shady, this is Lisa Marie. She's from San Francisco but is living here now, in Idaho Falls."

Despite the urgency of Sam's situation, and that she was now actively ushering people out the door too, Shady couldn't resist asking, "Really? Why?"

Shady adored California and that whole west-coast-beach vibe. She'd only ever visited for a week or a two at a time on family vacations, but there was something about it that got under her skin and remained there. She loved her hometown too—it was exactly that: home—but in her opinion, at least, it just couldn't compare.

Lisa Marie's laughter lit her from the inside out. In answer to Shady's question, she said, "Hey, it's not so bad here! It's cute. And, you know, it's only for a while. I work in pharmaceuticals, on a placement."

Ah, so she was smart *and* pretty—in many ways the archetypal Californian beach babe: petite, curvy, and with long blonde hair. Little wonder Ray was enchanted.

"Pleased to meet you," Lisa Marie continued, a hand reaching out toward Shady.

"Yeah, sure." Shady took her hand but only briefly, noting how cool it was, and smooth, an image forming in her mind, one that took her by surprise. Lisa Marie wasn't quite the perfection she portrayed. There was a tendency toward…what? Depression? Shady scrutinized her, noted blue eyes that weren't as bright as she'd first thought, with something else in them, something…shadowed.

Their hands parting, Shady was relieved. That insight, if that's what it was, was far from welcome. It felt like…prying. Nonetheless, when she spoke again, she noticed how her voice had grown softer, even sympathetic. "I hope you enjoy your time in Idaho Falls, and perhaps we can meet up if you have some free time. Grab a coffee or something."

"Really? I'd love to." Lisa Marie looked genuinely thrilled as she reached behind her to grab her coat. "That'd be so great." And then, as if remembering Ray, she added, "With you too, of course."

Ray looked a bit deflated at his sudden demotion to third wheel but nodded good-naturedly enough.

"We have to get going," Shady reminded them.

As they turned to go, Shady noticed what a good job Sam had done of rounding people up. The living room was now empty of everyone but a few slowpokes. The place looked like a bomb site, though, with empty glasses and bottles strewn everywhere, and so, ushering Ray and Lisa Marie out the door, she changed tack and returned to Sam.

"I'll stay behind, help out," she offered.

Sam waved a hand in the air, her hair, which was as dark as Shady's, swinging from side to side. "S'okay," she said. "I can do it. It's only the living room that's messed up. Good thing we'd only just got started, huh?" Sam, still a vision in tie-dye, seemed to have gotten over the initial shock of her parents' imminent return and was chill again.

"You sure you don't want any help?" Shady checked.

"It's fine."

Shady nodded, quickly embracing her friend before heading out onto the sidewalk, where Ray was still busy saying goodbye to Lisa Marie.

"You've got my number now," he said, "so let's up hook up. Soon."

"Sure, real soon." Noticing Shady, she added, "I'll get Ray to send you my details."

"Good idea," Shady replied, Ray looking once more a little crestfallen he wasn't receiving any special treatment.

When a Chevrolet Camaro in chic grey stopped beside them, his shoulders sagged even more. The passenger window rolled down, and a voice—a *male* voice—came from a neon-blue lit interior. "Lisa Marie, come on, sweetheart. It's late, I'm tired, hop in."

Poor Ray. His chances of anything more than a coffee with the new blonde in his life were becoming slimmer by the minute.

As the car sped away, he stood there. "She's got a boyfriend."

"Uh-huh. Looks like it."

"Strange. Ya know, I was certain...I was sure..."

"It could be the Californian way," Shady ventured.

"Cheating?"

"Flirting. Did she actually say she was interested in you—in that way, I mean?"

"Yes. Well...no."

"So, it was harmless flirting, then, huh?"

"Yeah, yeah. And let's face it, a girl like her wouldn't be

interested in a guy like me. Who am I trying to kid?"

Quickly Shady admonished him. Ray might not be Brad Pitt, but he was an honest, down-to-earth, loyal friend, and she told him this.

"I'd rather be Brad Pitt," he lamented, albeit with something of his trademark grin as they linked arms and began walking, away from the dispersing crowd until they were pretty much alone, taking the route back to the numbered streets around Kate Curley Park, where Shady lived with her parents. Ray's address was a fair hike from her, so she asked if he wanted to stay over.

"I made up the bed in the spare room earlier."

"What are you? Psychic or something?"

"There've been rumors."

"And your parents won't mind?"

"Course not, Ray. They love you."

It was true. They'd come to adore him in the months they'd gotten to know him. And so had she. They were friends, good friends, and although she'd made light of his disappointment regarding Lisa Marie, she sincerely hoped he wasn't hurt by it. She'd sort of known Ray in high school—they'd both attended Fairmont High—but really only on nodding terms. Now they were inseparable, the experiences they'd shared recently having bonded them tightly together—she, Ray *and* Annie. An unlikely trio, but a solid one.

"It's just so important to have friends," she said quietly, almost to herself, thinking of Lisa Marie again as they walked along.

"What's that? You say something?"

"Oh, I just..." Should she tell him about the insight

she'd gotten into the blonde? That she wasn't quite all she seemed, that she was…deeper. Feeling a little fuzzy-headed, she let it go. "I think Lisa Marie's new in town, and she's gorgeous, and she's smart, and she clearly has a boyfriend already, but don't let that put you off, Ray, not being friends with her, anyway. Call her and go for a drink, get to know the person beneath the exterior, what makes her tick and what doesn't." Ray was clearly confused by her words, making her rush to explain, "It's just, I think she'll be kinda…interesting to know."

"Yeah, yeah, I will. You gonna call her too?"

"Maybe." Changing the conversation, she inquired about his weekend plans.

"Working Sunday at the museum. Annie wants to visit a friend, so I'm covering."

"Oh, okay. I'm not on again 'til Monday."

"I know," he replied, smirking, "I'm in Monday as well, remember? Cataloging."

"It's odd, isn't it? For a small, privately owned museum in an out-of-the-way town, there's always so much to do."

"Never a dull moment."

"Not with the type of things Annie collects."

Their trek had taken them past a few stores, Shady breathing in the cold night air, filling her lungs with it. She regretted now that last full-strength beer—somehow, she'd managed to finish the bottle—and was glad she'd linked arms with Ray, leaning on him more and more.

"Long walk," she said, noticing wisps in the air as she spoke.

"Just another ten, fifteen minutes to go."

"We shoulda gotten an Uber."

"On our wages?"

She shrugged. He was right; their wages didn't cover traveling in cabs.

"Shady?"

"Yeah."

"You okay?"

"Just a little tired."

"And a little drunk?"

She laughed. "Maybe."

"Thought you were on the fake beer."

"I was. Mainly. Ray, can we stop for a minute?"

"You outta breath?"

"I just wanna get my head together, that's all."

They'd stopped by a thrift store—*Pre-loved*. Leaning against the windowpane, Shady shook her head as if trying to reboot it.

"You know," she said, frowning, "since becoming more aware of my abilities, it's gotten like this with alcohol, even the smallest amount. It's as if it…pollutes me."

"Don't drink, then," was Ray's advice.

"Yeah, there is that, I guess."

"You're not gonna hurl, are you?"

Shady snorted. "No, don't worry. I'm not that bad!"

"If you were, though, I'd hold your hair back for you."

Her dark eyes met the green of his. "You would?"

"Sure."

"Would you do the same for Lisa Marie?"

Shit! At once Shady chastised herself. Where had that come from? She sounded as if she were jealous, and she wasn't; Ray was only a friend, romantically not her type at all.

"Shady—"

"Sorry, Ray, like I said, the drink's getting to me. I'm talking shit."

She turned her back on him, mainly because she was sure her cheeks were glowing red beneath her upturned coat collar, but also because she felt *compelled* to.

Not just a flash of jealousy, other emotions rose in her— strange emotions, ones that made no sense, that normally she wasn't prone to.

Gazing distractedly into Pre-loved, she yelped. Not everything in there was shrouded in darkness. Her reflection wasn't, although, certainly, it was a dark thing.

My reflection?

It was a mirror she was looking into, vintage, as you'd expect from a shop like this, oval with a wicker-and-cane frame. Nothing fancy. Very ordinary, in fact. And pre-loved?

Shady didn't think so, not if the person staring back at her was anything to go by.

Not her own face, or at least she didn't recognize it as such, but a face twisted with so much fury, so much anger and hatred that it ripped the breath from her.

CHAPTER TWO

"We've come about the mirror you have in your window display. It's an oval mirror, one with a wicker-and-cane surround."

Annie Hawkins had listened intently to what Shady had to say about the mirror in Pre-loved, that the reflection staring back at her had not quite been Shady's own, nor the emotions that expression contained, and arrived at one conclusion: they had to buy it.

"It has energy attached," she'd said. "Whether intelligent or residual, we'll have to see."

Halfway through Monday morning, leaving Ray at the museum to curate and welcome any visitors—so many still drawn by the prospect of meeting Mandy the haunted doll, eager for the thrill of it—Shady and Annie had made their way to the antique store in downtown Idaho Falls and parked outside. The road was pretty empty, a hard frost covering the windshields of the parked cars and the sidewalk too, and Annie and Shady having to cling to each other before entering the somewhat dusty confines of the shop.

Annie had already instructed Shady not to look into the mirror again, not until it was back at the museum and she could do so under more controlled circumstances. Annie would deal with purchasing it, and then it would be neatly stowed in the back of Shady's Dodge Stratus as they drove out of Idaho Falls and back to Mason. When they'd ventured farther into the depths of the store, however, Shady couldn't help but glance in its direction, feeling again that compulsion and the desperation that emanated from it.

The person behind the counter—a somewhat elderly woman who looked as if she should be in a country kitchen baking apple pie rather than in a dusty store—smiled delightedly at them.

"You're my first customers of the day," she said in her sweet, crackly voice. "This weather does tend to make business a little slow."

Annie had duly smiled back at her, the pair of them exchanging a few pleasantries before she'd mentioned the mirror.

"Oh, taken a shine to it, have you? Folks never cease to surprise me."

"One man's junk," Annie replied by way of explanation.

"It's another man's treasure. I'm always saying that too, and thank goodness! My business depends on it." She held out a pale, freckled hand and continued in a singsong voice that sounded like a well-rehearsed greeting. "The name's Lucille Bonnet, and this is my store, but, please, go ahead and call me Lucy."

Despite the trepidation she felt on account of the mirror and what she might discover about it, Shady couldn't help but smile as both Lucy and Annie shook hands. One was so grandmotherly, so cutsie with a puff of white hair, while the other—Annie, who hailed from England but had lived in Idaho for many, many years—was anything but. Diminutive and in her mid-sixties—although Shady had never asked her exact age, and Annie hadn't offered that information either—there was nonetheless an air of authority about her, especially when she stood as she was now, straight-backed and dressed in her usual "Rhapsody in Brown," as Shady had secretly named it. It comprised a brown two-piece suit with a brown overcoat, her spectacles (also brown), perched on the bridge of her nose, and her hair (brown, of course) short and neat. Authoritative, no-nonsense, brisk and businesslike, the woman was on a mission in life, her museum testament to that, housing objects that could prove dangerous in the hands of those that didn't understand them or just wanted to exploit them. In a sense, she sheltered the items like a confinement building over a nuclear reactor, while also attempting to unravel what was so mysterious about them. Doing so, she reasoned, would help her to understand why the artifact had become so charged.

"There's always a reason," she would say. "Everything in the museum was owned, sometimes by one person, sometimes by several, and it's their energy which has attached itself, not always in a negative sense, but if that is the case, well, let's just say negative energy is harder to dispel. It can cling like a desperate thing, and it can also affect others, frighten or influence those who tune in to it, even if they do so unwittingly. That's where understanding helps. It dilutes the fear. It can dampen it."

As Shady remained resolutely where she was in the store, looking around at other supposedly pre-loved things—some felt that way, others not so much, although nothing, *nothing* compared to the mirror—Annie and Lucy made their way to the front, where the mirror was displayed in the window.

"It's a rather unusual design, don't you think?" Lucy asked Annie. "Not to my taste, a little too bohemian for me. For that reason alone, I'd say it was made in the sixties."

"The sixties?" Annie queried. "Yes, quite possibly. How long have you had it?"

"Oh, now, let me think. Not long, a month or two. So much comes through the doors, it's easy to lose track."

"I can imagine. Was it a local person that brought it in?"

"Actually, it was, a lady by the name of Glenda Staines. Said she lived locally, anyway. Funny that I remember her name—I don't usually. It just came to me as I looked at it. She said she'd had the mirror for a long while, kept it mainly under her bed as opposed to hanging on the wall, but the time had come to rid herself of it. Strange way to put it, don't you think? I gave her what I thought it was worth, but she handed the money straight back and said to give it to charity. We keep a box to support local concerns, so I popped it in there. It was very kind of her. Normally it's only quarters I put in."

Shady saw Annie peer into the mirror, noticed too that she didn't recoil.

"How much is it?" Annie asked.

"Twenty bucks. The wicker frame isn't in the best condition, I'll admit. It's unraveling in places. And the glass isn't as clear as it could be either. It's kinda hazy. Still, it's been in existence a long time, more vintage than antique. You really like it?"

"I...erm...yes. Thank you. Make it fifteen and you have yourself a deal."

As Lucy reached in to retrieve it, she quizzed Annie as to where she was from.

"England originally, a town called Lavenham in Suffolk, but I live in Mason now, just outside Idaho Falls."

"Mason? Uh-huh, I know it. It's in Bingham County, right? Passed through it a few times. Not much of anything there, if I recall correctly, apart from an odd little museum at the far end of town. Ever been in there?"

"The museum?" Annie repeated. "Oh, yes, yes, I have, once or twice. May I?" she continued, taking the mirror from Lucy and pressing it to her chest, mirror side inward, before calling out to Shady. "Would you take the money from my purse and pay the lady?"

Grateful for the protection Annie was providing, Shady duly obliged, Annie having conveniently left her purse on the countertop. Meanwhile, Lucy looked both amused and bemused as she headed back to the counter, muttering to herself all the while.

"From the way you're clutching that mirror, you sure weren't fooling when you said you liked it! Anyone would think you'd won the lotto!"

As Lucy took the money being extended, Annie, who'd stayed close to the door, backed out.

"Lovely to meet you," she said. "And thank you so much for this."

"You sure you don't want me to wrap it in newspaper for you?"

"No need," Annie assured her.

Shady, too, thanked Lucy and turned to follow Annie, herself a little amused now at the bizarre performance Annie was putting on as she dashed out of the shop and over to Shady's car, not worried by the ice now, apparently, only perhaps that Lucy might change her mind and call her back, deciding she didn't want to sell the item after all, that it might be more valuable than it looked…

Annie reached the car without incident, waiting patiently for Shady to open the trunk.

"Don't look at it," she warned, placing it facedown into the space there.

"I wasn't intending to, ma'am."

Not until they were safely back at the museum.

* * *

The museum basement was the arrival lounge for new objects and artifacts, the aim being to get to grips with them in a controlled environment, to get to know something about them before they went out on general display, if they ever could. It was here that Mandy had been kept for a short while, but now she was upstairs, in many ways the main attraction but safely sealed within a glass case. Whenever Shady worked alone at the museum, she'd spend time with the doll, releasing her from confinement to hold her, both attracted and repelled by her. The mirror, though, and what she'd seen in it, how it had made her feel, was something she couldn't imagine spending time alone with. Little surprise that its previous owner had wanted to off-load it.

Mirrors. Shady already had experience with them in her short career and was only too aware of how much energy they could retain from their previous owners. Before meeting Annie, she'd helped a few people out regarding objects they'd lost or had a feeling about, Gina Dawson being one of them.

Gina had called on Shady because she'd begun to have nightmares, terrible ones, and she wondered if Shady could help her understand why this was happening—she'd never had nightmares before in her life! Visiting her, Shady had immediately been drawn to a handheld mirror that Gina had only recently picked up in a thrift store, with a faux silver frame and a long, slim handle. That mirror—Jesus!— it had witnessed stuff, had been a focus for someone staring into it. A woman, Shady thought, pouring all her anger and hatred into it, the things that she wanted to do—which was primarily to hurt, to destroy. Not knowing what else to do, Shady had taken the mirror over to the kitchen sink and smashed it, bagging the remnants afterward, then taking it to nearby wasteland to bury.

Gina's nightmares had subsequently stopped. Job done. Or so Shady had thought. Unfortunately, the nightmares returned—with a vengeance. Worse still was knowing what she knew now, what Annie had taught her: that it wasn't always possible to dissolve the hold an object had on you by the simple act of banishing it. So she'd returned to that wasteland but for the life of her couldn't remember where she'd buried the mirror. Every inch of land looked the same, and she hadn't thought to leave a marker. Attempts to unearth it so far had failed, providing no chance to work backward with it, to connect further to its previous owner, to understand her, at least, and the torture she'd been in, to surround the object not in yet more dirt and darkness, but light.

All she could do was apologize to Gina, Annie further advising the woman to visualize white light at night, just before she went to sleep, a protective layer that would surround her, which negativity couldn't penetrate. Gina said it was helping, but only to a degree—whatever mojo had attached to the now missing mirror was as strong as it was bad.

And now there was another mirror to deal with, and more mojo.

"Are you ready, Shady?"

Shady nodded. She was as ready as she'd ever be, she guessed. Ray was with them too, having turned the sign in the window to "Closed" and locked the heavy oak door to the museum. When dealing with a new item, Shady was usually the star of the show, her abilities extending to include the gift of psychometry: being able to read a physical object. As willing as she was to do that, however, it could sometimes be unpleasant, even dangerous, and so it comforted her to have her colleagues with her, who surrounded her along with themselves in white light, ready to pull her back should old memories carry her too far.

Annie had propped the mirror up against the wall. The artificial lighting in the basement was bright, and all around her other objects seemed to creak and groan as if reaching out, as if wanting someone to acknowledge they were something more than inanimate. Full of energy, as Annie always said. Just as they themselves were. Pure energy, and energy that wasn't quite so pure.

Shady drew a deep breath as she moved closer to the mirror. She'd been tipsy two nights back when she'd first looked into the mirror. Approaching it stone-cold sober and by design rather than accident caused every nerve in her body to pulsate, the memory of the reflection she'd seen and the hatred it contained something visceral.

"Take your time, Shady. There's no rush," Annie reminded her.

"We've got nothing to do, no place to be," Ray added.

She'd kept her gaze averted on the approach, but now, standing before it, she looked straight at it, taking in the frayed cane-and-wicker frame that might have been considered fashionable once upon a time.

Annie and Ray had already taken turns looking into the mirror and, although both felt no fondness for the object, they'd felt no fear either. They'd seen what they expected to see, which was themselves, Ray goofing around, pulling silly faces and making them laugh, lightening, if only for a moment, the atmosphere in the basement that was always so heavy.

But Shady knew what she was about to see would be no laughing matter.

Lucy had described the glass as "hazy," and it was, as mottled as the backs of the old woman's hands. Shady saw her reflection in it, only her reflection, but then she adjusted her gaze again and stared deeper.

As she knew it would, her reflection altered, changed in ways that were, at first, subtle. Her jawline softened, the shape of her head was a little different too, and the color of her hair was no longer as dark.

It was another girl, a stranger, doing as Shady was doing and staring into the mirror. Whereas in Shady there was curiosity and trepidation, within this girl was a whole breadth of emotions that found release in her eyes, that had built up and continued to build, becoming explosive. It was a girl...just a young girl, although how young Shady couldn't tell, not yet. Would it help to step closer, to reach

all the big hotels were—the Hampton Inn, Hilton Garden, La Quinta, SpringHill, and—every town had one—the Super 8. More hotels were due to be built on this ground with construction scheduled to start soon, so the handheld mirror, if they couldn't find it, would be lost forever.

"Ah, this is nuts!" Shady said, sighing heavily as she gazed around her, the noise of cars from the nearby highway the only other sound to punctuate the day.

Immediately, Ray tried to appease her. "Shady, Gina said visualizing white light was helping, kinda. The nightmares aren't as intense now. Maybe if she keeps doing that, they'll continue to improve, whether or not we find the mirror." His voice grew firmer. "Shady, there are other ways to fight this."

"I know, I just…I wanted to get rid of the nightmares altogether, make it easier on her. I made a mistake, and I need to fix it."

"You know why you want to do that, Shady?"

"Why?"

"Because you're nice."

She smiled at this, albeit wryly. Often, she was described as nice, sometimes *too* nice.

Again, she surveyed the surrounding land. How much further and farther could they dig? "If only I'd met Annie before dealing with Gina and her mirror, I'd have known how to deal with it properly."

Ray frowned. "Apart from helping Gina—which, believe me, I know you want to do—is there…you know, another reason you're so desperate to find the mirror? Has it got anything to do with the other one, back at the museum?"

Ray was intuitive; she'd give him that. It did have

something to do with it. To Shady's mind, the energy attached to both mirrors was just so similar. Coincidence, perhaps? It could be. People stared into mirrors all the time and either loved or hated what they saw. Perhaps they even told themselves stuff, as if the person staring back at them were a separate entity somehow, a confidante, someone who would keep their deepest, darkest secrets, the *only* person who could ever be trusted with them. She was no different; she'd criticized her reflection on plenty of occasions, been dismayed by it, told it things too, her own secrets, upsets, and frustrations. If she could find Gina's mirror, she could sit with them both and put her theory about them being connected to the test, feed into the energy, into the demons that had tortured those who'd once owned them.

"Shady," Ray said, interrupting her thoughts.

"Huh? Oh…sorry. Yeah, Ray?"

"I just got a text from Lisa Marie."

"Lisa Marie?"

"You know, the girl from Sam's party."

"Lisa Marie! Yeah, of course. Actually, I think I just got a message too."

Retrieving her cell from her pocket, she checked the screen. Sure enough, there was a message from Lisa Marie: *You want to meet for coffee today? I get a break for lunch and could head downtown. I'd love to see you and Ray. Sorry for the short notice.*

Shady smiled at Ray and shrugged. "Shall we?"

"Hell, yeah! Have we got time to head home first, though, and freshen up a bit?"

"You really need to?"

"Shady, look at my jeans. There's mud all over them."

34

There was a speck of mud, nothing more, but she got it. He wanted to look his best, although as they walked back to her car, she not only pointed out they didn't have time to stop by Ray's place but reminded him Lisa Marie had a boyfriend.

"We don't actually know that," Ray said. "He could be her…uncle."

"I suppose. You really got the hots for her, huh?"

"You gotta admit, she's pretty special."

"Uh-huh." She was a ray of sunshine on a cold Idaho day, outwardly, at least.

"She's way out of my league, though," Ray lamented, both of them in the car now and driving toward the agreed coffee shop.

"Oh, come on, you're not starting that again, are you?"

"Well, ya know, just trying to be realistic here."

Vehemently, Shady shook her head. "How many times do I have to say it, Ray Bartlett? You're a catch for anyone. And you know why? Hey, don't do that, don't shake your head. It's because you're pretty special too, one of life's good guys. She'd be lucky to have you."

"Go tell that to my last girlfriend," he replied, sighing.

"Your last girlfriend? Who was she?"

"Alisha Adams. She lives in Idaho Falls too. She's a couple of years younger than us."

"How long were you together?"

"Almost a year, although we broke up a while ago now."

"Why?"

"Because she found herself a Brad Pitt look-alike, that's why. When it comes to personality versus looks, there's no contest."

Shady laughed. "Ah, Brad's too pretty for his own good. As for Alisha Adams, she's shallow. But, Ray, tread carefully, okay? Just in case Mr. Camaro was her boyfriend."

"Soon find out, I guess."

"You gonna wheedle that information out of her?"

"Or…you could?"

As Shady pulled up outside La Vanilla Bean on Park Avenue, she burst out laughing. "Yeah, I could, I guess."

"You would? You'd do that?"

They were on the sidewalk now, Shady still smiling. "What are friends for, huh?"

Ray's skin suddenly flushed red. "Oh, Shady, look! She's in there already."

She was, smiling and waving at them through the expansive glass frontage.

They entered the coffee shop by the corner door, the aroma of freshly roasted beans pungent. Shady inhaled, looking forward to something different from her usual caramel macchiato with soya; she'd go for coffee with pumpkin-spice syrup instead. Urging Ray to go right ahead, that she'd get the drinks—she'd already spotted Lisa Marie had a full cup in front of her, so there was no need to get her a refill just yet—Shady walked to the counter, turning her head slightly to look at the pair before ordering.

Lisa Marie really was quite dazzling, unlike any of Shady's other friends, who, like herself, were ordinary enough. With the exception of Sam Hope, that was, who tended toward flamboyancy on occasion while the rest of them dressed down in jeans, Converse and tee shirts—a kind of everyday uniform. Again, except for Sam Hope, most of her female friends didn't even wear makeup, not every day. And even then, glamorous Sam didn't quite have the natural sparkle that this one had. Maybe there really was something in the water in California, something that made you glow. This girl, in her early twenties, just as Shady and Ray were, stood out in Idaho Falls. And yet…Shady knew something about her was slightly off-kilter, that what was on the inside didn't quite match the confident and extroverted veneer.

Approaching their table with the drinks—and already regretting her pumpkin-spice choice, which she'd sipped and found far too sweet—Shady saw Lisa Marie was giggling. Even funnier, Ray was too. She set the drinks down in front of them, and Lisa Marie immediately reached out, taking Shady's hand in hers and declaring how lovely it was to see her.

Skin touched skin for the second time, and it was like being shot through with an arrow, for Shady, at least. The delighted expression on Lisa Marie's face didn't alter one bit, so she clearly hadn't noticed anything out of the ordinary. Shady, however, got another insight into the woman in front of her, the impression of a home, not a happy one, and the people in it—her parents?—shouting and screaming at each other, someone else crying, likely Lisa Marie herself. Alcohol. That played a big part. Drugs too. Addiction. Something Lisa Marie was used to, that she'd grown up around…oh God, that she had a problem with herself? Shady thought back to the party. A bottle of Coke had been in Lisa Marie's hand, not a beer.

As quickly as she could without seeming rude, Shady retracted her hand. The insight was too personal, too intrusive. Thankfully, that rarely happened—with people, anyway. She'd hate for it to become more common; it would be unfair to those around her. People were entitled to their privacy, and certainly Shady cherished her own, but with Lisa Marie, the connection was strong. Why? Was it because all the hurt, the pain, and the bewilderment she carried was actually very close to the surface, and all it took was someone astute enough to notice? If that was the case, then Ray was as far from astute as it was possible to get—Lisa Marie was dazzling, and, in turn, he was like a kid in a candy store, intent on gorging himself.

"So, yeah," their new friend was saying in response to a question Ray had asked and Shady hadn't heard, "it's pretty different here." She made a show of chattering her teeth. "It's cold, that's for sure. But the people are great. I met Sam right here, in this coffee shop. We swapped numbers, and she invited me to her party the other night, texted me while you were all at The Golden Crown, said it was kind of impromptu and to come along. I know Brett Easton too. He's one of your friends, isn't he, Ray?"

"Brett, yeah. How'd you meet him?"

"In the record store where he works. We got chatting about music. He was, um…"

"High?" offered Shady, before inwardly wincing. She might have meant it good-naturedly, even affectionately, but given Lisa Marie's background…

Lisa Marie only smiled. "He was, yeah. But we got along really well. He's a nice stoner."

"He's had it hard." Ray's jovial tone became more serious. "His dad left him and his mom when he was twelve, just walked right out on 'em. Hasn't been in touch since."

Lisa Marie looked far more somber too. "Jeez, that's harsh. Poor Brett."

"He's a good guy, though," Ray said. "Like you said, a nice stoner."

"Some aren't, I guess," she replied, Shady realizing there was no guessing about it: Lisa Marie knew full well there were some very unpleasant addicts out there.

Shady, stop it! Quit with the analyzing.

"You okay, Shady?"

Lisa Marie had noticed a subtle change, perhaps, in Shady's demeanor, which was probably coming across as slightly detached. Silently Shady admonished herself.

"What? Yeah, fine. Sure. And Brett, yeah, I like him too. How long did you say you were staying in Idaho Falls for?"

"I've been here a couple of months already, so not a bunch longer. The project I'm working on is almost finished. After Idaho Falls, I'm looking to head to Boise for a while. There's another placement there that interests me."

"You like to move about, huh?"

She nodded her golden head. "As much as work allows. If there are placements going, I take advantage of them."

"Your boyfriend travel with you?" There, she'd said it, noticing Ray's back straighten.

"My boyfriend?" Lisa Marie asked.

"The guy who came to pick you up after Sam's party."

"Oh, you mean Gregory! I'm renting a room in his apartment, and, yeah, I think he'd like to be my boyfriend, but, ya know…"

You have a problem with commitment because of your parents.

Again, the thought arrived unprompted in Shady's head, striking fear into her that she'd said it out loud. Only because Lisa Marie continued smiling did she realize she hadn't.

"Poor Gregory," she said instead, although his loss might be Ray's gain. Deciding to improve his chances further, Shady drained her pumpkin spice faster than it deserved and stood up. "It's been lovely to meet, but I've got to get going. I'm heading down to Mason, to the museum where Ray and I work. Got an afternoon meeting with the boss."

That wasn't strictly true. Annie hadn't called a meeting of any sort. Indeed, both Shady and Ray had the day off, hence why they'd attempted to exhume the remains of the mirror this morning. So, no, it wasn't Annie who'd initiated the thought of an afternoon visit; it was the cane-and-wicker mirror. Shady might have gotten nowhere fast with Gina's mirror, but with the other one, there was every possibility she could make some headway.

"See you again soon, I hope," Lisa Marie said, having also risen to her feet. Before she could reach out to Shady or hug her, however, Shady stepped back.

"Sure," she replied, noticing how hard Ray was blushing before getting out of there.

* * *

Annie looked up as Shady entered Mason Town Museum, peering at her almost owllike over the ever-present glasses.

"Hello, dear," she greeted. "I didn't expect to see you today."

"Can't keep away," Shady quipped, approaching the

counter Annie sat behind. "Busy?"

"Not overly. A couple of casual visitors this morning, but nothing since."

Shady glanced over to where Mandy resided within her glass case. "Not even the lure of a haunted doll can drag people out on a day as cold as this, huh?"

"Doesn't look like it," Annie replied in her clipped English tone. "It's always quiet in winter, though. In springtime it'll pick up. We'll get the usual tourists passing through, and they'll stop then, might even go out of their way to visit, having read about us on the net."

The website for Mason Town Museum was something Ray had also been working on quite successfully, having been surprised to find there wasn't one before. The overall premise was that it was the usual town museum focusing on local history, but he'd added—as Annie had instructed— that it had an infamous doll considered by some to be haunted. The museum had to make money—that was the long and short of it, especially if supporting two other staff members besides Annie—and Mandy would draw people, some just wanting the thrill of looking at a haunted doll, excited by the thought of it being evil. Others, however, would go one step further and feel sympathy for the doll, identifying more with the melancholy within it—feeding that side and helping her to grow, to become bigger and braver than she was. All three paid very close attention to people's reactions to her, and if they came in simply to leer or jeer, they were quickly discouraged.

But today was not about Mandy. Today was about the mirror and what was attached to it, Shady intent on extracting more information from it, to understand it further.

She told Annie her plans, and straightaway Annie offered to join her in the basement.

"You don't have to, you know, if you're busy."

"We can close," Annie assured her. "I doubt whether there'll be anyone else stopping by today. That's if you want me to accompany you?"

"I sure do."

Annie smiled. "Okay, then," she replied, coming out from behind the counter after grabbing a set of keys from the drawer below and heading toward the door.

Shady waited for her, and then together they walked past Mandy—and past other items in which memories stirred but that Shady had learned, courtesy of Annie, to filter out, surrounding herself in white light. She used to compare walking from one end of the museum to the other to running the gauntlet, but it was getting easier.

The basement, though, would be a different story. She'd have to shrug off that protective barrier to a certain extent, open her mind and expect the unexpected.

CHAPTER FOUR

Leave me... Done my bit... Wassat? What's going on? Take...with you. Please.

"Who's leaving? Who's staying? Tell me more, please."

The mirror was just an object, one of many in this building, and Lucille Bonnet was right: it was typical of something produced in the 1960s and sold everywhere throughout America. What clung to it could be residual rather than sentient, so there was little point in asking questions, not really; Shady knew that. But speaking out loud, and therefore keeping Annie in the loop, seemed the right thing to do, and so she continued.

"Here's what we know so far, okay? It's a girl or a woman who's looked into this mirror, and she hated what she saw, but it was...her circumstances that prompted that hatred, I think? Awful circumstances. The girl or woman was also fearful; she was sad, truly desperate. And she was abandoned, that abandonment tearing her apart even further." Solely addressing the mirror now, she went on. "This mirror contains your essence, something residual, but if we're wrong and it's more than that, let us know. Our aim is to find out more about you, to read you. And if we can, to help."

Could she do it, quiet the energy through validation? Would such a simple technique help to diffuse it? *I know you've suffered.* The mirror could then be what it was supposed to be, a mere object and nothing more. Until then, it would stay at the museum, which was a sanctuary for all things troubled, keeping not just the object safe but also the public.

Vital work, even if you couldn't tell your friends about it, who'd dismiss it as far too New Age for them despite tending toward New Age themselves, Sam Hope, for example, dabbled in oracle cards, and Brett Easton had a penchant for crystals. As for Teddy Cardenas—

YOU CAN'T LEAVE ME HERE!

Those words, heard the first time she'd connected with the mirror's energy, resounded again, causing Shady to inhale.

"Shady?" Annie queried, but Shady held a hand up, and Annie fell quiet.

You can't leave me with him!

"Him? Who do you mean? Is he someone you know, a boyfriend, a brother, a father?"

Residual, it could be residual, and yet the impact, the force of another person's emotions, was so strong.

Images formed in her mind: a doorstep. She heard the cheering and clapping of before—courtesy of a TV, perhaps? Envisioned a girl, just a kid, helpless, frustrated and scared, all the time. What was that like, living with constant fear, your belly full of it, gnawing away at you and never ceasing? There was fear in the girl, but something else too—determination? A refusal to let the situation she'd found herself in continue. And so, like the person who'd abandoned her, she needed to do some abandoning of her own. To stay where she was, with *him*, was a thought she couldn't bear. Things were bad now, but there were varying degrees of hell, and she could sink lower still.

Were those tears on the girl's face as she observed herself, or had her eyes remained dry? Perhaps she'd cried a river already, those tears no use anyhow. The girl's story was typical of so many in the States, neglect and abandonment so rife it was almost pandemic. But for Shady, with this kid, it was getting personal.

Shady's hands gripped the mirror's frame, the glass only a few inches from her face now. Before she'd started, she'd asked Annie to dim the lights, wondering if there was something to those urban myths, if the gloom, ironically, made it easier to see.

Her own face stared back at her, eyes wide and hopeful. *Come on, come on, let me see you.* Like before, would her reflection melt as someone else sought to replace it—a face from long ago? It was hard not to force it, to *imagine* as Ray had said. She had to refrain, let something supernatural happen naturally.

If I could see your face, properly see it, I could understand better. Who are you?

There! It was happening again, a slight haziness, Shady's features softening around the edges, the sound of clapping, of cheering, louder than ever. Her eyes were no longer as dark or as almond-shaped but rounder and lighter, her skin fairer too, and her hair frizzy. It was another girl's face, an echo, but Shady willed it to become clearer.

A young face, cheeks rounded, flesh plump. If she had to guess, Shady would say the girl was around twelve or thirteen, but it was so hazy still and therefore hard to be sure. Pretty, though, or she could have been if sadness hadn't marred her.

"Annie," Shady whispered, "I think I can see her, the girl."

"Okay"—Annie's voice was just as low—"but remember you can turn away at any moment, break the connection."

"She's just a kid."

"A damaged kid."

She shouldn't ignore the warning in Annie's voice, but Shady couldn't help it. She felt for this girl, for all those who were like her. This world, not just the USA, was full of them. Again, she realized how lucky she was, unfairly lucky, it seemed, prompting guilt.

You should feel guilty! You deserve to!

What? Where had that thought come from?

What makes you better than me? Why should you have all the luck?

As Shady continued to stare, more words—bursting with anger, spite and bitterness—filled her head.

You're nothing, d'ya hear? Just like me! You smile, you laugh, and you're loved, but it doesn't matter. You're still nothing! You act so high, so mighty—you'd look down on me, I bet. Go on, admit it, you would. I'm gonna make you realize what a mistake that would be, drag you down into the gutter. See what it feels like! I'm gonna make you suffer too.

"Shit!" Shady let go of the mirror, heard it fall back against the wall, not shattering, though; it remained intact. Annie had reached out to her—she'd felt the touch of her hand on her arm, but if she was also speaking, she couldn't be heard. The only words were those of the ill-formed face in the mirror, a face that—just before she'd let go of the mirror—had twisted and turned, no hint of prettiness anymore but something wretched. A monster, that's what it was, a creature from nightmares, the kind that would plague you after just one glimpse, embodying the darkness within us that we all feared.

Shady doubled over, a sharp pain in her stomach striking from nowhere.

"Shady!" At last Annie's voice overrode the other one. "For God's sake, what's happening to you? Away. Come away now. We've got to get you away."

* * *

Upstairs, toward the back of the museum, was a small room, a staff room where you could grab a coffee and some peace if you needed it. And Shady needed it. Big-time. She'd already told Annie what had occurred in the dimly lit basement, but as always happened with shock, she felt compelled to repeat it.

"The girl's full of terrible feelings, like there's a viper's nest inside her."

In front of Shady was a steaming mug of coffee, courtesy of Annie, and she picked it up and drank from it, welcoming its warmth when she had felt so cold and bleak.

"To be like that, Annie, so…devoid of hope."

Annie nodded in agreement, clearly trying to digest all that Shady had told her, to understand the pain Shady had been stricken by too. "Do you think she was hurt both physically and mentally?"

"I don't know. The pain in my stomach…it could be hers, I suppose. It was a stabbing pain."

"If not, then what do you think we could attribute it to?"

Shady shrugged. "The weight of her emotions?"

"You know, given her age, this person may still be alive."

Shady inhaled. "I know." A person who'd begged not to be left alone. "Annie, what are we going to do? That mirror can't come upstairs. It has to stay in the basement."

"Oh, it does, I agree, for now. Nothing comes up until we're sure that what's attached to it is on the wane, especially if that energy is as negative as you've experienced."

"We need to trace its prior owner," Shady said.

"Glenda Staines? Absolutely. A local lady, according to Lucy."

"That's right, and, Annie, this morning before I came here, me and Ray went to the place where I buried Gina's mirror. I wanted to find it because the feelings I get from the oval mirror are like those I got from that mirror too, and I just...well, I wonder if there's a link of some kind, a correlation."

"But you didn't find the mirror?"

"No, I didn't. And building work's due to start soon on that ground. What will happen if it remains in the soil there, pumping out all that negativity?"

Annie sighed. "It could well have an effect. Perhaps the hotel won't be as popular as others in Idaho Falls. There might be bad luck, for example, or plumbing issues. But you can't be blamed for what you did; you didn't know at the time there might be another way of dealing with the matter. If you think there is a correlation, it might be helpful to talk to Gina again. Get her to describe her nightmares in more detail, see what links might indeed emerge. But, Shady, remember this: there are many damaged people in this world, and many mirrors too, which have been party to that damage. The only link there may be is that this world is a tough place to live in at times."

She was right. For some people it was—it *obviously* was. You only had to look at them to see they'd suffered, the pain in their eyes almost as painful to look at. But with others, with people like Lisa Marie, either they hid it well or they'd overcome it and seized their lives back. No mean feat, and in Shady a new respect bloomed, not just for Lisa Marie but for Brett and so many who'd been hit by life but hadn't hit back, or blamed others, as the girl in the mirror had. It was possible she'd hurt people. Badly.

"Shady…" Annie's voice was much softer than before, clearly showing concern. "I think that's enough for today. You need to go home and get some rest. We don't have to rush into finding out more about the mirror; there's no deadline. It's been removed from the public, and that's what really matters. It's out of harm's way."

Shady nodded. There was comfort to be had in Annie's words, that the world had one less hateful thing to deal with. It had become their responsibility, and it could be investigated carefully, gradually, the mystery of it if not solved, then hopefully subdued.

After assuring Annie she was okay to drive, Shady went back to Idaho Falls and had dinner with her folks, keeping to herself what had transpired that afternoon, making everyday conversation with them instead, simple chitchat. After helping to clear the dishes, she retreated to her room toward the back of their single-story house, showered, and got into pajamas. She was exhausted, what she'd experienced today having taken its toll. It had been like dealing with a force of nature, a hurricane with a tidal wave of darkness riding on its back. One hand migrating to her stomach, she rubbed at the skin there. There was no physical pain, not now, but the memory of it lingered well enough.

Had Glenda Staines ever experienced anything even remotely akin to what Shady had? She'd been glad to rid herself of the mirror, Lucy had told them; she'd kept it under the bed, apparently, in her spare room. For how long?

Shady's eyes went to her laptop. She shouldn't fire it up, she should read a book instead, then get some sleep before another day dawned, but checking for any mention of a Glenda Staines on the net wouldn't take long. See if they could pay her a visit...

A few minutes later, Shady had located Glenda Staines on Facebook and sent her a private message, explaining she worked for Mason Town Museum and that they had in their possession her mirror, purchased from Pre-loved. She'd spun some story about it being a unique piece from the 1960s and that they simply wanted to find out a little more about its provenance, which, she figured, wasn't wholly untrue.

Her fingers still tapping at the keyboard, she couldn't resist doing a little more research. The subject? Haunted mirrors. Beyond the usual urban myths that all American kids knew about, she delved deeper into the subject of scrying—the ancient art of revelation. Once outlawed as the work of the devil, these days it was gaining in popularity. Her interest peaked when she read that Native Americans had used scrying too, as had the ancient Egyptians. The aim of it was to help people get in touch with their subconscious minds, their core needs, dreams and goals. Is that what the girl had been doing when she'd looked into the mirror? If that was the case, Shady couldn't help but think she'd done so unwittingly and in a somewhat twisted way, getting in touch with her nightmares rather than her dreams, giving vent to them, going one step further than that and *birthing* them.

Various articles also instructed on how to scry. There were several methods, and not all involved mirrors—like hydromancy, which used liquids—although mirrors were a popular choice, the technique involving relaxing your vision and staring into a mirror, waiting patiently for images and scenes to emerge.

Shady gazed over to her en suite bathroom. There was a mirror in there, a big one, fixed to the wall. She also had plenty of candles in her room, having a bit of a fetish for them, and so she could try it, look into her own mirror with perhaps more clarity.

Jumping up from her bed, she grabbed a few candles on the way there, unscented ones as opposed to those smelling of candied apples and bonfires. Once in the en suite, she lit the candles, flames immediately spluttering into life, orange and gold, before turning off the overhead light. On a deep breath, she leaned forward with her hands on the countertop and looked into the mirror, relaxing her mind, continuing to breathe deeply and evenly, relaxing her entire face also, feeling the muscles there go slack.

Shady had no idea how much time had passed; it could have been a handful of seconds or minutes. She felt calm, even practiced though she'd never done this before, as if it was yet another ability inherent in her.

As when she'd looked into the oval mirror, her face was now softening at the edges and becoming hazy. She continued to breathe deeply from the pit of her stomach, feeling also the first stirrings of excitement at what was happening. The goal, apparently, was to become a passive observer rather than an active participant, and this was something Shady found hard, impatience rising in her, wanting yet again to force something as opposed to letting it develop naturally. She held back, however, and let her mind wander, do its own thing.

The face in the mirror was so much like her own, it took a moment to register that it wasn't. She had, however, the same dark hair and dark eyes, the same-shaped face too, a strong jawline and long neck.

There were flames in the mirror, far gentler than the candles that flickered around Shady, and the woman danced around them, solitary, naked, her long hair flowing. The flames leapt as she leapt, keeping perfect time, other shapes beginning to appear in and amongst the flames, dark shapes, but they held back, not daring to approach her, afraid while also wanting to devour her.

Kanti. It had to be. Shady's maternal grandmother. Shady had never seen a picture of her, as Ellen didn't have any, not one—not because she didn't want a reminder but because Kanti had refused to have any photographs taken. She believed the process disrespected the spiritual world, as it could steal a person's soul. Not a modern Native American belief, rather, it was an ancient one that Kanti adhered to—one relating to mirrors that had extended to cameras, eventually, because of the mirrors in their mechanisms. Photos were themselves considered mirrors with a memory.

But Kanti was here now, in all her glory, keeping the demons at bay—in the afterlife, at least. How graceful she was, her limbs strong and sinuous. Gradually, though, her dance became frenzied, more passionate, the shadows in the background trying harder to push forward, their hands outstretched, clawlike, jagged talons desperate to inflict damage, to rent Kanti apart. Undeterred, she kept on dancing, smiling now, just as Shady smiled, triumphant.

Core needs, dreams and goals—this was all of those combined. Shady wanted to be like her, not broken as Kanti was in life but free as she was in death, to follow the path that was laid out before her, to embrace her gift, not deny it, fulfilling both their destinies.

As Kanti moved from side to side, so did Shady, wishing her grandmother wasn't a shadow in a mirror but someone she could reach out and touch and embrace.

Kanti, it's wonderful to see you!

In the mirror, Kanti stopped dancing. The flames died down, and the demons rushed forward to cover her.

Stunned to see this, Shady screamed, "Kanti! What's happening?"

Don't let your guard down. Ever.

That was the only answer forthcoming.

CHAPTER FIVE

"Glenda Staines? We're so pleased to meet you."

Annie and Shady had left Ray in charge of the museum while they paid a visit to the oval mirror's last owner. He'd wanted to come along too but agreed that three turning up at her house might be intimidating. The last thing they wanted was to alarm her.

Before they'd left the museum to drive the short distance to Glenda Staines' house, which was equidistant between Mason and Idaho Falls, Shady had asked Ray how the coffeehouse rendezvous with Lisa Marie had gone.

"Ya know," she'd purred, "did one coffee turn into two, then turn into beers and burritos at Jalisco's, perhaps? We know she doesn't have a boyfriend, so it's game on, I guess."

"Funnily enough," Ray replied, not amused by Shady at all, "it was you she talked about."

"Me?"

"Wanted to know how long I'd known you, what you were like. Guessed you had Native blood and said she loves all things Native, like, their spiritual ethos, the way they look at the world."

"Oh wow, right." Shady was a little nonplussed. "Um...sorry about that, Ray."

Ray scrunched up his nose in a gesture of defeat. "S'okay.

We still got on great, and, well, maybe next time we meet, I can sway her interest more toward me."

On the way over to Glenda Staines', with Annie driving, Shady was mulling over what Ray had said when a message came through on her phone. Sure enough, it was Lisa Marie: *Sorry you had to dash off the other day, we missed you! Want to meet again soon?*

Did she? She supposed it wouldn't do any harm. She'd invite Ray along too; it would just be easier if she did, a little less...awkward somehow.

Now was not the time to reply, however. She and Annie had work to do.

Last night after Shady's strange scrying experience, Kanti channeling it as a means of connection and either advising or warning her, Shady had blown out all candles and returned to her bedroom, trembling a little, if she were honest, wondering if she should tell her mom about what had happened or, again, just keep quiet. The subject of Ellen's mother was a sensitive one, her history not the easiest to come to terms with—Kanti had been raped, and the result had been Ellen, their relationship troubled right from the beginning because of it. That truth had been hidden from Shady until recently, as had any mention of her grandmother, who'd died when Shady was a baby. It was out in the open now, acknowledged, but it had to be treated sensitively. To go into Ellen's bedroom and say, "Hey, I was scrying in my bathroom, and whaddya know? Kanti came through, Kanti who looks so much like me, who was dancing wildly around the fire, naked, and, well, there were these demons in the shadows... She was sort of holding them back. Until the end of the dance, anyway."

Yeah, it wouldn't likely go down well, so she'd kept it to herself, checked her MacBook, and there'd been a message from Glenda Staines, who'd taken only minutes to reply. She had no hesitation at all in meeting them. *Sure,* she'd written, *here's my address. Is tomorrow okay, around noon? It struck Shady as slightly odd that such an unusual request hadn't been met with total bafflement, but if something was going to be easy, why knock it?*

And now it was noon, and they'd just driven under an overhanging sign welcoming them to Evergreen Ranch, a sprawling place, the nearest neighbor about a mile or so away. True to the property's name, even in the depths of winter, plenty of green remained on the hills and plains that surrounded them, the snow still temporarily at bay.

Glenda was waiting for them, standing on her doorstep in jeans and a navy fleece, indicating for them to go ahead and park right in front of the house.

"It's a beautiful day," she called out as Annie and Shady exited the car, "but, sure enough, it's chilly. Don't want you walking too far, now."

Her whitewashed home was beautiful, with gingham drapes at the window and a wraparound porch with two wooden rockers. Shady could almost taste the tang of the homemade lemonade that would be drunk there on summer evenings. To the right of them was a paddock with several fleece-blanketed horses idling, chestnuts most of them, although a glorious black stallion was visible too. As for Glenda, she looked like a homey, down-to-earth, no-frills kind of person. She ushered them into her home and toward the kitchen, where the aroma of fresh coffee and baked goods filled the air. When she told them what she was apart from homey, Shady's eyes widened, as did Annie's.

"I'm an empath," she said, pouring coffee into mugs and sliding a plate of oatmeal raisin cookies toward them. "Do you know what that means?"

While Shady stuttered, because of surprise more than anything, Annie replied.

"Yes, it's someone who is highly aware of the emotions of others, to the point where they're able to feel those emotions themselves."

Glenda smiled indulgently at Annie. "Right enough," she said. "Please, help yourselves. They're freshly baked."

Shady also knew what it meant, although it was only knowledge that she'd acquired recently, thanks to Annie, and something that could apply to herself too—especially lately, with Lisa Marie and the girl who, once upon a time, had stared into the oval mirror. She was able to read them, to connect with them, empathize, going one step beyond psychometry on occasion, going deeper.

Annie had taken a cookie, and Shady followed. She bit into it, and it was delicious, probably the best oatmeal raisin cookie she'd ever had, although there was no way she could tell her mom that, who considered herself something of a master baker too. While they settled in, Glenda went on to explain more.

"I had the mirror in question for years, and before you ask, because I know you will, I can't remember where it came from. When my husband and I first moved here at the beginning of the nineties, we had to tighten the purse strings, pour what money we had into the farm to get it up and running. In many ways, the house had to take a back seat. We shopped around for furniture in a whole variety of places, thrift stores, yard sales, you name it, filling this big old house of ours. We had three kids to feed and educate too, so back in the day it was a little hard going. You know, I have a sneaking suspicion it wasn't actually me that bought the mirror. I think my husband did, which is kinda ironic. As the years went by, as our income increased, I gradually got rid of a lot of the secondhand stuff, being able to buy the furniture I'd always dreamed of."

Glenda waved a hand around a kitchen that was impeccably furnished, resembling something from an interior-design magazine, Shady thought.

"What's the saying?" Glenda continued. "My home is my castle, or something like that. Well…that's true for the Staines family. This is our castle and our sanctuary, our refuge from what can often be an overwrought world. That mirror, though, I just couldn't part with it. Not then."

As she came to a natural pause, Annie filled the gap. "Glenda…if I may call you that?"

"Sure, go ahead. And, hey, you're English, aren't you? I love your accent."

Annie nodded and smiled before continuing. "As you know, we have the mirror in our possession. It's at Mason Town Museum, which I own and which Shady and another colleague, Ray, help me to run. It's a museum with a difference…"

As Annie said this, Shady sat up. "Annie?" she questioned. Was she really going to tell her what the museum in truth was? A sanctuary of a different kind. In reply, Annie simply glanced at Shady before doing exactly that. When she'd finished, Glenda was nodding her head, an expression on her face somewhere between surprise and awe.

"Well, well, well," she said, her coffee cup held tight in her hands, "sometimes I've wondered if such places exist, and now I realize they do, right here in Idaho."

"Ma'am," Shady ventured, "I, too, am an empath, and that mirror has a story to tell."

"Oh, it does! It does! It's witnessed the most heartbreaking of human emotions." Pushing back her chair, she stood. "Come with me. I'll show you where it used to hang."

Annie and Shady duly stood, following her out of the kitchen and down a light and airy hallway; colorful pictures hung on buttermilk walls on either side of them, as well as some photographs of the ranch itself. They were construction photos, faded for the large part, depicting the various stages it had undergone before becoming what it was today. Turning left, Glenda opened a door, and they found themselves in a bedroom, very inviting and very neat but with no real personal touches. A guest bedroom, maybe?

Glenda walked over to the far wall and pointed. "Here," she said. "This is where it was. And whatever guests used to stay here all said one thing when they came into the kitchen in the morning, always along the lines of 'Glenda, I look so tired today. That mirror you got in there, it's a little unkind, isn't it? Highlights every flaw.' It was the word *unkind* that used to stick in my mind. It got me thinking, you see. Originally, when I'd hung that mirror up, I didn't really give it much thought. It was cheap, it was functional, and it would do. But after a while, when the room was empty, I'd come in here, and I'd look into it, *really* look into it."

All the while, Glenda had been staring at the space on the wall, but now she turned to face them, a shine in her eyes.

"And I understood what they meant. You'd be feeling good about yourself, thinking you looked fine and dandy, and then you'd look in that mirror and something drab stared back. God, the feelings within me as I continued to stare! They were so strange, feelings I'd never had before. Thank the Lord. I admit it, I had a great upbringing, and then I bagged myself a wonderful husband, and together we had the loveliest children, never a day's trouble from one of 'em. I was blessed. Truly blessed. What looked back at me, however, was cursed. I'm not talking about ET and the like when I say this, but it was something alien. I'm an empath, as I've told you. I understand emotions, the good and the bad, but when they're bad, I've got my family for balance, to bring me out of the void and all the way back to the good stuff. With this mirror, it was different. Every time I looked into it, it got harder to return. It was like falling down a well. Eventually, Gerry, my husband, noticed. 'Glenda,' he said, 'something's happening to you. You're getting too attached again.'"

"Just to be clear, he knows you're an empath?" Annie asked.

"He sure does. There are no secrets in this family. One night, I brought him in here, asked him to look in the mirror and tell me what he saw or how he felt. He said nothing, but he became angry, and Gerry's the most mild-mannered man you could ever hope to meet; getting angry isn't his way. He reached out, took it off the wall, and I believe he was about to smash that mirror onto the floor, into pieces. I stopped him, had to wrestle it out of his hands, work hard to calm him down, to make him understand that was no solution."

Annie nodded. "Energy when it's negative has to be contained rather than randomly dispersed, adding to the already dead weight that exists."

"That's right!" Glenda also nodded enthusiastically at that. "That's what I think exactly. To keep the mirror, to harbor it, I suppose you could say, I had to agree to one thing, and that was not to keep it hanging on the wall." She pointed to the bed this time. "I kept it under there, gathering dust. For years, I did that, lost count of how many, but it's a bunch of 'em. We have several guestrooms in this house, and from thereon in, I housed friends and family in those rather than this one."

"Because of the mirror?" Annie checked.

"Because of the mirror," Glenda confirmed, nodding.

Shady was curious. "Did you ever look into it again?"

"Occasionally, but the effect it had could last not just hours or days but months."

"Again, for the record," said Annie, "could you explain that effect?"

The tears in Glenda's eyes broke rank, and she reached out toward a chair. On seeing this, Annie rushed forward to bring that chair closer so Glenda could sit.

"Shall I bring you some water?"

Glenda shook her head. "No, no, I'm perfectly all right, really. Or at least I am now."

Shady had spotted a box of tissues on a dresser and brought it over to Glenda, who duly took one and blew her nose. "Thank you," she whispered. "Thank you so much."

"We can stop if you like," Shady said. "We don't have to go on, not if it upsets you."

Glenda looked up, straight into Shady's eyes. "Upset me, sweetheart? The feelings in my chest whenever I looked into that mirror, whenever I touched it, did more than upset me. They damn near killed me! No one should have to feel that way, like their life doesn't mean a thing, like they aren't even worth a dime, that people exist only to use and abuse them. No one. And do you know why?"

"Why?" Shady felt cold suddenly, feeling the weight of the mirror and the energy that saturated it as if it was still in the room, as if it had never been removed.

"Because it's dangerous," Glenda replied. "Not just for them, but for all of us."

CHAPTER SIX

The drive back to Mason was a quiet one, Glenda having given Annie and Shady plenty to think about, not least why she'd eventually allowed the mirror back out into the world to endanger someone new. Her husband had once again been the driving force, insisting it finally be removed from the ranch or he'd smash it, and no one could stop him this time. And so, it had been deposited with Lucy at Pre-loved.

The reason Gerry Staines had finally gotten his wish was because his wife had attempted suicide. Homey, down-to-earth, no-frills Glenda, both successful and happy—ordinarily—had gone a step too far and identified too much. She'd taken pills, lots of them, washed down with whiskey. Thankfully, she'd been discovered in time and rushed to the hospital.

The tears had come as Glenda revealed this, and the apologies. "His mind was made up. The mirror had to go, become someone else's problem, not ours. I was in no condition at the time to prevent it, but, you know, I also had a feeling that if I were to put it back out there, then maybe, just maybe, the right person would find it, another empath, someone who was…stronger." One hand had risen to her chest. "It really was the strangest feeling, like a certainty, you know. What could I do but go with it? I prayed every day I was right, and then—" she paused for a moment and smiled instead of cried, her eyes on Shady "—you sent that message, and I knew, I just knew, I'd done the right thing. At the same time, I'm still sorry because…there's unfinished business where that mirror is concerned, I feel, business that has to come to a head."

In the car, Annie at last broke the silence. "She's quite right about the unfinished business. I'm not like you or Glenda. I'm not as sensitive. I don't think I could do my job if I was, but I just…instinct tells me she's right."

"Me too. But, with no clue where she got that mirror from, how are we going to trace more owners? It's from the sixties, right? Glenda's had it from around the time they moved into the ranch, in the early nineties, which leaves two decades unaccounted for. With Mandy, we had a more precise trail to follow. With the mirror it could stop right there, with Glenda."

They were just a few miles from Mason now, clouds bulging with snow although the forecast remained clear for the day. "Shady," Annie answered, "leave it to me for now, and I'll do some research. Take a break from the mirror, just focus on normality, as it were."

As she said it, another text came through, Shady checking to see who it was from. Lisa Marie again: *Not sure if you got my last text, just following up about a possible meetup.*

Shady raised an eyebrow. *She's eager!* Had Ray gotten the same text? She guessed she'd find out soon as the pair of them pulled up outside the museum and parked the car. As they opened the oak door to the museum, there was a wave of commotion, the chatter of voices from inside. It was midweek, post-lunchtime; the museum was busier on weekends, so it was with surprise that Shady registered this.

"Hey!" Ray waved from the counter. "Welcome back. Never been so glad to see ya."

"Where'd this crowd spring from?" Shady said upon reaching him.

"Been a steady flow of people all morning. I'm wondering if it's because someone's run another article on Mandy recently."

"Why don't we ask them?" suggested Annie, moving away from Ray and Shady and toward the group, who were indeed huddled around the glass case that Mandy was housed in. "Hello. How lovely to see you all! Are you visiting specifically because of the doll?"

The group, about seven of them and clearly all together, were polite enough, returning a wave of greetings. There were two older women, and the rest were youngsters around fourteen or fifteen. One of the women stepped forward.

"Hi there, I'm Lainey Granger," she said, "and this is my colleague, Rita Pryce. We're teachers at the Helen Rogers High School, just outside of Mason, and yes, you're absolutely right. One of our students came to visit Mandy with their parents and subsequently wrote a piece on her, a very thoughtful piece about, you know"—she lowered her voice slightly as if disclosing something of a dirty secret—"the paranormal."

"I see. And so you thought you'd come and see her for yourselves?" Annie inquired.

"Yes, and also bring a handful of our students along. It's an interesting subject, and, well...we encourage freethinking at Helen Rogers."

"Glad to hear it," replied Annie before one of the teens

spoke up, a girl.

"She's really cute. Got a cute name too."

"Oh, Mandy, you would say that," another girl said, pushing gently at her.

"Ugh," said another, a boy this time. "I hate dolls. No way she's cute, she's creepy."

His friend agreed. "There's a big dirty crack down her face. How'd she get that?"

Shady was standing with Ray, listening to the exchange of conversation, and smiled as he nudged her and nodded at the teachers. "Bunch of New Agers," he said.

"Gotta love 'em," and, like Annie, she meant it. It *was* best to encourage freethinking, to expose children to something other than the material because, like it or not, it existed, and it could affect you, in ways both good and bad. To understand at least something about it was the best defense. It could help to dissolve fear that could otherwise accumulate, fear of the unknown, mostly, which could otherwise cause the imagination to go into overdrive. It was also fair to say, though, that understanding required patience, persistence and time; it could be something of a journey.

"Children! Children!" The kids were growing yet more excitable about the possibility of Mandy being haunted, so the teachers attempted to rein them back in. Annie helped too, steering them toward other objects that weren't necessarily benign—none of them were, not at Mason Town Museum—but would perhaps provoke less of a reaction than a doll. Farm tools, for example, and domestic items including an old-fashioned sledge and snowshoes, as well as mannequins wearing jewelry and costumes from yesteryear. It was an eclectic mix the museum housed, for certain, yet Annie had managed to give it some form of cohesion. The children duly calmed, although many kept turning their heads to look back at Mandy, some fearfully, others with a little more sympathy—the doll, as usual, provoking all manner of reaction in people.

Annie looked back too, but at Shady and Ray. She winked and then headed to the staff room to hang up her coat. Shady, meanwhile, shrugged off her jacket and stuffed it under the counter while simultaneously asking Ray if he'd heard from Lisa Marie.

"Not yet, but here's hoping. Why? Have you?"

"Oh…no," she said, not wanting to upset him by saying she had.

"I might text her," he continued when Shady's phone pinged again.

Crap! Quickly she grabbed it, careful to conceal the screen from Ray, wishing Lisa Marie would back off a little. She was happy to meet her for a drink, or, rather, she had been before the hassling started.

But it wasn't Lisa Marie. It was Gina:

Shady, sorry to bother you again, but can we talk? Last couple of nights, the nightmares are the worst they've ever been.

* * *

When Shady got off work that day, she said goodbye to Annie and Ray, the latter climbing into the Ford sedan he'd borrowed from his mom for the drive back to Idaho Falls, and Shady getting into her Dodge. Annie lived here in Mason, so when all three were on duty, she was usually the one that locked up. Shady wasn't going home, though; she was driving straight to Gina Dawson's house, up near Rose Hill Cemetery on West 21st Street. A sizeable house, it used to bustle with family life, but with her husband dead and her children all grown up and moved out, only Gina lived there now. She seemed content enough—if it weren't for the influence the hand mirror held over her.

On the journey there—the clouds still loaded—Shady couldn't help but feel responsible for Gina, and guilty too. For the hundredth time she berated herself about losing the mirror the way she had, having only sought to rid Gina of it as quickly as possible, failing to realize at the time that once stuff got inside your head, it stayed there. If only you could unsee; if only you could unknow. It didn't tend to work like that, though, unfortunately.

If Shady was feeling guilty, however, Gina was oblivious to it, greeting her warmly enough and ushering her into the kitchen like Glenda Staines had, though compared to the ranch, the decor here was more homey than showcase. Gina offered coffee too, which she set about making, returning with full mugs and setting one down in front of Shady and then herself.

"Is the white light not helping?" Shady inquired.

"It was. Some nights I slept through peacefully enough, on other nights, not so much. It took the edge off my dreams, at least, kind of subdued them. Look, Shady, you know I don't watch or read anything scary, not even the newspapers or CNN." Here, Gina attempted a laugh, which went some way to softening the anxiety her expression was otherwise full of. In her late fifties and casually dressed, she was still very attractive, but she looked tired, her eyes red-rimmed, a hint of grey in her pallor. No wonder, really—what she'd seen in that mirror was disturbing, emotions belonging to the dark end of the extreme. And now Shady would hear all about the nightmares, the most recent ones, Gina clearly bracing herself at the prospect, as was Shady.

"It's like *I'm* a demon, you know?" Gina continued, her voice trembling slightly. "Before, I was surrounded by demons, but they were something external to me, hunting me down, chasing me. I was always trying to get away and hide."

As she spoke, Shady was reminded of what she'd seen in her own mirror during the scrying session, the warning—yes, it had to have been that—that Kanti had given her: *Don't let your guard down. Ever.* Kanti hadn't been able to erect a big enough barrier between herself and the darkness in life, but in death she was more in control. Shady would, of course, always strive to stay alert, but there would clearly be some junctures in life where she'd be caught off guard. In this world they lived in, there were plenty of monsters, lurking in the shadows and often in plain sight too, and striving to understand them seemed like such a strange thing to have to do when, like Gina, your instinct screamed at you to run from them.

Not only Gina's voice trembled but her hands as well. "We know that whoever owned the mirror before—a woman, not a man—was a depraved creature. We discussed that, didn't we? She looked into that mirror, and she poured all her terrible thoughts into it, what she wanted to do, how she wanted to lash out and inflict pain."

It was true; they'd had a discussion about that after Shady had gotten rid of the mirror, Shady concluding the woman must've been mentally ill, imagining her in a room somewhere, one as dirty and as cluttered as the woman's mind, a smell in the air that reeked. This was a woman to be terrified of, one seemingly without an ounce of humanity, but there was also something about her that Shady had felt sorry for—after all, who really wanted to feel that way? Was it because she was so unhappy, so fearful, that negativity had tightened its grip, expanding to become something more? Shady was no psychiatrist, but she could use her common sense, and that was where her thoughts were leading her.

Shady leaned forward and reached out to Gina, took one of her shaking hands in hers. "So, Gina, now you're the demon, and that's how the dreams have changed?"

"That's right." Gina's hand clasped Shady's, grateful for the gesture. "I'm no longer the one being hunted. I'm the hunter, and…and…it's worse somehow. I'm merciless."

Gina retrieved her hand from Shady's and covered her face as sobs burst from her.

Shady felt just as stricken. "Oh, Gina, Gina, I'm so sorry. I'll tell Annie about this. We'll get more advice. Annie told me once that she knows exorcists. I know that's kind of a scary word, a scary notion too, but Annie only knows good people, people who work with the light to dispel this kind of thing. We can help you; *they* can help you, honestly. We'll smash more than the mirror. We'll smash whatever's got a hold on you. Gina—"

Abruptly Gina's hand dropped, her tearstained face tortured but not in the way Shady expected. As she continued to observe the woman's face in front of her, Shady's mouth fell open in surprise and horror. Gina looked nothing like she normally did. Her eyes, a soft shade of blue, were almost black, the whites surrounding them yellow-tinged. Her expression, too, was something to behold. It was…lustful, a thing that wanted, that craved, whose appetite could never be satiated. It was opening its mouth, slowly at first but getting wider, Shady fearful that when at full capacity it could swallow her whole.

"Shit!" she screamed, jumping to her feet. "Where's Gina? What the fuck are you? WHERE IS GINA?"

"Shady? Honey?"

Shady had half turned, not to flee but to find something to protect herself with—a knife, perhaps, or a cleaver of some sort. At the soft mention of her name, however, she swung back to face Gina, though every sinew in her body, every cell, resisted.

It was Gina who sat before her, *only* Gina. No longer sobbing but contrite instead.

"Forgive me," she said, "for crying like that. I… It just happened. Oh, Shady, I really didn't mean to frighten you."

"Frighten me? You…you think your crying frightened me?"

On her feet also, Gina held out her hands in a persuasive manner, not just remorseful now but confused. "Well, yes, I know tears can have that effect, although"—she shrugged her shoulders—"it's mostly with men. My husband, Carl, he couldn't bear it when I turned on the waterworks, always pretended not to notice. That's men for you, I suppose—"

Shady couldn't help but interrupt her. "This isn't about you crying."

"It's all this talk of demons, then. It's as upsetting for you as it is for me. I'm sorry, I really am. I'll try harder with the white light, I promise. And maybe you're right, maybe I ought to see one of Annie's friends, see if they can help me further. The last thing I want to do is burden you…"

If Gina continued talking, Shady didn't hear. Instead, the stark realization hit her: When Gina said she was the demon now, the hunter, Shady had thought she meant only in dreams. And it was clear that Gina thought this too. She had no idea, none whatsoever, that nightmares and reality were merging, beginning to overlap, that for a moment—because, in retrospect, that's all it had been, a moment—Gina had gone.

The demon had broken through.

CHAPTER SEVEN

"Oh, that's bad, very bad."

As soon as Shady had reached home, she'd rushed straight to her bedroom, past a clearly curious Ellen. Calling Annie, she'd proceeded to tell her all that had happened at Gina's, stressing that Gina had no understanding such an event had taken place.

"And it wasn't my imagination," Shady also stressed.

"I wasn't about to suggest it was," Annie replied.

"But why? Is it the energy manifesting? Becoming stronger?"

"Yes, I rather think it is. You instructed Gina about the white light? Emphasized the importance of it?"

"Yes, I did, but...oh, Annie, I feel like this is my fault entirely."

"You mustn't continue to beat yourself up, really you mustn't. The fact Gina's unaware of what's recently happened is a good thing...for now, at any rate."

"I told her you knew people, people who could perform an exorcism."

"I do, yes, if it comes to that."

"Don't you think it has already?"

"My dear, exorcism is not something to be undertaken lightly. There are dangers involved in the period of extraction—or transition, as it were—terrible dangers, dangers that could prove life-threatening. For now, for a few days, at least, we ask Gina to work with the light because it really is powerful. We keep checking up on her to see how things develop. Meanwhile, I'll contact those you've mentioned and put them on standby."

The phone call ending, Shady lay back on her bed and mulled over all that Annie had said about the dangers of exorcism. Annie hadn't elaborated, nor had Shady asked her to. In the past, she'd seen films and documentaries on this subject and could imagine well enough.

Imagination. Annie had believed her when she'd said it hadn't been, but right now, doubt was creeping in. It was easy to question what she'd seen, or thought she'd seen, here in the relative safety of her bedroom, comforted by normality, surrounded by things she loved and objects that she trusted. It was easy to dismiss everything she'd experienced—every bit of feyness, every ounce of intuition—as pure nonsense. She was made of flesh and bone and lived and belonged in the material world only. If she could truly believe that, just for a moment, that the paranormal was a man-made concept and nothing more, it'd give her brain a rest, that was for sure. Currently, her mind felt bruised.

"Shady?"

Her mom was at the door, knocking tentatively.

"Hi, Mom. Come in."

"I don't want to disturb you, honey, and dinner won't be long—we're having your favorite tonight, mac and cheese with a garden salad. But first I've got a little something for you."

There was something in her mother's hands, wrapped in tissue paper.

Curious, Shady sat up. "What is it?"

Rather than answering, Ellen sat down on Shady's bed and handed her the package.

"Mom?" Shady took the package and, slowly, somehow wanting to savor the moment, realizing how significant it was, began to peel away at the paper. A scrap of leather was revealed, soft to the touch, with several shapes etched upon it.

"It was Kanti's," Ellen told her. "I don't have any photographs of her for you, but I have this, at least. I put it away years ago, after Kanti died. I didn't keep many of her belongings, something I now regret, but..." There were tears in Ellen's eyes, eyes so different from Shady's and Kanti's, that were the brightest blue rather than the darkest brown, the eyes of her father as opposed to her mother, unfortunately. Taking a deep breath, she continued. "Anyway, I kept this. In truth, I was drawn to it, couldn't bear the thought of parting with it. See those shapes she made on it? Do you know what they are?"

Shady studied them. "Stars?"

"That's right. And in Cree, stars represent guidance. Shady, I know Kanti is with you, but take it anyway. She'd want you to have it, I think."

"This was Kanti's," Shady said, barely able to believe it, the stars upon it crudely drawn, perhaps, but by Kanti's own hand, and because of that she found them brighter than a comet. Bringing the piece of leather up to her nose, Shady inhaled deeply. It had been put away for many years, and yet it was still fresh, still pungent, a slight muskiness to it that she was sure was also unique to Kanti, that made it even more precious.

"Oh, Mom," she said eventually, still clutching the scrap of leather as she threw her arms around her and hugged her close. "This is just…amazing." More than that, it had been given to her when the time was precisely right, filling her with confidence when she'd faltered, dowsing the fear that had ignited, strengthening her barrier of protection.

Ellen held her, the intuition that she denied clearly having kicked in. The timing of the heirloom was no coincidence.

"Thank you, Mom," Shady whispered. *Thank you, Kanti.*

* * *

Shady woke on Thursday morning, stretched and yawned before getting up to look out the window. It had snowed overnight, but only a little, not the deep swathes they'd endured a month or so back—and nothing like last November when they'd been in the depths of Canada, searching for clues about Mandy's heritage. There, the weather had been so dramatic, so extreme.

As she and Annie had agreed, she texted Gina to ask her how the night had gone, her hand reaching out to clutch at the patch of leather that she'd kept by her bedside throughout the night and holding it to her chest as she waited for a reply. It came almost straightaway: *I had another terrible nightmare. I woke from it around 3am and didn't dare go back to sleep. You know, it's as if things are coming to a head somehow. Don't ask me how I know that, but it's a thought I can't seem to shake. Perhaps I'm overreacting, I don't know. Thanks for keeping in touch, Shady. I do appreciate it.*

Shady frowned as she finished reading the message, the idea of something coming to a head tying in with what Glenda had said about unfinished business.

Kanti, guide me, give me an idea of what to do.

Should she go back to the soon-to-be building site and continue digging? Unearth every inch of land there? Impossible.

Stupid, Shady, stupid, stupid, stupid!

She couldn't help but continue to blame herself for the predicament Gina was in. Like the oval mirror, there were no clues to follow. Gina had told her the thrift store it had come from, at least, and soon after she'd buried it, Shady had gone there, curious about its previous owner. The person that ran the shop—which was similar to Pre-loved, minus the charm of its proprietor—had made no attempt at remembering either the object or where it had come from. He'd looked at Shady as if she was mad for asking, which was probably understandable. As she mulled all this over in her mind, another message came through—from Lisa Marie. Shady didn't even bother to read it, growing more peeved, if she were honest, by her dogged persistence.

"Shady!" her mom called. They were due to go grocery shopping this morning, after which Shady would head to Mason to work the afternoon shift.

"Won't be long, Mom," she called back. "I just need to get ready."

Fifteen minutes later, having showered and pulled on jeans, a snug-fitting sweater and her boots, Shady joined her mother in the kitchen, and together they left the house.

As they drove to Walmart, Shady thought of how pretty the snow made everything look. The streets were clean and white, everything sparkled, but it was no match for the stars Kanti had drawn to light the way—not for herself but for Shady.

"Skies look clear now," Ellen commented. "Don't think we'll have more snow today."

"Probably not. It's still freezing, though."

"Yeah, it's pretty cold. You got enough sweaters, honey? Need to get some more?"

"I'm fine, Mom, and if I run out, I can buy my own."

"On your wage?"

Shady smiled. True, it wasn't a living wage. Annie simply couldn't afford to pay her and Ray that much. Even Brett earned more than them, working in a record store downtown, but Shady didn't care. She was meant to be at the museum, with Annie and Ray by her side, and so she'd take the deal, she'd continue to live at home; her folks were delighted about that, anyway. And she would learn, soak up as much knowledge as possible regarding her new calling, not only because it was vital—what had happened to Gina Dawson proved that—but in honor of Kanti and their shared heritage.

Walmart was busy, more so than usual.

"It's the weather," Ellen muttered derisively as they entered the store. "People panic."

Shady wasn't so sure that was true but noticed her mom immediately start to throw more cans than usual in their cart, guilty of stocking up on a little extra too. It was normal for it to snow in Idaho Falls throughout the winter months, around two or three inches at a time, but hopefully they'd already had the worst of it. Although, down in Boise she believed it was really heavy, like record-breaking heavy, eleven or twelve inches.

Snow was pretty, snow was cool, but it could also be disruptive, and, given Gina's situation, what Glenda had said too about unfinished business, Shady was developing a sense of urgency, like a kettle coming to a boil. Something was going to happen, and soon. If that was the case, Shady thought, barely listening as her mother read out the next item they needed from a previously prepared list, she'd need to keep her wits about her, practice visualizing white light. Keep that patch of leather close at all times, praying for guidance…

"Shady, will you stop daydreaming and help?"

"What? Sorry, Mom. What is it you want me to fetch?"

"Skip up the aisle and grab some canned vegetables, corn, tomatoes, oh, and artichoke hearts always come in handy. If they have canned pumpkin, we'll have some of that too. I'll make us pumpkin pie. I know Halloween's long gone, but what the heck?"

Dutifully Shady moved up the aisle, knowing her mom favored organic if she could get it and the prices weren't too astronomical. Bending to retrieve the pumpkin, which was on the lowest shelf, she moved sideways at the same time, taking no notice of where she was going and colliding with someone, who yelped.

"Oh, I'm sorry," Shady said, immediately straightening to see an older woman by her side and a can rolling toward her own feet—a can the woman had been holding, perhaps, that Shady had caused her to drop. "Here, let me get that for you."

"There's no need—" the woman began, but Shady reached for it anyway. It was pinto beans, Walmart's Great Value brand, and that fact made Shady feel guiltier, organic not being an option for some. "Here you go," she said, smiling as she handed it over.

The woman reached out too, and as she did, their fingers touched. It was Shady who yelped now, like she'd been hit by a gigantic bolt of lightning.

Although the woman was around a similar age to Annie, perhaps a little older, late sixties as opposed to mid-sixties, she hadn't fared as well. In Annie's eyes, and in her smile, a spark of youth was evident, something that time could never chip away at. In this woman, however, something *had* eroded, badly, various emotions surging within Shady that weren't her own but which she was familiar with all the same.

Ugly. All of it...so ugly. Hate. Hate you. Me. Hate that I'm here. That there's nowhere else to go. HATE!

Despite the force of what hit her, Shady didn't break their contact. Instead, she gripped the woman's arm.

"What are you doing?" Shady heard her say. "Let go!"

Through her, Shady was experiencing so much hatred, so much anger. So much...fear too. She looked deeper into the woman's eyes. They were blue but a dark shade, the surrounding lines so deeply etched in her skin that they might as well have been scars. Shady was spellbound. Totally. People bustled all around them, and there was baby-boomer nostalgia muzak being pumped into the air, something like Billy Joel, meant to enhance the shopping experience, to make you hum along, linger that bit longer, spend more... Shady, however, was aware of one thing and one thing only: this woman.

"I know you," she breathed.

"You don't! I've never seen you before. Stop it. Leave me alone."

"It is. It's you."

"Stop it or I'll call security."

"I'm Shady."

"Shady? Shady who? Let go of my arm!"

With a strength that Shady wouldn't have guessed she possessed, the woman finally reclaimed her arm. She then dropped her basket and let it clatter to the floor. Behind her Shady heard her name being called, a question in it. It was her mom, most likely, but she didn't turn to check. The older woman had backed away, her eyes on Shady all the while, wide open, full of alarm yet curious too.

"Who are you?" she muttered. "Just who the hell are you?"

She eventually turned and walked hurriedly onward.

"Shady! What are you doing? Where are you going? Did you get the pumpkin?"

That was definitely her mom's voice, but Shady ignored it, almost drinking in the woman, committing to memory how slight she was, her body probably painfully thin beneath her heavy coat, hair once blonde but now straggly with large amounts of grey.

Despite the bombardment of negative emotions that had emanated from her, Shady couldn't help but pity the woman. Her coat was almost threadbare, and her boots were scuffed. She was downtrodden, beaten by life, not someone to be frightened of, not now.

As Shady followed her, she pleaded. "Please, wait. I'm

sorry about what just happened. Of course you don't know me. It's just…I feel I know you. I do, in a way. If you give me a chance, I can try to explain. I didn't mean to scare you. Wait. Please. Wait!"

If the woman heard, she gave no sign. Instead, she carried on hurrying, turning right, then doubling back down a chilled aisle, a waft of icy cold air making Shady feel even bleaker than when she'd gripped the older woman's arm. She hated to pursue her like this, but there was no way she could lose her either. Shady had connected with the mirror, and she'd connected with the older woman, and it was the *same*. From having absolutely no trail to follow regarding the oval mirror's provenance, the hand mirror too, there was sudden hope. Understanding this connection was essential if she was to help Gina before she fully realized what was happening to her. This was also no coincidence; she was being guided. She had to see it through.

"If you'd only let me explain…"

They'd reached the entrance to the supermarket now, people still pouring in, shoulders hunched against the weather, and only two people hurrying out: Shady and the mysterious woman. Shady was catching up with her, though, closing the gap. Soon she'd be able to reach out, touch her arm, and continue pleading with her. *Listen to me.*

Just a few more feet… If only there weren't so many people descending upon Walmart, but it was midmorning, a popular time. From having gained ground, she was now losing it. Too many people were getting in the way—every time she dodged someone, she ended up face-to-face with another, as if they were actively trying to stop her. And now that they were outside, there were cars to contend with too, pulling into spaces or exiting them.

Shady quickened her pace. There was no way she could lose this woman. Idaho Falls—if she indeed lived here and wasn't visiting from out of town—was a big enough place. Shady may never find her again. Then what would happen to Gina? How could they help her then? The energy intent on possessing her, not just in dreams but during waking hours, was something that knew itself inside and out, was so certain of itself and the power it could wield, the destruction it could wreak. It was feeding on Gina's fear, scornful of her attempts to prevent it. And it was insidious, always there, in the shadows, waiting to strike.

"YOU HAVE TO STOP!"

Shady was shouting now; she was running. Tempted to push people out of her way, she only just stopped herself. In this sudden sea of collaborators, the mysterious stranger had disappeared. *I'm not going to let you get away. You can help us. I know it.*

There she was! Just up ahead. Not getting into a car—instead, she was about to cross the road, heading for the bus, perhaps? Certainly, a bus was waiting to carry cold shoppers weighted with bags back to their homes. If the woman got on it…if the bus pulled away…

Not just running, Shady broke into a sprint. "Wait! Please wait."

The woman was about to cross, and the bus's engine revved, a burst of smoke erupting from its exhaust.

Shady had to do something besides shout as she closed the gap between them. Pull something else out of the hat. Something…special.

"Wait! Oh, please wait."

Damn it, but she wasn't listening! *What can I do? How can I stop her?*

A word came to mind, not one that Shady expected: *gold*, was that it?

Gold. Golden. Goldie.

"Goldie! Wait. You have to."

The command burst from her mouth before she could either stop or consider it, incredibly achieving the effect she'd wanted. The woman in front of her stopped in her tracks, came to a halt, just like that, stone-dead, and swung herself around to face Shady, not just horror on her face but surprise too. Shady's heart leapt in triumph to see it, and then it raced faster than she ever could.

"No, no," she shouted. "Get out of the way. Move now!"

A car full of kids came screeching around the corner, music blaring through wound-down windows. They were playing Justin Bieber, she was sure of it, the kids singing along with him. All had beaming smiles on their faces, not concentrating on the road ahead or fully registering how busy it was at the store today, how many people there were—one woman in particular, who was standing where she shouldn't be. In the road. Directly in their path. And all because Shady had called her Goldie.

Shady's scream joined those of the teens, and Bieber was drowned out.

CHAPTER EIGHT

The paramedics were called and the woman rushed to Eastern Idaho Regional Medical Center. That Shady had learned that much was a miracle because what had happened after the crash was a blur.

The woman—Goldie—had been hit, her body crumpling in front of Shady after the driver of the car, only eighteen, had slammed on the brakes but not quickly enough. On icy roads the car had slid and collided with her, hitting though not running over her. Shady was thankful for that, at least. She wasn't dead. But she was badly hurt.

Ellen had caught up with Shady, although as she drew nearer, her attention was on the drama unfolding rather than her daughter, her eyes as wide as Shady's and her hand to her chest as she whispered, "Oh my God! What happened?"

Shady hadn't rushed forward, not at that point, shock having rooted her to the spot. Other people had, though, an entire crowd of them, most tending to the woman on the ground, others seeing to the teens, two of which were crying hysterically, clearly in shock. Soon, sirens filled the air as ambulances arrived at the scene, paramedics jumping out and police clearing the crowds, beginning to establish facts. Finally deemed safe to move, the woman had been whisked away, Shady darting forward to ask where she was being taken. And now she was on her way there too, Ellen driving her, their cart of groceries still at the store, the only thing on their minds the welfare of the injured stranger.

"They won't let us see her," Ellen warned Shady. "Don't think they will."

"But we have to find out how she is. We can't go anywhere until we do."

"Shady, it wasn't your fault what happened! This woman has nothing to do with you. I don't even know why we're doing this, chasing after her. She's a stranger, for God's sake. Why'd you run off in the store anyhow? What's this all about?"

Shady turned to her mother then, noticed how worried she looked, repeatedly glancing at her daughter and then at the road. "Mom?"

"Yes, darling."

"Do you trust me?"

"What? Yes. Of course."

"Then trust me on this. You're right, I don't know that woman, but I think I know something about her. It's to do with a mirror I found in a store in town. A secondhand mirror."

"Oh," was all Ellen said in response, shifting slightly in her seat. That she wanted to say more was obvious, but she was able to resist. And how Shady appreciated it, for the freedom she was giving her, for refusing to make it any harder for her daughter to walk down a path that was already difficult enough.

And Shady *would* tell her all in time. Right now, however, she couldn't explain even if she wanted to. Why had the woman reacted like that when she'd called her Goldie? So dramatically! And how come the name had popped into Shady's head in the first place? Was it the woman's Christian name? Anyone less like a Goldie—a name that seemed frivolous, somehow—she couldn't imagine.

They reached the hospital parking lot and hurried to the reception area. A young man behind a desk noted their approach, his dark hair neat, and his smile fixed.

"Good afternoon," he greeted. "How may I help?"

"Shady, let me deal with this," her mother whispered before issuing a greeting of her own. "Hello there, I'm Mrs. Ellen Groves. A terrible thing has just happened. We'd just finished grocery shopping at the store and were walking back to our car when we heard brakes squeal. A woman was hit by a car and brought here to the ER just a short while ago. A woman we know, actually. She's, um…a neighbor."

Quickly the receptionist arranged his face into an expression more suitably somber. "I am so sorry to hear that, ma'am." His fingers started tapping at a keyboard in front of him. "What's the woman's name? I'll check admissions for you."

"Her name?" Ellen faltered. "Um…"

"Goldie," Shady intervened. "We know her as Goldie."

"And her surname?"

Now Shady faltered. "That we don't know." She attempted a small laugh. "We just…never thought to ask. Please, is there any information on her already? Is it possible we can see her? Not right away, I realize, but soon?" She glanced over at a waiting room that was by and large empty. "We can wait. Or, Mom, you go home, and I'll wait."

Again, addressing the receptionist, she added, "I don't mind how long."

"If you'd like to take a seat," he responded. "I'll see what else I can find out."

The minutes ticked by. The receptionist left his station, disappeared into another area of the hospital, and then came strolling back at a leisurely pace. Shady jumped up.

"Have you found anything out about Goldie yet?"

The receptionist shook his head. "There's no one here by that name."

Ellen rose from her chair too. "What about an old lady recently admitted?"

"I'm sorry, you said you were neighbors?"

"Yes, that's right," answered Shady.

"Then I'm afraid that information is confidential. It's her family we need to contact."

"She doesn't have any!" Shady burst out, suddenly confident of that fact.

The receptionist's gaze was cool. "That's something we'll need to check."

"We're good neighbors," Ellen said in her most persuasive tone.

"Nothing I can do, I'm afraid, not right now."

Briefly Shady closed her eyes, frustration overcoming her...and fear. "Tell me she's still alive." *Please.*

"There've been no fatalities reported at the hospital this morning," was his reply, muttering under his breath as he turned from them to retake his seat, "for once."

Both Shady and Ellen also retook their seats, Shady picking at already short nails in an agitated manner. "Mom, you don't have to stay."

"*We* don't have to stay," Ellen amended. "Shady, this may have nothing—"

"It has," Shady interrupted. "It does."

More minutes ticked by, Shady noticing it had begun to snow, another light flurry. If the grocery shopping had gone to plan, she and Ellen would have been home by now, filling cupboards, the refrigerator and the freezer. Ellen would then point to the window at the snow, declaring she'd make hot chocolate for them, which they would sit with at the kitchen table just as they'd done since Shady was a little girl, feeling warm and cozy. Now, however, in the clean but stark surroundings of the hospital reception, she was consumed with nothing but worry. If the mystery woman died, Shady would feel at fault, and for good reason. If that name hadn't popped into her head, if she hadn't yelled out... And the woman's secrets would die with her too, and then there'd be no hope of...what? *Salvation*? It was another word that came to mind, adding to the confusion.

"Shady?"

So lost in thought, Shady turned to her mother first on hearing her name. Ellen was staring straight ahead, however, with a smile on her face. Shady adjusted her gaze, and there in front of her stood Lisa Marie, conservatively dressed in a navy pantsuit and heels, but even they couldn't make a dent in the golden vibe she exuded.

"Lisa Marie!" Shady said, back on her feet. "What are you doing here?"

"This is where my placement is. Remember me telling you?"

"What? Oh yeah, your placement, sure. I... It's nice to

see you. Um…this is my mom, Ellen. Mom, this is Lisa Marie, a friend of Sam and Brett's. We met at a party recently."

Ellen, who was also on her feet, looked delighted to meet her—not just smiling, Shady noticed, but beaming, a fact that fascinated Shady. This girl, this woman who'd endured a rough ride in life, lit something in other people too. It could be just the simple fact that she was pretty, but Shady didn't think so.

With Lisa Marie standing there expectantly, Shady explained what they were doing at the hospital reception, ending with an apology that she hadn't yet gotten around to replying to her texts about meeting up.

Lisa Marie waved a hand in the air. "Don't worry about that. You seem to have enough on your hands. This lady, though, you say you don't know her, but you seem pretty upset all the same."

"It's because…because—" Shady glanced briefly at Ellen before continuing "—when she stepped into the road, I noticed the car coming toward her, and that she *hadn't* noticed, and so I…um…called out, tried to stop her. If I hadn't, she might have gotten across safely."

"You feel responsible?"

Shady swallowed. "Yes. I do."

Ellen didn't contradict her this time, and for a moment Lisa Marie was quiet too before inclining her head to the left. "There's a café here, would you like—"

"Oh, well, I can't…my mom…"

"Shady," Ellen countered, "don't worry about me."

"No, I mean both of you," Lisa Marie assured her.

"You know what, we really need groceries," Ellen said.

"Shady, you go for coffee with this lovely young lady while I go back to the store. I can come pick you up after."

It was a plan—a good plan—Shady not ready to leave the hospital just yet, not so empty-handed. Ellen looked eager for her to accept that plan, as did Lisa Marie, whose blue eyes glittered even brighter than they had just a fraction of a second before.

"Shady?" Ellen prompted, and Shady nodded.

"Sure," she said, turning to Lisa Marie. "Lead the way."

* * *

"So, how come you're called Shady? I've been waiting to ask. It's an unusual name. Really pretty, though."

There *was* a story behind it, Shady telling Lisa Marie the bare bones of it. "Mom called me Shady because I was born as the sun was setting."

"A time of shadows?" asked Lisa Marie, causing a shiver to run down Shady's spine.

"No, not shadows," she said, "not as such. A romantic time is how Mom describes it, her favorite part of the day. But there's also a song, 'Shady Grove.' It's not quite my name but near enough. It's an old song, a folk song, so that played a part in it too."

"Cool. Guess why I was named Lisa Marie."

"Nothing to do with Elvis Presley, I suppose?"

"Yep, Mom and Dad were real fans." She averted her eyes as she said it, Shady imagining she could hear the inward sigh that accompanied those words. She brightened quickly enough, however. "How nice to bump into you today, though. A real bonus."

Shady smiled. "What do you do here, exactly?"

"I work in the labs, vaccine research and development. It's a job that could take me all over the world, but so far, I've only worked between California and here. In the future, though, I'd love to go abroad. Got that itch, you know, to travel."

"Wow! You really have it together."

"I've worked hard to get where I am." Again, the light within her dimmed momentarily. "What about you, Shady, do you enjoy your work?"

"In the museum? Yeah. It's…different. I'm sure Ray's told you, but the museum's just a small-town affair, about thirty miles outside the city."

"Yeah, he mentioned that, said you're a lot of fun to work with."

"He is too. I was thinking of becoming a teacher, but…"

"You got sidetracked?"

"Something like that. So, you'd like to travel abroad, huh?"

"After Boise, yeah."

"Not gonna head home?"

"To San Francisco? No."

"Don't you like it there?"

"It's a great city, don't get me wrong…"

"But that travel bug."

Lisa Marie laughed. "It's bitten hard."

There were a few people in the café, medics and those visiting family and friends. Shady and Lisa Marie were sitting at a table by the window, the snow continuing to fall outside but no heavier than before. As Shady turned her head toward it, a sigh left her body, and her shoulders slumped.

"Shady." Lisa Marie's voice was much softer this time. "What is it?"

Shady turned back to face her. "That woman," she said. "I feel so...bad."

"Hey, come on, it was just an accident."

"Maybe. Maybe not."

To her surprise, and alarm, tears pricked at Shady's eyes, hot tears that stung. Quickly they broke rank. "Shit," she exclaimed, raising a hand to wipe at them. "I'm so sorry. I'm just...I wish I could say sorry to her too."

Lisa Marie reached out again, taking hold of Shady's free hand and clasping it.

"Oh shit!" Shady repeated, not just because she was embarrassed and ashamed of how she'd pursued the older woman through the store and out onto the streets, but because more visions were filling her head—they were *pouring* into her mind, revealing once again more than she ever wanted to know or, more pertinently, what Lisa Marie would want her to know. *How do I stop this?*

The visions were even clearer than the woman's face opposite her. And she could also hear snatches of what had been said in the past, words that had been hurled, used as weapons.

You're a drunk, Bobby Lyons, a useless, waste-of-space, stupid drunk!

And you're a bitch. Should never have married ya, let a pretty face reel me in.

Leave, then! Go on. Walk out the door! We'd be better off without you anyway. Don't you get it, Bobby, I want you to leave. I hate the look of ya, the smell of ya. Just go!

There was the sound of a hand connecting with flesh—not just once, over and over.

Screams. Tears. A daily recurrence. The very walls that contained these people would shudder as if a hurricane were tearing through it, one fueled not by nature but by so much pain, by frustration, anger and despair, an endless cycle. Shady quaked to witness it, as the child would quake, the beautiful, blonde-haired cherub that had witnessed everything. She—Lisa Marie—was aged how old in the visions? Four or five? She would try to find new places to hide so that the tsunami wouldn't encompass her too. And all the while, her parents continued to yell.

If it wasn't for her, I'd be long gone, you know that?

You're sticking around 'cause of her? Don't. There's no need. She hates you too!

Another slap, another scream. Lisa Marie crying, wishing she could get away, escape. Hence the travel bug, perhaps, as if…as if she was still running.

Still the visions kept coming. A child going to school, not quite the golden girl she presented as now, but unkempt, her hair greasy, the sweater she wore with a hole in it, the skirt crumpled and ill-fitting. She was a girl who sat alone, that others laughed at, pointed at, whispered about. Kids could be cruel. This girl, though, she persevered and worked hard. A bright kid, dedicated to a plan of escape, shrewd enough to know that education would provide that opportunity. A kid who'd return to a cluttered house after school, to a kitchen that remained cold and unused, cupboards barely stocked.

She'd go to her bedroom, open her library books and carry on studying.

As the years passed, her determination increased.

There were more fights. Again, Shady could hear echoes of Lisa Marie's parents screaming at each other, the same old arguments, the same accusations flying.

You been with another woman?

Course I ain't.

What's that I can smell on ya?

Just my own sweet perfume, darlin'. You damn near put me off women for good.

I hate you, Bobby Lyons! Why don't you just leave?

You'll be out the door before me, be damn sure of it.

But Lisa Marie was the first one out, not them. A straight-A student, gaining one qualification after another and no one to praise her, no one to attend her graduation either. Others still pointing at her, still whispering, not laughter or smugness on their faces now but bitterness and resentment. How could a kid like that ace them out?

A potted history: tragedy turned into success, Lisa Marie moving out and never looking back. Not once. Leaving the people who'd spawned her but done very little else. Lisa Marie's heart—despite her relief at severing the connection—cracking a little more.

"Sorry," Shady whispered again, her cheeks still wet from tears.

"Shady, seriously, what happened to the woman *wasn't* your fault."

"It's not just about her. It's what happened to you too."

The words were out of her mouth before she could stop them. She winced, cursing herself for thinking out loud, for slipping up.

Lisa Marie's back straightened as her hand released

Shady's. "What do you mean?" she asked. "When what happened to me?"

"When…when…" Shady's tongue darted out to lick at her lips, a nervous gesture. What could she say? How could she possibly explain?

"Shady?" Lisa Marie prompted, and there was that determination Shady had witnessed in her visions, not just curiosity in her voice but a demand.

Shady looked around as if seeking an escape of her own, felt her face flush hot and cold, had to force herself to look back into Lisa Marie's eyes. "I…" *Damn it!* "Sometimes I get an impression of the past. When I hold objects, I can sense the history of them, energy that's still attached. There's a name for it, it's called—"

"Psychometry. Yes, I know."

Shady's eyes widened. "You do?"

"Of course."

"But…do you believe in it?"

"I believe that energy can be transferred or soaked up. The more paranormal side to the subject, however, is open to—" she paused "—a somewhat lively debate. So, yeah, I know about the practice of psychometry. What I don't understand, though, is why you're sorry for what happened to me. How do you even *know*? You can't."

"I…" Shady sniffed before wiping at her eyes, trying to buy more time, basically. "Like I said, I can read objects sometimes, not always, but…more and more often, I can. And…um…something else has been happening lately too. With certain people, again not everybody, hell no, not by a long shot, but with some…there's a connection."

"A connection?"

Shady nodded. "And I seem to be able to read them too."

There was a moment of silence, almost perfect in its completeness, and then Lisa Marie stood, an abrupt action, her chair scraping against the linoleum as she did so.

"I have to go," she said before turning just as abruptly.

Shady shot to her feet. "Please. Wait."

Heads turned as Shady hurried after her, Lisa Marie setting quite the pace. They were out in the corridor, Shady not wanting to reach out, to touch her again, but afraid that if she didn't, she wouldn't be able to stop her.

Proud. Oh, Shady could sense that all right. Lisa Marie was very proud, very determined, and very scarred by the childhood she'd received at the hands of her parents. She *hated* anyone knowing about it, wanted them to believe in Lisa Marie the reinvention, the golden girl with the glittering career, not the shitshow that had preceded it.

"I didn't mean to pry," Shady desperately attempted to explain. "I'm not like that, it just…it happens, and I don't know yet how to stop it. It's all so new." She swallowed hard, noting the unforgiving look in the other woman's eyes. "I'll take advice. I'll learn how to control it. But for now…" Briefly she lowered her gaze. "I'm awed, actually, by just how determined you are. You're young, but look at what you've achieved already—"

"I don't want your sympathy—"

"It isn't that," Shady assured her. "Truly, it isn't. You know, I've had such a privileged upbringing, but until not so long ago, I worked at a burger joint, dreaming of being a teacher, but that's all, just dreaming. Whereas you've taken your life and you've run with it. Don't get me wrong, I'm happy with what I'm doing now—like I said, I love the museum. But maybe, just maybe, I've had it too easy. And in some way that's stripped me of the same kind of drive that you have. I'm making a mess of this, I know I am, and I'm sorry for that too. For everything. Okay? I'm just…really sorry."

There was yet more silence as the two girls held each other's gaze, such pleading in Shady's eyes, such steeliness in Lisa Marie's. And then, by increments, her steeliness softened, became less glaring.

She opened her mouth to speak, and Shady braced herself.

"You want to see this woman that came in, that you feel so guilty about?"

Surprised by this offer, Shady could only nod in reply.

"I'll be in touch," Lisa Marie said before continuing on her way.

CHAPTER NINE

"The thing to do, Shady, is not panic."

"But, Annie, this isn't something I want. If I'm honest, it frightens me. I don't need that kind of insight into anyone."

It was Friday; the day following the incident with both Goldie and Lisa Marie, and Annie was pouring Shady a mug of coffee in the staff room at the museum, Ray remaining out front to greet any visitors.

Placing the mug in front of Shady, she eyed her solemnly before also taking a seat.

"Shady," she said, straightening the glasses perched on the bridge of her nose, "your gift is immense. In some ways you've only scratched the surface of it, but I agree, you need to be in control of it, rather than it being in control of you." She paused, a look of contemplation on her face. "In fact, it's imperative. You need to learn how to filter, I suppose. A little like you do with objects whose energy reaches out to you."

"Certain objects," Shady reminded her.

Annie agreed. "And it may only be certain people you form a connection with."

Her words had a calming effect on Shady. She had said as much herself to Lisa Marie, thinking back to the recent gathering she'd been at with Ray, at Sam Hope's house after the meetup at The Golden Crown. She'd touched people that night, either on the arm or by hugging them, and she hadn't been assaulted by visions of their past. It truly did seem only *certain* people affected her in this way: the woman now lying in a hospital bed, and Lisa Marie.

Shady lifted her hands to rub at her scalp. "Oh, Annie, if it wasn't for me, Goldie—or whatever her name is—would be at home right now, just going about her daily life. But when I accidentally touched her, the images, *the feelings*, matched those of the mirror."

Annie nodded. "Yes, yes, you've said. It's most intriguing."

"Annie"—even to her own ears, Shady's voice sounded subdued—"they're bad feelings. Unnerving. And then…and then…with Lisa Marie, there are similar emotions but not as drowned in the darkness."

"Drowned in the darkness?"

"That's the only way I can think to describe it. Lisa Marie hasn't had the easiest of lives, but there's so much more that's positive about her. She turned her life around."

"And this other woman?"

"I don't think she ever did."

Voices drifting toward them caused them both to turn their heads.

"Sounds busy out there," Shady finally remarked.

"Yes, we'd best go and pitch in. But, Shady, about what's happening to you, it's important to put it into perspective. Maybe…maybe you connect with certain people because you're *supposed* to. In that respect, the mirror could have set something off."

The mirror that resided beneath her feet, in the

100

basement, that she could feel the pull of, as if the energy drenching it was magnetic. But filter it she must, as Annie had said, be in control of it rather than the other way around. Something her grandmother, Kanti, had never achieved. Taking a last mouthful of coffee, Shady remembered what her mother had said about Kanti, how her gift had, in essence, broken her: *Because of the type of thing she could sense and see. She was weighed down by darkness, to the point where she…became it. It took over. And it broke her.*

She mustn't allow that to happen to herself. Ellen wouldn't allow it, and, from afar, neither would Kanti. As for Lisa Marie, she was an example of how you could overcome the darkness, push back against it and succeed. Shady hoped they'd meet soon, was sure they would because there was a pull there too. She felt a spark of shame that her persistence had once irritated her.

Standing up, her hand went to her jeans pocket, where the leather patch with the stars engraved upon it was safely stowed. Having loved it from the first moment she'd set eyes on it, right now it bolstered her; touching it was like receiving a warm hug from a woman she'd never known but who was nonetheless very much a part of her.

She took a deep breath. "How much do you want to bet it's another school group out there?"

* * *

The Mason Town Museum was heaving, Shady's prediction of another school group correct, and Mandy, as usual, the attraction that had drawn them.

"Who doesn't love a haunted doll," the teacher overseeing the group had said, a tall man, bespectacled and lanky, who must have been in his mid-to-late twenties but looked considerably younger, much like an overgrown kid himself.

"Some people are terrified of haunted dolls," Ray pointed out.

"Yeah, sure," he replied, "but come on, she's not really haunted, is she? It's just a clever hook." He tipped his head to the side. "A unique selling point, you could say."

If you only knew, thought Shady, steering a bunch of kids, preteens this time, away from Mandy and toward other objects, aiming to give them a fair shot also.

Period costumes drew some interested glances from the girls, at least, equipment that trappers once used more fascinating for the boys. There was Native jewelry too, coins, china, silver and glass, and a Linotype machine that dated from 1906, upon which the *Mason Observer* was once printed. Annie had taught both Ray and Shady the narrative concerning more significant pieces, which Shady recited now, embellishing it only a little with some insights of her own. The energy attached to most of the artifacts that had made it upstairs was, on the whole, faint, wanting attention but not seeking to dominate Shady's mind—the information she received being shadowy as opposed to sharp-edged. She was able to pick up an emotion here and there rather than being overwhelmed by it: the joy at receiving a piece of jewelry from a lover, perhaps, or the concern etched into a surviving and much-loved family object from the Great Depression, or the wristwatch of a US airman who had borne witness to the bombing of Japan in 1944.

Like other kids that had attended the museum recently, glances kept returning to Mandy, to what was magnetic in her. Even so, Shady's audience listened attentively enough, the teacher who'd brought them nodding his head approvingly at the impromptu—for the museum staff, at any rate—history lesson his pupils were being given. Getting into her stride, Shady was enjoying herself, loving how she could combine her past ambition of teaching with more recent aspirations, the kids completely engrossed and firing questions at her: *Does the Mason Observer still exist? When was gold first discovered in Idaho? Was life for everyone much harder back then? It looks like it. Even people with money. What do you mean there were no dishwashers?*

There were nine in her group, nine in Annie's and nine in Ray's. As they moved from section to section, Shady tried to keep up with their inquisitiveness, enjoying too how much their positive energy lifted the atmosphere, allowing them to touch certain exhibits, laughing at their screwed-up noses as they handled a purse made of crocodile skin that was at least one hundred years old, or tried on a traditional snowshoe, comparing it to what was available in the sports stores now. It was all good fun, all educational, a boom of laughter from Ray in the distance showing he was having a good time too, while Annie had her group hunched over a glass cabinet full of curiosities as she pointed to each in turn.

So absorbed was Shady in what she was doing that she barely registered two of her charges were whispering. Kids did that kind of thing all the time; it didn't concern her. But it took even longer to notice something else: that after a while, the whispering had stopped, and her group of nine had become less.

Shady frowned. "Two of you are missing. Anyone know where they've gone?"

The remaining kids looked at each other, then shrugged.

"O-kay," Shady said, stretching the word out in a puzzled manner before glancing over at Annie's and Ray's groups and performing a head count. Nothing untoward there. They had nine each, which meant two were still unaccounted for.

Excusing herself, she dashed over to the teacher. Ed his name was, Ed Owens. Perhaps he would know of their whereabouts.

"Hello," he said as Shady approached him, large brown eyes containing as much eagerness as a puppy. "Gotta thank you for this tour. It's all going great, isn't it?"

"Yeah, it is. The kids are really nice. Thanks for bringing them along."

"Places like this bring the past to life. There's so much interesting stuff here, *unusual* stuff—you know, besides Mandy, I mean. And I like the personal touch, the way you interact with the kids. It really gets them going. Yeah, it's great. All great."

"Thanks," Shady repeated before getting to the point. "Two boys, Aiden and Christopher, if I recall correctly, were in my group. They…um…well, did they ask you if they could use the bathroom or something?"

"Aiden and Christopher?" Ed asked, looking over Shady's head to where the rest of her group stood waiting. "No, they didn't."

"Oh." Shady was nonplussed. Where could the boys have

gone? Ed had been standing by the counter, which was fairly close to the museum's combined entrance and exit, so, trying not to panic, she asked him if he'd seen them heading this way.

"Going out the door, you mean? No way they could have snuck past me."

Something Shady felt only partly relieved by.

Annie had noticed something was wrong. "Shady," she called, "do you need help?"

Before Shady had a chance to answer, however, Annie detached herself from her group and headed their way. Ray, too, joined them.

Quickly, calmly, Shady told them about the two boys, realizing—perhaps belatedly—that they'd been the ones whispering to each other. They'd been doing something else too… What was it? Shady tried to recall. Had they been…pointing?

The memory returned. Yes! They had! They'd been pointing to…

"Shit!" Shady turned her head toward the back of the long hall-like building, to the spiral staircase that led down to the basement. On their tour they'd been very close to it, which was fine; the kids' attention had been on her and what she was saying, or so she'd thought. For two boys, however, those metal treads descending into somewhere unknown had clearly proved irresistible. Again, fine, if it wasn't for what was down there…

Shady broke away from the adults and walked past clusters of children who were now engaged in chatter with each other, her pace quickening until she was practically at a run.

"Shady?"

Calling after her, Ray was no doubt following her too, although she didn't turn to check. What if...what if one of the kids was sensitive to what the basement held?

Just a few steps from the open staircase, she heard something, a noise rising from the depths of the museum, a bloodcurdling wail.

Having reached the top of the stairs, Shady flew down them, her hands sliding along the winding handrail so fast it caused a friction burn. Annie made a point of keeping the lights on in the basement, not wanting objects to fester in the darkness, an attempt to combat what was attached to them, to wear it down, but right now that light seemed to have lost its edge. Its somewhat comforting glow was subdued.

"You did that somehow! You...you tricked me!"

"I didn't! I swear. Why would I want to do that anyway? What's the point?"

The boys came into view. They were at the rear end of the basement, facing each other, accusing each other, one boy lifting his hand and starting to jab at the other.

"You did do it! You tricked me! You stood behind me and pulled a face, a wicked face. That was you in the mirror! Not me."

The mirror?

Her gaze left the warring boys and traveled to the object behind them—the mirror, of course, its dustsheet having been yanked off, the glass within glinting. And there was something else. A shadow? Was that it? Right there, in the mirror. One that lingered when it shouldn't, long after the boys had turned away, that made the hairs on Shady's arms

106

rise and stiffen. It *was* a shadow, the shadow inside us, perhaps, which the mirror drew out, which it magnified.

Finding her voice at last, Shady shouted across to them.

"Come here, boys. Get away from that mirror. Come on, now, come here."

Cajoling words, calm words, but with a distinctive plea in them.

"Boys, will you come here? Please."

The boy who'd been accusing the other, who'd been jabbing the other—Aiden, if Shady remembered correctly—turned his head only briefly to look at her. Christopher did too, but then his eyes were back on his opponent, round and fearful.

As Aiden and Shady's eyes met, Shady could understand the other boy's fear. What had lingered in the mirror was also presenting on his face, just as it had presented on Gina's. It was stuck there, like a mask, hiding what was good, what was innocent about the boy, and maybe not just hiding but attempting to smother it.

Although aware of movement at her back, Shady didn't turn her head.

"What is it? What's happening?" asked Ray.

Annie was with him and no doubt Ed, Annie not asking questions, but trying to take it all in, to understand, just as Shady was doing.

"Boys!" shouted Ed, doing his utmost to capture their attention, but there was too much distance between the adults and the boys to stop what happened next.

Aiden flew at Christopher, his hands held up, such menace, such intent in them.

"What the hell…?" It was Ed again, bewildered.

From the top of the stairs came whispers and bouts of giggling, the children having gathered, not able to see what was happening from their position but feeding off the energy such a conflict had created, the raw-edged excitement of it.

"Aiden, don't. Get off!"

Christopher was pleading with his friend, was begging him to retreat, but Aiden's hands were around his neck now and beginning to squeeze. All the while, he continued to scream at his friend, calling him a liar, a *dirty* liar, a trickster. "It was you in the mirror, not me!"

What had Aiden seen in himself that set him off like this? What...*possibilities?*

Shady, Annie, Ray and Ed bundled forward, Shady still in the lead and reaching the boys a moment before the others. Her hands were outstretched too, and she placed them on Aiden, trying to separate him from the other boy, aware of just how hard Christopher was struggling and that his eyes were bulging, his mouth open as if trying to scream, to plead some more for release, but only able to choke and splutter. Shady considered herself relatively strong, but up against Aiden, a child of no more than twelve, she was proving ineffective, something that baffled her. Aiden was slight, smaller than Christopher, but fury had made him superhuman.

"Shady, move. Let me," Ray insisted, and Shady duly complied, watching, just as Annie and Ed were watching, with something akin to desperation as Ray tackled Aiden.

Helpless. That's what she felt, a bystander, almost as if she were watching a movie. If only it was that and nothing more. She was also aware some children had crept down the metal treads, their eyes on the scene in front of them, more confused now than amused.

"Just…stop it, let him go… You have *got* to let go."

Ray was tall, he was sturdy, and yet he was panting, beads of sweat appearing on his forehead. Slight Aiden was surpassing him in strength, or, rather, whatever possessed Aiden was, a trickster more sinister than his friend could ever be.

She didn't want to look at the mirror. She shouldn't—not now. Her attention should be on the boys only and Ray's efforts to separate them. Perhaps she should wade in again. There was no way Aiden could be a match for them both. Get Ed involved.

She was about to do that, to step forward and urge a stricken Ed to do the same, but her head turned almost of its own accord back to the glinting mirror, to the source of the trouble, the very thing that had encouraged it. The energy attached to it was resilient, embodying a strength of feeling that hadn't yet dissipated. Whoever had looked into it and had felt that way *still* felt that way… The energy had a channel, and therefore something to feed off.

Goldie's energy—the old woman.

Goldie.

As Ray let out a yell of triumph, the mirror cracked.

CHAPTER TEN

A couple of hours had passed since the dustup between Aiden and Christopher, but Shady was still shaking, something that hadn't escaped Annie's and Ray's attention.

"This has been quite a day for you," Annie remarked, eyeing her sympathetically.

The mirror had remained intact, but a long, jagged crack had appeared from top to bottom just as Ray prized Aiden off Christopher, Ed rushing forward to catch Christopher before he could collapse to the ground. The fact that the mirror had cracked at that precise moment was further troubling Shady. Like it was mocking the triumph.

After the incident, with Ed consoling Christopher, Annie had crossed over to Aiden, a boy who looked, if such a thing was possible, even more upset than the one he'd attacked, who was staring at his hands as if they were something quite apart from him. Annie had talked to him, her voice low and soothing. She'd then reached out for him and, just as the other boy was sobbing in his teacher's arms, he'd clung to Annie and sobbed in hers. Shady, meanwhile, had grabbed the dustsheet and thrown it over the mirror, not sure that Annie or Ray had noticed the full extent of what had transpired.

Before Ed and his class of schoolchildren left the

building, he'd taken the other adults aside, issuing a strict warning for his charges to stay by the entrance of the museum while he did so, Aiden and Christopher assigned friends to flank and look after them.

"The boys..." he began, still red-faced and flustered, "they're not bad boys, not at all. Mischievous, yes. Occasionally. Certainly, they shouldn't have snuck off like that, but—" he paused, still trying to explain it to them and, no doubt, himself "—I guess kids will be kids, and there's something about basements, isn't there? They're tantalizing."

There *was* something about the basement at Mason Town Museum, Shady felt like saying—or, rather, what it housed—but she resisted, allowing Annie to answer instead.

"Children will be children, I agree. I'll also admit that we should have a barrier across the stairs, one that says 'Private,' and I'll rectify that as soon as I'm able to. But, Mr. Owens, just because we were giving the children a tour doesn't mean that you shouldn't have kept a keen eye on them, especially those you describe as...mischievous. They remain your responsibility, not mine."

A light bulb went on in Shady's head. Annie was shifting the blame, not because she was one to shy from ownership but because she wanted to move the emphasis from what the basement contained and the energy that existed there, that could influence the impressionable, the mirror in particular.

Ed was definitely curious about the mirror and why it had prompted such a reaction, but...after Annie's barely disguised threat—that Ed had been idling by the counter, on his phone mostly, glad of a few easy working hours while others took care of his class—he let the matter drop. Instead, he thanked Annie, rather profusely, gathered the kids and beat a retreat.

Questions, however, were dominant in Annie's and Ray's minds, especially when Shady told them that the mirror had cracked—and precisely *when* it had. On hearing that, rather than venture back toward the counter and begin locking up for the day, all returned to the basement, staying close to the bottom of the staircase while they considered the events that had so recently taken place.

There were many items in the basement, ranging from small to large. They called to Shady, not specifically wanting her attention but anyone's, none more so than the mirror. That she'd found it independently of Annie, brought something so dark into the fold, made her feel guiltier still. When she apologized, Annie was dismissive.

"It's a problem that needs dealing with. That's all there is to it."

A problem that was now theirs, Glenda Staines having done her stint.

Ray was the first one to say what was on everyone's lips: "What now?"

Annie raised an eyebrow. "What indeed."

"I need to look into it again."

Both Annie and Ray turned toward Shady as she forced these words through gritted teeth. In all honestly, it was the last thing she wanted to do, but in the absence of any other plan, it seemed like the only option available.

"Shady…" Annie said as Shady walked toward the mirror, but when her voice trailed off, Shady understood why. To go on to say what she'd likely intended—*you really don't have to do this*—although true to some degree, wouldn't offer any solutions. And solutions were what the newly formed museum staff were all about: finding out about something, understanding it, and that understanding, that validation, hopefully helping to subdue it.

Just a few steps from the mirror, Shady's determined strides ended. Ray was close behind her, as was Annie, and she could feel their energy too, strengthening her own.

All she had to do was reach out and remove the dustsheet, look into the mirror again and try to see the face that had looked into it years before, the girl or woman who'd poured all her hatred, anger and pain into it, that imprint remaining long after she'd walked away.

Shady's hand shook at the prospect of revisiting evil, but therein lay the issue. Was it truly evil she'd witnessed? Could it be defined as simply as that? Evil was complex, multilayered, not just a product of nature; nurture had a part to play in it too. Events in life—unfair events, unfortunate—could mold you into something you otherwise were not. And it could happen to anyone, because that depth of feeling, that variety, was all there in every person's heart, each emotion a tectonic plate and constantly shifting. That's what frightened Shady most: what she, too, was capable of.

"Shady, would you rather I did it?" asked Ray, sweet Ray, who considered himself not as susceptible as her. But it was untrue. Aiden had proven that. A kid, a preteen, but already darkness had formed in his heart, the mirror able to pick up on it.

"I'm okay," she replied, her hand inching closer.

"We're surrounded in white light," Annie assured her.

113

"Nothing can harm us. The light is stronger than the dark. Always."

"Always," Shady repeated, her hand making contact with the dustsheet at last and beginning to pull. Off it came, little by little, the wicker-and-cane frame the first thing revealed, but soon the mirror itself would be too. Would what she saw in it this time be worse than any Candyman with a hook for a hand, ready to impale you? Yes, worse, because it attacked all the complexities you were comprised of and apparently knew your soul.

The dustsheet was off, the mirror exposed. There wasn't just her reflection in it, but Ray's and Annie's too, on either side of her.

Her eyes flickered to their reflections first—they looked normal, themselves—and then returned to her own face. That was where the crack was, running from top to bottom, straight through her reflection and dividing it. One half was her—definitely her—her eye brown, her hair long and straight, her skin its usual dark tone. That was fine, all good. But the other half…

"Oh shit…"

"Shady?"

She glanced at Ray and registered his concern before being drawn back to her own face, the other half. The side where the eye was not just dark but black, where half her lip was twisted and her skin raw and puckered.

Good wolf, bad wolf.

It was Kanti's voice in her head.

What do you mean, Kanti? I don't understand.

You do. Good wolf, bad wolf. The choice is yours.

* * *

Lisa Marie had said she'd be in touch, and she was true to her word.

Annie had decided that enough was enough with the mirror for that day; it was time to close the museum and for everyone to return to their respective homes. Shady had, of course, recounted what had happened while looking in the mirror, Annie nodding emphatically all the while.

"Your grandmother's quite right," she said, "we do have to choose our side, and we have, you, me and Ray. We fight on the side of the light. Saying that, the darkness is seductive. It can look like the easier choice, but ultimately it will eat your soul."

It had startled Shady when she'd said that. They were such dramatic words, such...*un-Annie* words. Even Ray had looked surprised, but Annie shrugged and turned away, denying any opportunity for further questioning. Before heading back out into the cold, Shady had gone up to Mandy, kissed two fingers, and pressed them against the glass case, feeling the doll both yearn for such a gesture and recoil from it. She and Ray then drove back to Idaho Falls in their respective cars, planning to fit in a drink in The Golden Crown before home.

It was there, while Shady was nursing a Coke, that a message came through from Lisa Marie, Shady grabbing her phone from the table in front of her and reading aloud for Ray's benefit too:

Hi Shady, the woman you wanted to know about isn't called Goldie. Her name's Joan Parker, and she's 67 years old. She lives in Idaho Falls but on the outskirts. Not sure of the area, but I looked at it on Google Maps, and it's just over the Snake River, close to the airport. Seems like she not only lives on her own but is on her own completely, as no next of kin has been found. She's alive, Shady, but in pretty bad shape. Right now, she's in a coma. I know you feel bad about what happened to her, but it's not your fault. Accidents happen. I can most likely get you in to see her, just for a few minutes.

Her eyes lingering on that last sentence, Shady's back straightened.

"I can see her," she breathed, feeling a little like the Mandy doll herself now, both yearning for and appalled by the prospect. She turned to Ray. "What time is it?"

"Late, nearly eight o'clock. Shady, you can't go now."

"Can't I?" she said, her fingers busy texting a reply.

Not even a couple of minutes later and she got the green light from Lisa Marie, a somewhat surprised Ray offering to drive her to the hospital, picking up Shady's car on the return journey. Shady was about to agree when Brett walked in.

"Hey, guys, good to see ya! You're not going, are you? Come on, I'll buy you a beer."

Ray was about to refuse, but Shady stopped him.

"Ray, it's fine. Stay and have a beer with Brett. Lisa Marie said I'd only be allowed a few minutes anyway. Reckon I've got to play the worried-neighbor card again. That'll be the only way they'll let me in, and it'll probably be just me, not the pair of us."

"You sure?"

"Sure, I'm sure. Stop looking so worried. Oh, hang on…" A grin lit up Shady's face. "You wanna tag along because you get to see Lisa Marie? Is that it?"

At first Ray denied it, but then he started grinning too.

"Technically, this is work, so…"

"Yeah, yeah, I get it. Keep me in the loop, okay, and, ya know, remind her I exist."

"Will do, Ray, will do." Saying goodbye to him and Brett, Shady made her way out of the bar and back to her Dodge. Before firing up the engine, she sat there, taking a few deep breaths. She had no idea what to expect from her visit to Joan Parker, but she was nervous; she couldn't deny it. Worried, guilty and sad too—the woman was in a coma. What if she didn't recover? Shady could hardly bear to contemplate that possibility, refused to. She'd be all right. She had to be. *Get on with it, Shady.*

After nudging the car into drive, she pulled onto the road. It was so cold, the sprinkling of snow having stopped but the clouds ever threatening. Shady drove in silence with the heater cranked right up, praying all the way for the recovery of the woman and wondering at the sadness she felt, which was quickly becoming the dominant emotion. It was like a weight almost, bearing down upon her chest. Why did she feel this way? It wasn't just for obvious reasons; it felt...deeper than that, more ingrained, tears welling in Shady's eyes, one or two spilling over.

The woman had no next of kin that the police had been able to find. She lived on her own, on the outskirts of town, and she was full of...hatred. That was all Shady knew about her so far, and yet, in the confines of her car, she was crying about her, wanting desperately to see her again and not just due to guilt but something else too. Fascination? Shady had to admit it. The woman fascinated her. The mirror did. And the possible link between shared emotions. Plus, there was Gina to think about and the parallel with her. If there really was a link, then she had to find it, do whatever it took.

The parking lot at the hospital was relatively empty, Shady choosing a space close to the entrance and locking her car before hurrying into the building. Lisa Marie was waiting for her at reception, dressed more casually this time in jeans, sneakers and a pale blue sweatshirt. Her eyes not glowing quite as bright, tiredness danced around their edges.

"Thank you for doing this," Shady said. "I've been so worried."

"It's fine. And this is a good time to visit, actually, as it's relatively quiet here tonight. I've explained to the nurse on duty that you're a worried neighbor, that okay?"

"Uh-huh."

"To be honest, she seemed relieved someone was concerned. And, well, you certainly look the part."

Shady attempted a laugh. "You're right there."

"You're also nervous, aren't you?"

Shady nodded, eliciting a look of sympathy from Lisa Marie. She had the impression that Lisa Marie might have reached out to her at this point, touched her arm in a comforting gesture, but had stopped herself, not wanting to be "read" again.

The two women fell into step with each other, Shady then following her up a flight of stairs and down a series of well-lit corridors to a waiting area just outside the ICU.

"Jeez," Shady said, coming to a standstill. "Just how bad is she?"

"I've already popped in to see her today. She doesn't look bad, not at all, just...like she's asleep. True, her head is bandaged because of the trauma she received, but otherwise there are no cuts or bruises that you can see."

"What's the prognosis, though?"

"At the moment I'm not sure, but it's a condition in the ICU that you err on the positive."

"Where there's life, there's hope, huh?" Or at least there had better be.

In the waiting area, which was comfortably furnished in an array of soothing colors—pinks, yellows and greys, all pastel in shade—Lisa Marie asked Shady to wait while she double-checked with the nurse if it was okay for her to go into the ward.

A few minutes later and she was back, holding the door open and indicating for Shady to come on through. It was quiet within, a corridor linking separate rooms, most of them with glass panels, but Shady was unable to see into them as curtains had been pulled shut for the evening. The only sounds to break the silence were monitors beeping or the soft footsteps of a nurse or doctor as they passed by, clipboards or bottles of meds in hand.

Lisa Marie led her to a room at the far end of the corridor, three or four yards past the nurse's desk. "She's in there." Lisa Marie's voice was barely above a whisper. "Would you like me to accompany you, or should I wait out here?"

Shady didn't want to go in alone; she wanted to turn and run, forget about Joan or Goldie or whoever she was and mirrors with jagged cracks down them. In fact, she didn't just want to turn and run, she was suddenly desperate to. It took a supreme effort to not only stay where she was but respond to Lisa Marie's question.

"I'll be okay."

"Sure." And now Lisa Marie did reach out, just briefly, her touch warm and reassuring, Shady wanting it to linger, to combat some of the fear that had risen up.

Lisa Marie retreated, however, Shady taking another deep breath as she pushed the door open.

You're a bad wolf, Goldie.

The question was, how bad?

CHAPTER ELEVEN

Fuck him. He's no use. Never has been. She left him, and so will I, in this dump of a house, in this dump of a neighborhood. Will he care? No. He's like her. Never cares a damn thing about anyone, or he cares the wrong way. I have to get out. Escape.

The woman whose hand Shady held—Joan Parker—looked so small lying there in that hospital bed, hooked up to various machines. She looked…frail. But that was now. When she was young, she'd been someone quite different.

Her eyes were closed, and her lips couldn't move, but nonetheless she had a story to tell, and when their skin had first made contact, Shady's fingers closing around hers, the visions—the *insight*—had been intense, quickly engrossing her. The girl Joan had been was every bit as determined as the girl Lisa Marie had been.

Don't care if there's nowhere to go, I'm still going. I swear if he looks at me that way again, if his hands reach out, grubby fingers stained with nicotine… No! I'll sleep on the streets, it don't matter. Take my chances. Damn him! And her too, for leaving me like she did, with him. Where is she? I could try to find her. Where would a woman like her go?

At first Shady had thought Joan—or Joanie, the name she was getting now—was talking about a husband or a lover. It took a little while to work out it was her parents, one of whom she was leaving and the other who'd already left her, who'd disappeared. Joanie wanted to find her momma but had no idea where she'd gone.

Not gonna find her! Don't want her! Hate her. Hate him.

How quickly she changed her mind, descending into hatred that was almost pure. Strange to describe it as that, but it was true. This woman, this *girl*, had pure hatred running through her veins, and it burned like fire.

A story. So much to tell, to extract, Shady getting somewhere at last, but then it changed as if…as if the woman had realized what was happening, like she was fighting back against Shady's efforts, angry about it, furious, seeking to stop it at any cost.

"I'm sorry," Shady began. "It's just…I'm trying to help—"

It was as though any further words were snatched from Shady's mouth, as if her mind was seized too, this woman able to penetrate just as Shady could, twisting the visions, manipulating them, her fingers grabbing back when before they'd been limp.

You want to know about hatred? I'll show ya!

Evil was a blackened thing; it was a pit into which she was being pushed, falling deeper and deeper into a cauldron of agony and hopelessness.

There was a cacophony, high-pitched screams and grunts so low they were guttural. There was pleading and begging and cruel, cruel laughter. Faces. So many that Shady felt like she was being attacked by them, each one devoid of any trace of happiness or lightness of being—misery was all they knew, that somehow nourished them.

Hands clawed at Shady too, not just the older woman's hand but a mass of them, ripped and yellowed fingernails sharp and tearing at her, tearing *into* her, aiming for her beating heart, wanting to squeeze it to pulp.

"Stop it! Stop this now!"

Shady was sure she'd shouted these words, screamed them, even. Someone was bound to hear her—Lisa Marie, who was waiting outside the room. She'd burst through the doors and save her, but no one was forthcoming. Had her voice, so wracked with shock, been nothing more than a ragged whisper?

"You have to stop!"

Just like a boy should have been no match for her and Ray, a woman in her late sixties, in a coma, should have been no competition either. Easily, Shady should be able to break the hold that Joan Parker had over her, sever the connection. She couldn't endure any more of these visions. What was the woman trying to do to her? Kill her?

You're an old lady. How are you doing this?

If only Annie were here, and Ray too; they'd help her. White light. That's what Annie would say. *Send out a tide of it. Push the darkness back. The light is so much stronger.*

Did this woman even know what the light was?

Goldie. You were called Goldie once, weren't you?

"Aargh!"

Shady screamed as the woman's grip became tighter still.

That's it! That's my name! Who I really am.

No longer falling, it was as though Shady was on a carousel, a nightmare ride, shadows riding beside her. And all of them like Goldie, cut from the same cloth.

A group that had found each other, that had banded

together. Like calling to like.

The shapes were drifting closer to Shady, reaching out…

"This isn't real, none of it. You can't hurt me."

How they laughed at those protests, Shady trying harder still to weave a blanket of light around herself, to follow Annie's advice but failing. In the presence of what was so dark, so…merciless, it was just too difficult to summon.

You've got to try, Shady!

"Goldie, let go of me!"

The voice that answered back was scathing:

But you wanted to know! That's why you came.

"I did, yes. But only to help, I swear it."

I don't want your help!

"You do! You can't go on like this."

You could never help.

"Joan. Joanie. Goldie. Keep those others away from me. Don't let them hurt me."

Oh, we're gonna hurt you, all right, real bad! That's what evil does, you see? It goes around and around. Once you're on the ride, ain't no getting off. You get stuck there.

"Okay, okay." How she cursed the tremor in her voice. "You're hateful, I get it. But…you're also terrified, and…and that's why you're doing this. You want me to be terrified too. You don't want me to see because…" She floundered. Why didn't she want her to see? *Think, Shady. Think!* "Because you're ashamed, that's it. So full of shame."

NOOOOOOOOO!

The woman's denial was only in her head, but that didn't make it any less ear-shattering. Shady feared for her own sanity so much that it gave her the strength to finally retrieve her hand, the effort so immense that she tipped back in her chair, sending both her and it crashing to the floor. *Shit! Shit! Shit!*

As Joan's denial continued to echo in her mind, as it bounced off every wall in the room, growing louder, Shady scrambled to her feet. She kicked the chair away and started to retreat, only dimly aware that a door had opened behind her, that someone was responding at last.

"Shady? Are you okay?"

It was Lisa Marie, but Shady ignored her, focused only on the woman lying in the bed, a woman still silently screeching.

Run, little girl. While you can!

Still Shady begged her. *What are you so afraid of?*

Run or see if I don't send the darkness after you.

"Shady!" Lisa Marie's voice was more urgent now. "What was the commotion in here? What did you do?"

Finally, Shady faced her.

"What did *I* do? It was *her*."

CHAPTER TWELVE

"Jeez, Shady, that's terrible. There's no way you can see her again."

"I have to, Ray. I have to find out more. It's all connected—her, the mirror, and Gina's mirror—I swear it."

"But she said she'd send the darkness after you!"

"She won't. She can't. We've got the light on our side, remember?"

"Jeez," Ray repeated. "She sounds like a real wrong 'un."

"I think she is, or was, or whatever. But, Ray, this is Annie's mission, what she set out to do. This is what we signed up for." When, on the other end of the phone, Ray remained quiet, she added, "Joan's nowhere near as frail as she looks. She's a scary lady, that's for sure, but she's also frightened."

"No wonder! If she's at death's door, she probably thinks hell's waiting for her."

"Maybe. Maybe not. There could be another reason too."

There was sarcasm in Ray's laugh. "What other reason could there possibly be?"

"I don't know, but I have to find out. It's not just her wellbeing I'm thinking of, it's Gina's, because although Gina doesn't realize it yet, not fully, the darkness is on her case too. We have to solve this problem. I really don't think we've got much choice."

Ray sighed heavily. "Okay, okay. No one ever said this job was gonna be easy, but, man, does a stint at a diner or a supermarket look good right now! What's the plan?"

"Lisa Marie has managed to find out her full address…"

Poor Lisa Marie. She'd gotten Shady out of Joan Parker's hospital room, taking time to upright the chair before the pair of them scurried back to the soothing atmosphere of the ICU waiting area. It was empty, so they could talk there in private, Shady guessing she owed her an explanation.

"I…um…kinda tuned into Joan too."

"And?"

"And…" Again, Shady had hesitated. "She's got a colorful past."

"You saw it?"

"I saw echoes of it." Which had been enough, for the time being, at least.

"Shady." Lisa Marie had reached out and touched her, something Shady had been grateful for, hating to think she'd put her off, that Lisa Marie would see her as some kind of witch or a voodoo queen to be avoided at all costs. "You look really shaken."

"Honestly? I am. Thanks, you know, for getting me out of there. For getting me in there in the first place. For…not being put off by me."

Lisa Marie had been quiet, but only for a moment. "Are you reading me again?"

"Nope. Too wiped out, I think."

"Come on, let's go to the café, grab some coffee."

Once there, they'd sat on chairs opposite each other,

Shady also grateful for the warmth of her coffee, feeling so cold after what she'd seen, visions meant to scare her away.

Just like Ray was asking now, so had Lisa Marie: "What's the plan?"

Shady had shrugged. "If I could see her again, that would be some kinda plan. But it's like she wants to block me."

"People don't appreciate being read, I suppose."

"I get that, but there's something in her past…" Shady had wondered then: Should she tell Lisa Marie the true nature of her job at the museum, about the mirror that now had a crack in it, and of Gina's mirror too, the parallels and how Joan Parker fit into all this? She decided against it. It sounded mad, and, as friendly as Lisa Marie was being, she likely thought Shady insane enough already. "I just want to help her," she said instead. "I believe she needs help."

"I don't under—"

"No, I know you don't," Shady rushed on. "But it really is all that I want. Look, I'm not crazy, I'm really quite ordinary and down-to-earth."

"Aside from your ability."

She nodded. "Well, yeah, aside from that."

There was silence before Shady spoke again.

"Joan could die."

"As I said, the ICU prefers a more positive approach—"

"But she could."

"The doctors won't admit it, not yet, but yes, of course she could."

"And then there really would be no way to help her."

"Maybe she's happy with that.

"And maybe she's not."

"Like I said, what's the next step?"

"To find out her exact address."

"With a view to doing what, exactly?"

Shady shrugged again. "I guess I could visit her house, look through the windows, touch the walls, retrace her footsteps to the front door, basically try and learn more about her."

"You're not thinking of breaking and entering, are you?"

"I'm no criminal."

Lisa Marie finished her coffee and then placed the disposable cup on the table in front of her. "You know things about me—like you said, you can read me. I don't feel particularly happy about that. The past is the past, and that's where I'd like it to stay. I dragged myself up and set my own goals. I have parents, but this is my life, and it's me who'll choose how to live it. I'm my own person. I've had to be. I'm better than them." As she said this, her voice cracked slightly, but quickly she regained control. "There's a saying, isn't there, that what doesn't kill you makes you stronger. I tend to think that's true. I've suffered, Shady. Maybe Joan Parker's suffered too. I've already told you there've been no next of kin found, no family, basically. I'm not sure about friends, but this woman seems to be on her own. I guess what I'm trying to say is, I believe you, and that your intent is good."

"I can't read everyone," Shady was at pains to reiterate. "It's just…certain people."

Lisa Marie laughed. "Should I be flattered?"

Shady smiled too. "There's no need to worry, not where you're concerned."

"Okay. Like the ICU people, I think I'll err on the positive regarding that. So, yeah, you've got this insight, a *psychic* ability, it would seem, but I've got something too, a well-honed instinct. I've had enough bullshit in my life, so my internal detector is very well-developed. I don't want to have to endure any more of it. Ever."

"Lisa Marie—"

"No, wait, let me speak. I like you, Shady. I really like you. And I know you're genuine. As long as we don't stray too far into criminal realms, I'll help you with whatever you need to do. I'll find out her address. And, well, we can take it from there."

We. Her use of the word was not lost on Shady. Lisa Marie wanted to get involved. And she liked Shady, *really* liked her, Shady feeling both confused and grateful of that.

They'd parted soon after, Lisa Marie promising to deliver the goods, which she had, less than an hour later, via text. That's when Shady had phoned Ray and told him what they had to do.

"We gotta go there, Ray, to Joan Parker's house."

"It's after eleven."

"Doesn't matter. We have to go. Now. Oh, and Ray?"

"Yeah?"

"Lisa Marie's coming with us."

* * *

With the three of them in the car, they ventured out of Idaho Falls and into its outskirts, Shady at the wheel and Ray graciously riding in the back so Lisa Marie could have the front passenger seat. Boy, he'd been excited to see her again, chattering excitedly with Shady before picking her up but a little subdued afterward—succumbing to nerves, most likely, or trying to play it cool. Lisa Marie had been polite to him, but, Shady had to admit, most of the girl's focus was on her rather than Ray, including thanking her for being able to tag along.

"Sorry about the late hour," Shady replied.

"No problem," Lisa Marie assured her. "Guess you gotta strike while the iron is hot. Besides"—she glanced sideways at Shady, her smile bright even in the dark confines of the car—"it's kinda exciting. I'm as interested in Joan Parker as you guys now."

Shady had already briefed Ray about the conversation she'd had with Lisa Marie, about what the girl knew and what she didn't, and that she'd placed her trust in their motive, which was a desire to help Joan. At Lisa Marie's words just then, he'd shuffled a little in his seat but hadn't commented, whereas Shady continued to contemplate her use of the word *exciting*. She could hardly be blamed for thinking that, but if she knew the true extent of what Shady had experienced while in the hospital room with Joan, she might think again. Shady was far from excited; she was anxious about what she was doing but felt it necessary. The mystery surrounding the mirrors was plaguing her, and she needed to understand what was behind it, just as she'd done with Mandy.

The GPS showed they were close to their destination, only a couple more miles to go. They certainly were on the outskirts of Idaho Falls, an area that Shady had never been to before—farther out than the airport, with houses in existence but few and far between, as were stores and businesses. Really, there was just a whole lotta...nothing.

"Ray," she said, "have you been here before?"

"Nope. Look around. No reason to, is there?"

"None at all," Shady agreed.

The roads were largely deserted, cars parked here and there but most of them looking as if they'd been abandoned. The whole neighborhood did, come to think of it, although lights behind windows showed at least some evidence of life. It was almost as if this place hid from plain view, and, in turn, so did the people who chose to live there. Which again begged the question: Why?

"Her house should be coming up soon," Lisa Marie said, "in the next few yards. Four twenty-nine Sandborne. Yeah, look, that's it, I think," she added, pointing.

"What a dump," Ray said from the back.

He was right about that. Of all the run-down properties they'd passed, this was by far the worst. A single-story house with a porch out front, there was no cute rocking chair to sit on; instead, boxes were stacked on top of each other and no doubt bursting with junk. The property truly looked as if it should be condemned. A quick glance at Lisa Marie showed that she, too, was shocked someone could actually live there, taking it upon herself to assure them that she'd double-checked the woman's address.

"Do you think it's safe to even get out of the car?" she asked.

"You don't have to—" Shady began, but Lisa Marie interrupted her.

"Are you getting out of the car?"

"Yes, of course."

"Then so am I."

"Don't forget about me," Ray reminded them. "I'll protect ya."

Shady also scanned the neighborhood. "Doesn't seem to be anyone lurking."

"Just us three amigos," Ray said even more chirpily. If he was at all nervous, he was doing a good job of hiding it, again, most likely for Lisa Marie's sake. Shady winced a little inside at all the effort he was going to, especially as Lisa Marie appeared oblivious.

"Okay, come on," she said, shoving the door open, the coldness of the night air momentarily stealing her breath. "Shit, it's freezing out there."

"I don't know how you guys stand it," said Lisa Marie.

"We're born to it," Ray said. "Don't you get snow in California?"

"Not in San Francisco usually, but in the Sierra Nevadas they do, around Mammoth Lakes and Mount Whitney, a whole ton of it."

"Ever been to the Sierra Nevadas?" Ray asked, coming to a standstill beside her on what was supposed to resemble a sidewalk. "Family vacations, that kinda thing?"

Lisa Marie's reply was curt, as Shady knew it would be. "No."

Lisa Marie was actually the first one to venture forward, pulling a dark green puffer jacket tight around her as she did. Ray caught up with her, Shady at the rear.

"Remind me again why we're doing this," Ray muttered, but the question was merely rhetorical. He knew well enough why—they *had* to—but even so, close to midnight and being in a previously unexplored, run-down part of town made her feel antsy too.

Lisa Marie, however, was braver than both of them.

She reached the front steps to the porch and, without

hesitation, started to climb.

"She lives alone, right?" Ray checked.

"Apparently. There are no lights on inside," Shady said.

"Just making sure no one's gonna come rushing out the door and shoot us, that's all."

"This job, eh?" Shady tried to joke.

"Yep, fraught with danger, supernatural and otherwise."

"We'll be careful, Ray."

Standing on the porch, in amongst the clutter—which not only included boxes but items of furniture that had long outgrown their use—Lisa Marie looked around her. "All this," she said, "resembles her state of mind."

Shady nodded. That would make sense.

"So, if it's like this outside, what it's like on the inside?" Ray wondered.

"It'll be worse," Lisa Marie answered. "No doubt about it."

In an attempt to put that suspicion to the test, Shady pushed her way through the debris to a window. While she peered in, Ray looked outward, no doubt endeavoring to make sure there was no one nearby who would spot them. Thankfully, no houses were immediately opposite or adjacent. It was just them…and the house that Joan Parker lived in.

Her forehead touching the windowpane, Shady lifted both hands so she could block out the glare from a nearby security light. There were sheer curtains at the window, and, although tattered, they still made it impossible to see beyond without any light from inside. Lisa Marie was clearly having the same problem at the window on the other side of the door, finally taking a step back.

"Can't see a damn thing," she said.

The porch wrapped around the side of the house, Ray suggesting they follow it. One after the other, they picked their way through yet more rubbish, Shady imagining the critters that probably lived amongst it, rats probably, and wondering whether they might disturb a nest, causing hundreds to come scurrying out, rushing over their feet, climbing legs, biting... As well as trepidation, a huge wave of sadness swept over her, an all-too-familiar feeling lately. She couldn't help it, she felt sad for Joan Parker, responsible for her, and marveled that she should—that a woman so full of hatred should prompt that.

"I've got to get in there," she said, more to herself than the others. Even so, Lisa Marie glanced toward Shady, a slight frown on her face. "It's the only chance I have of understanding her," Shady continued, her voice just a little louder.

Lisa Marie, who'd been leading the troop, reached the back door, her hand, after just a moment's hesitation, reaching out to clasp the door handle.

"Lisa Marie?" Shady questioned. Even Ray looked surprised by what she was doing. Lisa Marie had probably already broken the law by sharing a patient's address, but then visiting the empty property while that person lay in the hospital was something else entirely.

The door—already in a decrepit state—yielded readily to her touch and creaked open.

"I thought you said you wanted nothing to do with breaking and entering," Shady said, not just stunned by her actions but also by the fact that the door wasn't locked. They'd already established this was a tough neighborhood.

Wasn't Joan Parker afraid of who'd come calling, or was she past caring? Would anyone in their right mind do so anyway?

Lisa Marie answered while stepping inside. "You want to understand the woman?"

"Yeah, sure—"

"It's hardly breaking and entering if the door's unlocked."

"It's trespassing, though," countered Ray, looking decidedly uncertain, especially as at that moment they heard the sound of a cop car's siren, but it was far in the distance, just an echo, really, the police called to some other incident elsewhere in the city.

Before going any farther, Lisa Marie stopped and looked at them fully. "Shady, Ray," she said, "what we're doing, it's for the purpose of good, right?"

Shady glanced briefly at Ray, who in turn nodded at her.

"Yes," Shady answered, her eyes back on their intrepid friend. "I've said that it is."

"Then that's good enough for me." Facing forward, she walked farther into the gloom of the house, Shady and Ray, who were still at the door, gasping on hearing her next words:

"Shit, this place. It's full of mirrors!"

CHAPTER THIRTEEN

I love it here! I belong! It's such a strange feeling, to belong, to feel…accepted. He makes me feel accepted. Doesn't matter I'm not the only one for him. He loves me. He said so. Last night. He made me feel so special. Ain't ever felt like that before—like I mattered. He says I'm different. I'm one of them. He wants me to join them. There are other girls too. We'll be a family. A real family. We've chosen each other, we who are different. Together we're strong. This is our time. A good time. I'm happy. Never been happy either. He says he hasn't been happy, not 'til he met us. This is new, exciting, incredible!

I ran, and it was the right thing to do because look where I arrived.

Lisa Marie was right. Inside Joan Parker's house there were many, many mirrors. Some lying around on surfaces, others hanging on the wall. They were every shape and every size, including jagged shards of mirror that had no frame at all, that looked lethal. All had one thing in common, to Shady, at least: they told a story, albeit in fragments.

"It stinks in here!"

Ray was the one complaining, but it couldn't be disputed—the smell was of all things dirty, all things old, the interior, as Lisa Marie had predicted, worse than it was outside, cluttered with junk, plastic bags as well as boxes filled with rubbish, and not just rats amongst them, there were bound to be spiders too. If Lisa Marie was also right about it being a reflection of its resident's mind, Joan Parker was tortured indeed.

When they'd entered the house, they'd stepped into a short hallway, no carpet beneath their feet; kicking junk out of the way revealed only floorboards. There was a semblance of a kitchen to the left of them and a bedroom to the right. Shady never got that far, however, remaining stuck in the hallway, looking into one mirror and then another—the woman's life having to be pieced together.

As Lisa Marie and Ray had started exploring, Shady had looked into the first mirror and sensed not something unpleasant but…hopeful, that of a new life unfolding. The girl that Joan Parker used to be had escaped from an unhappy home, that was evident, ending up somewhere that made her more content. Shady was curious: Who was the person that made her feel part of this new family? An odd family if she were not his only partner but one of many. Also, how old had Joan been? Or rather, how young?

Bolstered by this experience, relieved that looking into her past was not as traumatic as she'd feared it to be—not yet, at any rate—Shady looked into another mirror, Lisa Marie and Ray still poking around. The next mirror was hanging haphazardly, as they all tended to be. She not only looked into it but gripped it too.

A new person. A new identity. Here you can be whoever you wanna be. You can be free. "Just follow me," he says. Like the Messiah, the Son of God, and we are his disciples. I'd do anything for him! Anything! And he'd do anything for us. Our family, the other girls included, is devoted. I'm supposed to love them, and I do, but...some of them, they're jealous of me. I'm younger. I'm pretty. Not all of them are pretty. Does he tell them they are anyway? If he does, it's only because he's kind. That's what he is: the very embodiment of kindness and love. There are more joining us. Every day they come. Other girls. Some guys too. The girls serve the guys, but that's the way it should be, he tells us. It's the natural order of things. He speaks only the truth, and I admire him for it. He held me tonight. Just me. He loved me until I thought I'd go mad with longing. And then he said I was to love the other men too, in that special way. Doesn't matter that I only want him. His will be done. In all things.

"Shady?" Ray was back by her side. He looked...unsettled. Nervous. "This place," he continued, "these mirrors...what can you see?"

"Ray," Shady whispered, looking over his shoulder and spotting Lisa Marie returning also, "keep your voice down. She doesn't know, remember?"

"All righty, sorry. But...are you okay?"

Something had caught Lisa Marie's eye, and she'd stopped, reaching out to pick it up—a vase, it looked like—turning it over in her hands. Instead of answering Ray, Shady took the opportunity to look into another mirror, intrigued by these remnants, these random scraps of life, which in some ways was like listening to a snatched conversation.

This mirror was different from the other two. Its backing was tarnished, sprayed gold once upon a time; it had since blistered and peeled. They hadn't turned any lights on upon entering the property—the last thing they wanted was to attract attention—but the night wasn't overly dark, the nearby security lamp providing illumination enough.

Shady stared into the mirror, intending to do so for just a few seconds, enough to snatch another snippet of information and learn more about this new family. When she'd looked into previous mirrors, her reflection hadn't changed as such, but it was as though she'd seen beyond it, into not just another life but another world.

This time, perhaps because of how mottled the glass was, like the glass in the cane-and-wicker mirror, her face appeared darker than before, and blurred too.

UGLY!

The word seemed to be screamed at her, so hard that it was like being slapped across the face. Visibly she flinched and stepped back, heard Ray's concern as he spoke her name. Lisa Marie had noticed too, but Shady, transfixed, could not turn her head.

The world. People. Me.

All of it…so ugly.

Jesus, the vehemence behind those words! The same words that had entered Shady's head while looking at the oval mirror in the basement of Mason Town Museum, the *exact* same. What had happened to hope, and the wonder of acceptance?

Hate you. Me. Hate that I'm here. That there's nowhere else to go…

"Joan, what happened?" Shady whispered, unable to care if Lisa Marie heard now.

Nowhere to go. Not me. Can't be me. Have to stay. Be someone else.

"Who, Joan? Do you mean Goldie?"

HATE! HATE! HATE!

Shady yelped. Again, each word was like a blow, filled with such loathing. *You're like a pendulum, swinging from one emotion to the other.* Unstable. Yes, that much was clear. And so, so damaged. She had no one to talk to. Was that why she had a fascination with mirrors? An obsession? No one to tell her innermost feelings to…except herself.

Able to turn her head at last, Shady swung around. Both Ray and Lisa Marie were by her side, reaching out to her.

"We should go," Lisa Marie said.

"Come on, Shady," urged Ray. "It's time to quit."

"No!" Her voice was louder than she'd intended it to be, but they had to listen to her. It was time to go, she *wanted* to go, to get out of this grim, sordid ruin of a place, but to leave like this, so confused? What if…what if there was more to learn—something vital, a bigger insight leading to greater understanding? If Annie were here, she'd perhaps force the issue, but she wasn't, only Lisa Marie and Ray, both looking bewildered by Shady and what she was doing: pushing past them, heading toward another mirror…and another…so many memories filling her head, and all belonging to someone else.

There were hands. Shady felt them as though they were on her own body, violating her. *It is your duty to serve!*

Was this some kind of cult Joan had gotten herself involved with?

I love him. Only him. Not these others. What they do to me, to the other girls too… There's no tenderness, none at all. Relax. Enjoy it. I have to try. This is what being part of our family means. At least I'm wanted. I'm serving a purpose. A divine *purpose.*

Divine? It sounded far from that. It was profane. Why did she stay? She had run once. She could run again.

This is the way we live. The only way. Listen to him! To his words. He still loves you. His love is infinite. And you said you'd do anything…

Whirling around, Shady looked from the mirror in front of her to yet another, bent down and picked up a jagged piece from the floor.

As soon as her hands closed around the shard, she heard laughter. A sound that should have inspired relief—it was Joan laughing, wasn't it? But there was an element of something else other than enjoyment—insanity? Was Joan insane?

I love it here! I do! I love him. All of them. My family. This is better. So much better! Happy. How could I have thought otherwise. I wouldn't betray him. Never! This is what I want. Exactly what I want. My family is all I need.

Shady was bewildered. What was going on? The woman traveled between despair and ecstasy, to and fro, to and fro, like a yo-yo bouncing on a piece of string.

The heat of the desert. Limbs. All of us entwined. His hands upon me. His lips. He is the Messiah. A god. Worship him. I do. Don't question him. I won't. You're special. Am I? A kindred spirit. That's why we're together. Like calls to like. Don't question it. Ever.

Shady dropped the mirror, was swaying, she realized, from side to side. Feeling not frightened or confused or sad or betrayed. She was content. Just that. Inhaling deeply, smelling not the rot that had assailed her when first entering the house but something earthier than that, more pungent still.

Voices called to her, but they seemed so far away—Ray's and Lisa Marie's, and another voice too, that of Kanti?

"Stay back. Just wait."

Had she uttered those words or just thought them? She couldn't tell; the world she'd lived and breathed in just a few seconds before was becoming a memory also. This was a different world she'd entered, a world in which harsh lines were no longer straight, in which thick walls were not solid. On the contrary, everything was fluid here, with no dullness at all. It was all so vivid—even in the gloom it was vivid, all the junk that littered the floor and every surface a treasure, the mirrors especially, glinting and catching her eye.

Look into them. Go on. Look and see.

"Shady!"

Aware of the alarm in Ray's voice, and despite the fog she was suspended in, Shady picked up the pace, running into a room and closing the door behind her, then just as quickly dragging over a table to block the door, preventing anyone from following.

There were mirrors in the room. More of them.

Someone to talk to.

That was it: their definite purpose. There was a burst of laughter as she thought this, the same as she'd heard before—utterly devoid of joy.

Talk to me, Joan. Show me who you are.

There was banging on the door and a voice shouting. Ray's, although it sounded distorted, as though reaching her from the far end of a long, long tunnel.

"Shady! What's in the way of the door? Come on, let us in. What's going on?"

A female voice joined in.

"Shady, honey, come on. We have to get you out of there."

And then a whisper, in her head, not her own, although it repeated words she'd used:

Show me who you are.

The mirrors swayed like she was, and each and every one of them had something in them—a shadow? Was that it? Or a facet? Was that more likely? Remnants of a woman that had fractured, and so easily. That was the thing. It was just so easy to shatter.

Are you the same as me?

The whispering in Shady's head was able to drown out the other voices.

No longer swaying but staggering forward, as if she was high, or drunk, or both, Shady reached one of the mirrors, the shadow in it coming forward too, eager to look into her eyes, to reach out to her, mouthing words at her, words that she had also said:

Who are you?

Shady swallowed. *Who am I?*

Like calls to like.

What?

The room swung on its axis as Shady shook her head. "I'm not you! I'm not!"

Good wolf. Bad wolf. There was supposed to be two. But what Shady saw staring back at her—her own face, her own eyes, her cheeks, nose and a mouth that was wide open now, that was emitting a wounded, howling sound—was bad through and through.

CHAPTER FOURTEEN

"What the hell was all that about, Shady?"

A visibly shaken and angry Ray asked this, but right now Shady didn't have the words to tell him, to even begin to explain.

All three of them were back in her car, speeding out of the neighborhood, Ray at the wheel as there was no way Shady could drive. She was shaking too, and her hand was damaged, wrapped in a kitchen cloth and held close to her chest. Neither a big drinker nor a drug taker, all Shady had ever done was a bit of weed; she'd certainly not taken something like LSD. She had friends, however, who'd indulged—Brett, for one, Sam and Teddy Cardenas too, the latter having once described an experience to Shady, the "trip" he'd been on. From the back seat of the car, Shady now recalled what he'd said, finding similarities with what had just happened to her. She'd taken a trip, in that run-down house in a run-down part of town, right into the psyche of Joan Parker—or Goldie, as she'd become, having left home, having escaped, and consequently reinventing herself.

"Shady, are you okay now?"

Lisa Marie's voice was far gentler than Ray's. Both were concerned, Shady knew that, but in Lisa Marie there was no anger, at least.

"I'm so sorry," she muttered in reply, "you know, for what happened."

"What did happen?" Ray still demanded to know. "I had to practically break the living room door down to get to you. She's going to know now that someone's been in her house, if she ever makes it home, that is. You went…wild in there."

She had. She'd not only howled in shock and pain and terror, she'd run at the mirror, desperate to destroy what it had shown her, someone evil and not Joanie this time but herself. A lie! An utter lie. Shady was nice, everybody said so. Heck, she even used that insipid word to describe herself. Cameras didn't lie. Nor did mirrors. But that mirror had. And so she'd run at it and smashed the glass with her bare fist, not even registering at the time the damage that she'd done to herself, the shards that had bitten back, every bit as ravenous as the wolf she'd seen.

She'd then whirled around, as fast as a dervish, intent on destroying the entire room and everything in it, the other mirrors in particular, when Ray, having managed to get the door open at last, rushed inside and stopped her.

Lisa Marie had been close behind him. Although clearly horrified by what Shady had done, she'd grabbed her hand and examined it, then dragged her out of the room to where there was more light pooling from the security light, to get a better look.

"Superficial, I think. But we'll have to make sure. We'll have to go to the hospital."

"I can't!" Shady protested. "She's there!"

"Joan Parker?"

"Yes. Yes. Her. Goldie."

"But we need to see to your hand, make sure there's no glass in those cuts."

"Can't you do it? At your place?"

"I...I..."

"I can't go to the hospital. Not tonight. Please. And I can't go home either. Mom will hit the roof, so will Dad. Can we go back to your place, Lisa Marie? Can you fix it up?"

Lisa Marie hesitated before carefully releasing Shady's hand and rushing into the kitchen. "More fucking mirrors," Shady heard her say, Ray still in the living room, trying to make good the damage there—the sound of more police sirens in the distance perhaps spurring him on since one might be coming for him, after all.

Lisa Marie returned quickly enough, clutching a kitchen cloth, distaste on her face. "It's the only thing I could find. It's not overly clean, but...it'll have to do. You're dripping blood."

"We'll have to clean it up," replied Shady.

"Not now we don't," Lisa Marie said before calling to Ray. "Come on, we're going back to my place."

Ray appeared in the living room doorway. "This mess, though?"

"Can wait," Lisa Marie insisted. "We need to treat Shady's hand. Besides, who's to say it's us responsible? I don't think they'd tolerate video surveillance in this area. It's a case of what goes on in Vegas, stays in Vegas. Without witnesses, no one can prove a thing."

As they entered a more familiar part of Idaho Falls, visions of Goldie and the life she'd fallen into continued to torment Shady, as did the vision she'd had of herself, which had been a deliberate image to taunt her, she knew it, and yet…were the mirrors possessed by energy more intelligent than residual? If they were, it wasn't by someone dead, not this time, but someone living, a woman hanging on to life in a hospital bed, who yet again, in whatever way possible, was trying to discourage Shady from unearthing the truth.

Ray brought the car to a halt at last as Lisa Marie spoke.

"Here we are. That's my apartment block, or at least where I rent a room in an apartment. Gregory will be asleep by now, so we have to be quiet. Don't worry too much, though. He's a great guy with a weed habit. When that man sleeps, he really sleeps."

"A weed habit?" Ray raised an eyebrow. "And he works at the hospital too?"

"Hey, don't judge," Lisa Marie reprimanded. "He works in pediatrics. Just yesterday he had to tell the parents of a twelve-year-old boy that their son wouldn't see thirteen, had to stand by as they sobbed their hearts out. Whatever gets you through having to do stuff like that on a regular basis, you know? And a smoke last thing at night gets him through."

Ray nodded before killing the engine. "Got it," he said, clear remorse on his face.

There were flakes of snow in the air again as they trudged from the car to the apartment block, the three of them riding the elevator three floors, then trudging some more down a long tiled corridor. Once in the apartment, Lisa Marie led them through to the kitchen, where she sat Shady down on a bar stool before rummaging through some cupboards. At last she emerged with a first-aid box, impressively stocked.

Placing it on the countertop, she took Shady's hand in hers and carefully removed the cloth, giving it to Ray with instructions to place it in the trash can.

"I'll take it out later and dump it down the chute. The incinerator's the best place for that piece of rag. I'm just sorry it was the only thing I could think to use, Shady."

"No problem," Shady assured her. "Just as long as I haven't caught botulism from it."

"Can't guarantee that," Lisa Marie said, but she was smiling as she set to work clearing the wound, that smile drawing Ray's gaze to it and finally melting some of his anger.

"Ray," Shady said, "I'm sorry. I know you're mad at me."

"I'm worried." His eyes were back on Shady now. "You locked us out, and you flipped in there, totally. I…God, I was imagining all kinds of things. Not least what Annie will say when she finds out what we've been up to."

"Yeah, Annie won't be impressed, that's for sure. Ow!"

Lisa Marie was the one apologizing now. "I gotta make sure the wound's clean."

"And is it?"

"Yeah, yeah. No need to get the needle and thread out. Butterfly closures will do."

Shady heaved a sigh of relief. "Holy shit, I'm thankful for that."

Ray made them a pot of strong, hot coffee. Once Shady's hand was cleaned and dressed, all three huddled around their cups instead.

"I suppose I'd better explain," said Shady.

Lisa Marie didn't know the full story; would now be the

right time to enlighten her? Did they owe her that much at least for the support she'd shown?

"Shady," Ray said, seeming able to read minds too on this occasion, "I think it's okay…you know…"

Shady nodded and started right at the beginning, with Gina's mirror.

* * *

Shady opened her eyes to see strains of light coming through the bedroom window—not hers, but the window in Lisa Marie's room, where she, Ray and, of course, Lisa Marie had crashed after the three of them had talked into the early hours.

Lisa Marie had already known that Shady could read objects and sometimes people, but not to what degree. Part of Shady was nervous what her reaction might be, but she needn't have worried. Lisa Marie had listened patiently as she'd explained not only about Gina's mirror and the mirror from Pre-loved that was now in the Mason Town Museum basement, and what the museum's function really was, but also what had happened the previous year with a doll called Mandy. There'd been only fascination in her eyes, no reproach, no scorn, and not one ounce of disbelief.

"And Mandy's kept at Mason Town Museum too?" Lisa Marie had asked.

"She is, locked in a glass case. Only me, Ray and Annie have the key."

"You're both extraordinary people," she'd gone on to say, and how Ray had blushed!

"You're pretty great too," he'd mumbled.

"As for Annie, I'd like to meet her. She sounds like quite a character."

"Oh, she's great," Shady agreed. "She's wise, kind...heroic."

"A caretaker in the true sense of the word," Lisa Marie mused.

"A keeper," Ray added, "in every way."

After a slight pause, Lisa Marie nodded toward the fridge. "I'm not a drinker, but there's a cold bottle of wine in there..."

"Guess we could use it," Shady replied, shrugging.

She poured them all a large glass. When that was drained, she suggested opening a bottle of Tennessee whiskey. "It's Gregory's, just like the wine was, but to hell with it. I'll replace them both tomorrow." And they got stuck into that, Lisa Marie then wanting to know more and more, trying, as she put it, to combine science with faith.

"I do believe in the spiritual world," she professed. "I believe there are those that guide us. We can't see them, but if we listen carefully, we can sometimes hear."

At her words, Shady thought of Kanti and the patch of leather in her jeans pocket, the stars crude but distinctive. Her very own guide. What would Kanti make of what Shady had seen in the mirror? She'd dismiss it for the trick it was; there was a certainty in Shady's heart about that. *You're the best of us,* she'd say. *Don't be fooled.*

Shady then went on to tell Ray specifically that some of the words that had formed in her head while staring into the mirrors were exactly the same as those in the basement with the oval mirror. "The memory was the same," she said.

"And you're sure it's not, you know..."

"My own mind embellishing things? Because I'm desperate to make a connection?"

Ray had blushed, making Shady smile.

"Ray, I get it. I know what you're trying to say. But it was the same words, the same emotions, the same...*everything*."

Finally, tiredness had overcome them, and they'd crept into Lisa Marie's room, Shady sharing the double bed with Lisa Marie, Ray sleeping on a makeshift bed on the floor.

It had been cool, like being kids again, camping out, seriousness and astounding revelations giving way to messing around and hushed giggling fits. Ray had reverted back to the kid he'd been in high school, a clown, keeping them all highly amused with tales of his boyhood antics. A clown, yet there was a deepness to him, which Shady had discovered when she'd first been up-front with him about Mandy. But his lighthearted side, she loved it—at one point he'd made them laugh so much, she and Lisa Marie had clutched at each other, Shady trying not to read her, to give her new friend the privacy she deserved, but sensing how much this evening meant to her.

Lisa Marie had accepted them for who they were, and, in return, they'd accepted her too, without question, and she relished this, she *loved* it, being part of something when she hadn't even been a part of her own family, not truly. At school, too, she'd been an outsider. When their hands had touched, Shady felt a warmth that she immediately reciprocated. They might all have experienced very different childhoods, they might *all* be considered loners to some extent—neither Shady nor Ray had been members of the cool gangs at school—but now they had found each other, confided in each other, and, subsequently, a bond had been forged. Misfits together.

Fully awake now—her two friends still slumbering—Shady realized she was smiling. Last night had been traumatic, and her hand throbbed from the injury she'd suffered, but she was still basking in the glow of friendship. They hadn't gotten around to drawing the shades last night, so she could see that snowflakes continued to drift down, perhaps covering the roads again, the sidewalks and buildings, making everything glisten.

Her cell phone was in her backpack on the floor beside Ray. Like everyone, her morning habit was to check it for messages and emails, but Shady resisted, just enjoying a moment of peace and contentment. Funny that she should feel this way after enduring what she had, but she didn't question it too much or mind the fact that her head was throbbing along with her hand, the effects of wine and whiskey. The headache was sure to last all day, but hey, this time it had been worth it.

At last the sound of movement broke the peace, but not from anyone in Lisa Marie's room, which was large and spacious and boasted an en suite where Shady hoped she could grab a quick shower before leaving. The sound had come from outside in the living room—Gregory, no doubt, getting ready for work. Shady sincerely hoped there'd be no bad news for him to break today, not wanting to imagine the pain he'd also endure at having to do so.

How was Goldie? she wondered. That name seemed more real to her than Joan Parker. The gang she had run with, the people she'd chosen as her real family, there was something wrong with them. Very wrong. The warm feelings she'd experienced at first with them—the same kind of feelings that Shady had experienced last night, she supposed, the joy of acceptance—hadn't lasted long but given way to something else: disappointment, disillusionment, and even fear. But then those feelings had been…*quashed*, was that the right word? They'd been quashed because the need to belong was dominant in her, but could she be blamed for that? Wasn't that the case for everyone? After all, who was really happy being an outsider? Who was content with another day when nobody called? Very few, that was for sure. Everybody sought validation from someone, be it a parent, a mentor, a friend or a boss. It was knowing that you were loved and appreciated that helped you get through.

She'd have to go and see Goldie again, perhaps even return to her house under cover of the night to make some attempt at cleaning it up. The thought made her heart race.

You're not alone, Shady. Ray will insist on coming with you, maybe even Lisa Marie. And Annie. And Kanti is always with you. Don't be scared.

Even so, that contentedness she'd felt this morning, it was on the wane.

The door to the apartment closed. Gregory had clearly left. And she would as well. But she wanted just a little more time, to bolster herself if nothing more, closing her eyes, listening to Lisa Marie's rhythmic breathing, to Ray's slight snuffling.

The sound of her phone vibrating in her rucksack interrupted such musing.

"Damn!" she whispered, shuffling over to the side of the bed, then leaning over to pull her phone out of the bag.

Noting the caller ID, she saw it was Annie. She had to answer it, but not in here. With Gregory no longer in the apartment, she could sneak into the living room. Swinging her legs onto the floor, she tiptoed across the room.

By the time she was alone again, Annie had hung up.

Before she could return the call, however, a text came through, also from Annie:

Call me as quick as you can. I've just heard that Gina's had an accident. She's in the hospital, and she's asking for you.

CHAPTER FIFTEEN

Shady raced to the hospital in her Dodge, cursing the traffic whenever it held her up, tempted to run every red light that conspired against her. Ray stopped her from doing so, reminding her that if she gave in to temptation, they'd all end up as patients at Eastern Idaho Regional Medical Center, either that or in the morgue.

Lisa Marie hadn't come with them. She'd had to shower and get ready for a full day's work, but they promised to catch her up with news of Gina as soon as they could.

At the door, waving them off, she'd first kissed Ray on the cheek and then Shady, her lips lingering a second longer on Shady's cheek, feeling electric almost, which amused and baffled Shady but not for long, her mind too preoccupied with more urgent matters. Shady had, of course, spoken to Annie straight after the text.

"How'd you know she's asking for me? Who got in touch with you?" she'd asked. Sure, Annie knew Gina; in fact, Shady had met her through Gina. When Annie had been looking for someone with psychic ability to help with Mandy, Gina had recommended Shady after she'd dealt with her mirror the first time around, having thought she'd solved the problem. If only. En route to the hospital, Shady recalled the incident in Gina's kitchen, when her face had changed and become quite grotesque, with Gina unaware, totally unaware...

"Shady, calm down," Annie had replied. "Gina's in the hospital, and yes, she's very shaken, that's true too. But she's conscious. She couldn't remember your number. Her mind just went blank, but thankfully she remembered mine. She's not in mortal danger, far from it, but—"

"The accident she's had, it's to do with a mirror, isn't it?"

"Yes, it is."

"Christ, what's happening?"

"I don't know. We're in the thick of the mystery, but we'll unravel it, Shady."

Now, though, there was Gina to see, Annie on her way to the hospital too, meeting Shady and Ray there.

The snow that Shady had been watching earlier had indeed left a light layer upon the ground, but it had since stopped falling, happy to just tease the folks of Idaho Falls for now and remind them to be grateful. Parking the car, both she and Ray had their hands stuffed deep into their pockets as they made their way to the hospital entrance, Shady muttering under her breath, "Feels like I've moved into the goddamn place."

Annie was waiting for them in reception. On spotting them, she hurried forward.

"There you are! My goodness, are the pair of you all right? Shady, you've hurt yourself too. What happened?"

"It was just an accident," she replied, not wanting to get into it. She'd tell her later, of course, tell her everything, but right now Gina was their priority. "Where is she?"

"I've already checked," Annie said. "She's in accident and emergency."

Shady glanced at the receptionist, a young woman this time, not the man she'd encountered when she'd tried to see Joan Parker. "We can go through?"

"We can," Annie said, turning from them to lead the way.

Gina was in her own room just off the ER, sitting up in bed, one hand wrapped in bandages and held to her chest in a sling. Whereas her face had been grey-tinged the last time they'd met, now it was devoid of all color. She was paler than milk, every line on her face pronounced.

Shady rushed up to her, desperate to know what had happened, impatient for information, knowing that Joan Parker was in this building too, the links that had seemed so tenuous before growing ever more entwined.

"Shady," Annie said, trying to calm her enthusiasm, "let's sit awhile, give Gina a moment to…explain."

Ray pulled out three chairs, and Shady sat, although all she wanted was to throw her arms around Gina, who looked not like a woman in her mid-fifties but a lost child.

Before Ray sat, he offered to get some coffee, but heads shook, notably Gina's, who, beneath her shocked demeanor, appeared as keen as Shady to make sense of it all.

"I was up early," she began, a tremor in her voice. "I couldn't sleep, or, rather, I'd been sleeping and yet again having nightmares." There was a brief silence before Gina could continue. "I was tired, groggy, needed coffee to get me going, like we all do, so was about to head to the kitchen and make some, but…I just sat there, on the edge of my bed, clutching at the neck of my nightdress, unable to move. As if…I was still dreaming."

"But you were awake?" Annie checked. "I only ask

because dreams can seem so lucid."

"I was awake," Gina confirmed. "But not...functioning properly."

"If you've had little sleep..." Ray suggested.

Gina nodded. "Yes, interrupted sleep can definitely make you feel otherworldly. Never had a problem with insomnia, though, always slept so well, until...until..." At this point, Gina looked upward at the ceiling, something in Shady jolting. Where was the ICU, exactly? Mentally she recalled the route that Lisa Marie had taken her, down corridors and up a flight of stairs. Was it directly above them? Something in Gina sensing that?

"Gina," Annie prompted when another wave of silence wrapped itself around them.

"Sorry," Gina said, her eyes back on them now and such a haunted quality to them, squeezing Shady's heart, making her feel so sorry and even guiltier...

A tear slipped down Gina's cheek, eliciting sorrow from Annie too.

"Your hand," Annie said, "it must hurt very much."

"It does," Gina replied, noticing for the first time, perhaps, that Shady's hand was bandaged too, although nowhere near as spectacularly. "What happened to you?"

"It's just a scratch," Shady told her, avoiding Annie's no doubt inquiring gaze. "The bandage is overkill, to be honest."

Gina seemed to accept this without questioning, sniffing as she continued. "I needed coffee, no doubt about it, needed to wake up, you know? Shake myself out of the daze I'd fallen into. Eventually, I got to my feet, fixed everything in my head, like, *The kitchen, Gina, you're going to the kitchen.* Simple enough, huh? It's what I do every morning, start my day in there, plan what it is I'm going to do and who I'm going to see. All so normal, so humdrum, just another day to get through. But..."

Ray's eyes were on stalks as Gina paused again.

"I never made it into the kitchen," she said, a frown and so much confusion on her face. "I went right, and into the bathroom. Oh dear!"

As Gina fully broke down, Annie sprang from her seat, closing the gap between them so she could comfort her. "Gina, I'm so sorry for what's happened and how upset you are. But, you know, it'll help to talk about it rather than keep it bottled up. And we'll help, I assure you. We'll do our utmost to get your life back on track."

Damn this guilt in Shady's throat; it was almost choking her.

"Gina," Annie said, pleading with her, "tell us what happened."

"I don't remember."

"Gina—"

"Annie, it's the God's honest truth. I don't remember! Not all of it. I know I never made it into the kitchen, that I went into the bathroom instead. It was morning, early morning, as I've said, but for such a bright room, it didn't seem that way. It was dark, hazy. Please, listen, I wasn't dreaming, I wasn't sleepwalking, I was awake, okay? Awake."

"We believe you." Annie took a step back to allow Gina some breathing space.

"I was awake, but everything was different. *I* was different. Heavier, like...there was something inside me, dragging me down. All the way down." As Gina took a deep breath, she tilted her head to the side, still confusion on her face but also a glimmer of understanding. "You know, that could be why it was so dark in the bathroom."

"How do you mean?" asked Annie.

"When you feel that way, heavy, I mean, it's difficult to recognize the light, to let it in."

Beside Shady, Ray murmured to himself, "Yeah, yeah. I s'pose."

"I entered the bathroom, and I walked over to the mirror. I'm sure that's what I did. I walked over to it, and…it got really dark. Really heavy. I must have raised my hand, I must have smashed the mirror, but I don't remember doing it. I don't."

The tears were back in Gina's eyes, were falling down her cheeks, but Annie seemed determined to keep her distance, surely wanting to comfort her some more but also not interrupt her, not this time. Gina was in the flow, caught up in events, the past, and maybe, just maybe, she might get an insight into what had possessed her to do as she did—to smash that mirror to pieces with her bare hands, a rage inside her, a fury from nowhere.

Fury.

Shady got this insight, not Gina, her eyes drawn upward again to whomever lay above them.

Goldie, what have you unleashed?

* * *

The nurses were nothing if not vigilant at the Eastern Idaho Regional Medical Center. Two of them heard Gina sobbing and came rushing into the room, declaring she was tired, she needed some time to rest, and that her visitors must leave.

Annie stood her ground. "Aren't you going home today, Gina? Because if you are, we could return with you and settle you in. Or…you could stay at mine. There's plenty of room, no need to go back at all, not just yet."

"I am leaving today," Gina assured her, "but—" she shrugged as the nurses continued to fuss around her "—not until this afternoon. And I'm going to my sister's house. She lives just over the border in Montana. I'm heading there for a few days."

"Okay, I see. That sounds like a good plan. I'll call you later this evening to see how you are. Or you can call me, call *us*"—here Annie motioned to Shady too—"at any time."

Shady nodded. "Keep in touch, Gina. And…regarding this, I've already made progress. I'm getting there."

As the nurses shooed them out of the room and into the corridor, Annie eyed Shady curiously. Glancing only briefly at Ray beforehand, Shady blurted out what had happened the previous night, the truth about how she'd gotten her injury too.

"You went to Joan Parker's home?" Annie looked incredulous. "You broke in?"

"Not technically," Ray denied. "The kitchen door wasn't locked."

"If you'd been caught…"

"We weren't, though," Shady replied. "Not many houses in her neighborhood. No one, really, to see."

"But you saw?" Annie continued. "Quite a bit, by the

sounds of it."

Where they stood, nurses and doctors were brushing past them, going briskly about their business.

"Look, there's a café here," Shady said. "Why don't we go there and talk? Somewhere a little more comfortable."

"Yes, let's do that," Annie agreed, Shady sighing in relief as they left behind the somewhat frenetic atmosphere of the ER.

The last time she'd been in the café was with Lisa Marie, who was also elsewhere in the hospital by now, Shady hoping her hangover wasn't too bad and resolving to text her later. First, though, there was more explaining to do.

"I kind of flipped out, I suppose," Shady told Annie. "Not at first. At first, when I looked in the mirrors, the ones lining the hallway, at least, I saw stuff but nothing particularly bad." She shrugged, a wry gesture. "It wasn't great either, don't get me wrong, but Joan had found what she called a family, people who made her feel she belonged, one man in particular."

As soon as she'd revealed this, Annie's back seemed to stiffen. "A family? As in a group of other people, friends?"

"I think so, yeah. She loved this man; she was obsessed with him. I think he was, like, the head of this family. To be honest, from what I could make out, he sounded totally full of himself, an asshole, who thought he was on par with Jesus Christ. I got the impression lots of girls were obsessed with him. They all shared him, you know, in the bedroom."

"Was he a Mormon?" Ray asked, only half joking, it seemed.

Shady shook her head. "Don't think so. He might have likened himself to Jesus, or Joan likened him, but there was

163

nothing religious about this guy, nothing…sacred."

"How old was Joan in the visions?" Annie looked not just uncomfortable but as if she was hot, loosening the scarf at her neck as a ragged sigh escaped her.

Again, Shady shrugged. "Can't be sure, but young, I reckon. Very young. It's like she hadn't formed a personality of her own yet. She was…impressionable. There weren't just women, well, *girls* in this guy's entourage, there were boys too, and, well, I think the women had to sleep with all of them, not just the main man. They had to, like…service them."

When Annie failed to respond, Shady prompted her. "Annie, are you okay?"

"I'm just doing the math, that's all."

"The math?"

"Yes. Joan Parker is in her late sixties?"

"Yeah. Lisa Marie told me that, according to records, she's sixty-seven."

"Right, if she was in her mid-teens when she met this man you've seen in visions—"

"I didn't actually see him, only Joan referring to him."

"Okay, well, even so, she would have met him some time in the 1960s."

"A swinging time," murmured Ray, but no humor at all in his voice now as he gazed intently at Annie.

"Indeed," she replied. "I witnessed something of that time myself. It was…an *amazing* time. The world was changing. Dramatically. People were changing. They were throwing off the shackles of restraint that post-war society had bound them in, protesting about the Vietnam War, finding themselves, and becoming free."

"Sixty-seven was the Summer of Love," Ray said. "It was all happening, especially in San Francisco, the Haight-Ashbury area."

"San Francisco?" Shady said.

"Yeah," he answered. "Why?"

"I was just… Lisa Marie's from San Francisco."

Ray frowned. "So?"

Again, Shady stuttered slightly. "There just seems to be…so many links. So many coincidences."

"Between what?" asked Annie.

"Between everything. They're random, but, at the same time, are they? Gina, Joan, the mirrors, Lisa Marie too and the insights I get into her background—it kinda corresponds with Joan Parker's background, you know, but it's different too, their reaction to it. And now there's San Francisco, where Lisa Marie's from, the Summer of Love and…this guy."

Annie seemed perplexed as she leaned forward. "Shady, when you entered the living room and locked the door behind you, what made you flip, exactly?"

"By that time, well, it was like I was on acid. My head was all over the place. I couldn't think straight. Goldie's energy is strong; her memories are so alive. She's told these mirrors everything about her life. *Everything.* It's like they're her confidantes. Maybe that's why she's so obsessed with them, because she can unburden herself and what stares back doesn't judge. She's a mixed bag of emotions, dark emotions, but there's sadness too, and there's unhappiness. They underscore everything. Even the joy of acceptance wasn't complete."

"So, what happened? Why did you smash the mirror?"

"Because…because this time when I looked into it, I didn't see visions. I just saw me, or at least…I think it was me. I'm not so sure now. It was dark in Goldie's house. There was some light from outside, in the hallway, at least, but not in that room. In that room there's barely any light at all. Ah shit, I'm trying to get this straight in my head, but it's difficult to remember, like it was for Gina. Best way I can describe it is this: Back at the museum, when the mirror cracked, I looked into it and saw my reflection split in half. One half was me, just normal, the other half was…bad. Good wolf, bad wolf, you know? But in Goldie's living room, it was different. I looked into the mirror there, and what I saw was…shit, it was horrible! Could it really be me? Somebody I was capable of becoming if life had turned out differently?"

Annie shook her head. "It could be that you saw him."

Shady was confused. "Him?"

"Yes, through Joan's eyes. And if he's who I think he is, he's a very bad wolf indeed."

CHAPTER SIXTEEN

Cults…the sixties were full of them.

"I'm not talking of a satanic nature," Annie was quick to point out, "although heaven knows there must have been plenty of those too, but groups of people who drifted together for various reasons, political and social upheaval being one of them. You see, in the days when Joan—sorry, Shady, let's refer to her as Goldie for the moment; somehow it seems more apt. In the days when Goldie was young, no more than a teenager, there was so much unrest in America. We had the civil rights movement and the Vietnam anti-war movement, JFK, RFK, all to the soundtrack of Dylan, Janis Joplin and Jefferson Airplane, and, well, cults sprang up to fill the void, all over the place, a charismatic leader at their helm feeding off that desire for freedom of expression."

They'd finished their coffees and returned to the museum in Mason. It might be Saturday, but they still had to open, although all three doubted it'd be busy, not today, with no curious schoolchildren led by even more curious teachers. Plus, the weather sucked. It was sleeting as opposed to snowing but still so cold, the sky with no color in it at all.

As they'd guessed, there were no visitors waiting and no one on the streets of Mason either as they'd approached the museum. Technically, it was Shady's and Ray's day off, but as Shady had insisted they give sanctuary to the mirror from Pre-loved, they had a responsibility to deal with the consequences. Knowledge was armor—that was a favorite saying of Annie's. They had to know about the mirror, about Goldie, Annie fueling them with yet more coffee, bringing a pot out to the main counter of the still-deserted museum as the discussion continued.

"Even today," she said, "there are thousands of cults in America. It really is a hotbed. And to be fair, some are harmless, but some can be very dangerous indeed."

"What's the attraction, though?" Ray asked. "I mean, I don't have a degree in the subject or anything, but from everything I know about them, they suck you in and then you have to abide by a strict set of rules. There's nothing 'free' about them at all."

"So many people are lost." Annie adjusted her glasses to sit perfectly on her nose. "And in a country as vast as America, it's easy to drift. Many do. Which is fine, in theory, it's their prerogative, but actually, picking up on this good-wolf, bad-wolf theme you're talking about, Shady, so few of us are lone wolves. Few wolves are either. Because, like wolves, we're a pack animal, and we want to belong. Even if it takes time to admit it."

"No man is an island," muttered Shady.

Annie nodded. "That's right, or, rather, very few are. Cults are actually a fascinating subject. Take one charismatic leader, a transcendent belief system that offers all the answers to life's questions, a solution that can only be gained by following the leader's rules, then chuck in a bit of brainwashing, and there you have it."

Ray's expression as he held on to his mug of coffee was nothing less than intrigued. "Wasn't there a cult that all committed suicide together? Down in Waco, Texas?"

"Wacko more like," Shady said, raising an eyebrow. "But yeah, there was. I remember watching something on TV about it a while ago. Jeez, it was sinister."

"That was David Koresh, leader of the Davidian Seventh-Day Adventist Church," Annie elaborated, "and yes, it is something of a sinister tale. Strictly speaking, they were a religion, not a cult. That definition became an interesting debate at the time. Theirs wasn't a suicide pact either but a standoff with the FBI, who'd swooped down on them at the ranch they occupied because they suspected them of stockpiling illegal weapons. The standoff lasted a very long time, over a month, and then there was a shoot-out, resulting in many lives lost."

"But there *were* cults that committed mass suicide, right?" Ray asked.

Annie nodded again, this time more solemnly. "Yes, there were. In San Diego, in the late nineties, members of Heaven's Gate performed a mass suicide, believing the earth was about to be recycled, but not to worry: a spaceship would land and whisk them all away. The catch? They had to shed their earthly bodies to board the spaceship. Cue a cocktail of phenobarbital and applesauce for their members. There was also the Reverend Jim Jones, who set up the Peoples Temple in the mid-fifties. He was seen as a beacon of peace across the racial divide and attracted many followers because of it, leading his members to Guyana to create a 'socialist paradise.'

"When the cult attracted unwanted attention, including

suspicions that some members were being held against their will, a death followed—not his, but that of a congressman who was hell-bent on investigating them. Members of the cult ambushed and shot him several times. Others were injured and killed alongside him, including members who were trying to defect." Annie sighed. "It's all such a fearful waste of life," she said before continuing. "Fearing retribution for the congressman's death, Jones led almost one thousand followers into a mass murder-suicide, which later became known as the 'Jonestown Massacre.' Many died by drinking cyanide mixed with Flavor Aid."

"I don't get it," Ray declared. "I mean, why would you do that? Follow so blindly?"

"Because you believed, that's why," Annie answered. "They brainwashed you into believing. And you wanted to belong. You'd do anything to belong."

"Are you anti-religion?" Ray asked her.

"No. I very much believe in the goodwill and good intent of those that follow it, the ordinary people of faith. What I'm constantly saddened by is the politics and hypocrisy of those that hold its power."

There was a pause in conversation, Shady, for her part, ingesting all Annie had said. She already knew some of the history of the hippie era and how it had ended badly, seen TV documentaries, perhaps even discussed with her high school friends the nature of cults and the people who joined them, but, to be honest, it wasn't a subject that had over-occupied her mind. Sixties music was the catalyst for the social landscape of the time, and that music wasn't hers, even if her own name came from it.

"Annie," she said, "when we were at the hospital and I

told you about what happened at Goldie's house, you said that I saw 'him'—'a very bad wolf indeed.' What did you mean? Who do you think I saw?"

From staring into her almost empty coffee cup, Annie fixed her gaze on Shady, those brown eyes of hers almost opaque in the somewhat dull light of the museum.

"Look," she said, "the subject of cults has always fascinated me. I'm British, and we have cults too back home, I'm not saying otherwise, but in America, they can be far more extreme. I'm also not intending to deny, or *decry*, other people's religious beliefs. Who's to say that Marshall Applewhite, the Heaven's Gate leader, was wrong and I'm right? Was he evil? I don't think so. I think he truly believed he was saving people. Perhaps the earth *will* be recycled at some point, and we're going to have to jump ship if we want humanity to survive. Head via spaceship to the kingdom of heaven."

"Cool," Ray said, grinning.

"People are entitled to live according to their religious beliefs and the teachings of those that they consider divinely inspired. The Heaven's Gate pre-suicide address is still there on YouTube for all to see. That's the wonderful thing about a country like America—we have that right, that freedom, and long may it continue, but in turn, those that don't have specific beliefs have the right to live peacefully too, not to be…terrorized or constantly evangelized.

"Shady, the man I'm referring to as the bad wolf is, of course, Charles Manson, arguably the most famous of cult leaders, responsible for the brutal deaths of nine people."

Shady's jaw dropped. Charles Manson? Just like every kid in America knew about the Candyman, they knew about

Manson and what he'd done, or, rather, what he'd instructed members of his "family" to do.

"Family!" she said at last as Annie's words sank in. "That's what Goldie said she was a part of, the leader a man that she loved. They all did, the women especially. They were like…slaves. Willing slaves. Shit, Annie! Are you saying Goldie was a member of the Manson Family?"

Annie looked as ashen as Gina had in her hospital bed. She didn't answer immediately, didn't hold Shady's gaze either, but stared into the distance, teeth gnawing at her lip. Ray was quiet too; he simply placed his mug on the counter and stood there, his expression as shocked as Shady's.

Annie? Jesus, the silence was intense, as if everything around them, every single energy-charged object that the museum housed, was waiting also. *What are we dealing with here? Goldie… They all had nicknames, didn't they? Manson's Family. And Goldie was Joan's, a sweet name, cute, and therefore not appropriate at all.*

Finally, Annie spoke. "We mustn't jump to conclusions—"

"But you think she was, don't you?"

"I don't know. All I'm saying is, the timeframe fits. And the story—what we know of it so far—fits. But I could be wrong. I'm just piecing things together in my mind."

Shady placed her mug on the counter too and started to wring her hands together. "I'm just a girl, an ordinary girl. I…I don't want to know about stuff like this! It's…too dark. Too…shocking. I shouldn't have insisted we bring that mirror back here. Should have left it where it was. Some things…you don't wanna know about."

"Shady," Ray said, reaching out for her, but she backed

away.

"No, I can't do this. I can't. Because if it is Manson I saw, then...I saw the devil."

Annie was trying to calm her too. "Shady, dear, perhaps it was wrong of me to voice my suspicion, because, really, that's all it is. As I've said, there are many, many cults, both now and historically. I just...I happen to think it's important we discuss our ideas and our theories, that we're open, honest and truthful with each other. You're *not* in this alone. Never think that. And it's your choice to have nothing more to do with this case. We can...keep the mirror here, down in the basement, covered. You never have to look in it again. It's out of harm's way, at least, which is something to be grateful for. There really is no evidence I'm right, but even if I am, it's not Manson we're dealing with, it's one of his disciples, a woman who's not dead, who's still clinging to life, and a woman who, despite everything, needs help. Perhaps...perhaps we're the only ones able to give her that. But if you decide against it, that's fine. The last thing I want you to do is panic. What I'll continue to reiterate is that you're not alone. We're with you."

Shady knew that, had no doubt about it, and a problem needed resolving, but to resolve this? Still retreating, she picked up pace, Ray beginning to follow her, pleading with her.

"Shady, it's a lot to take in. I know it is. But Annie's right—we're in this together. We can sort it out."

"Sort out a problem like Manson?"

"It is *not* Manson we're dealing with," Annie continued to insist.

Shady halted for a second to glare at her. "By proxy we are! His energy, it would have tainted hers…Joan…Goldie…whatever."

"Maybe, but it's still important to remember this isn't about him. He's dead. And—" Annie faltered, but not for long "—he wasn't the devil. He was a man, just a man, albeit very damaged. I've read about him before and the type of background he came from—"

"Lisa Marie came from a bad background." As Shady said it, she noticed Ray further surprised by this revelation. "But she's done so much good with her life! She fought against the damage and turned it around, worked hard at school and got herself a profession, a fricking good profession, one that's enviable. She's sweet and she's kind. Not everyone who's damaged turns out bad. It's a choice, Annie, a choice!"

Annie was nodding as furiously as Shady. "It is, Shady, it is. But by the same token, not everyone is able to make the right choices either. The world simply doesn't work that way; if only it did. Some people's inner demons prove too strong."

"And that's our problem now, is it?"

"Sometimes, yes."

Shady had heard enough. Shit, if her mom knew about this latest case, and her dad, they'd drag her out of the dusty surroundings of Mason Town Museum, lock her in her room and throw away the key! No way she could deal with this. No way. Manson was huge. Not just a man, despite what Annie said. He was something far darker.

She had to get out of there, go for a walk, try to clear her head.

"Shady!" Again, Ray pleaded as Shady, having turned her back on them, reached the door and yanked it open. She heard Annie pleading too, not with Shady this time but with him, to leave her alone for now, to give her the space she needed.

And boy, did she need it. Out in the open, the door closing behind her, she raced down the steps, glad she'd kept her jacket on. Stuffing her hands into her jeans pocket, she felt the patch of leather, the softness of it, recalled the stars etched upon it, symbolizing the light that was supposed to lead the way—a light that right now seemed so far away.

If Annie was correct, she'd become entangled with the biggest badass wolf of all. And anyone guided by him was, in turn, bad through and through. They had to be.

She's just a frail old woman.

Vehemently, Shady shook her head.

Age doesn't excuse what you were once capable of!

Shady continued down the path that led away from the museum, the voices in her head continuing to war with each other. Positioned on the edge of town, Mason's one street of stores, bars and restaurants was behind her. In front was only wide-open space, which was exactly what she wanted, a wilderness in which to escape the human race.

The state of Idaho was full of vast stretches of land, sometimes mountainous, at other times flat plains that stretched on and on. There was woodland too, acres upon acres, up ahead an area where trees bunched together, where she could hide if she wanted to.

The air was cold and the clouds low as she quickened her pace, an urgent need in her to be amongst those trees, the pines, the firs and the cedars, so verdant despite the winter weather, their green, leafy smell drifting toward her, enticing her further.

Shady loved the outdoors, the wilderness, felt both awed and excited by it. When she, Ray and Annie had been trying to find out about Mandy's history, their journey had taken them into the depths of Canada—the Saskatchewan province, a snow-covered terrain of utter wilderness covering miles and miles with no sign of human life at all, only a glimpse of moose here and there, and birds of prey swooping low. It was in Canada that Shady had discovered something about herself too: her Cree heritage courtesy of Kanti, something else that had awed her. She belonged to one of the largest groups of First Nations in North America, a group split into several subgroups, including the Woodland Cree, Plains Cree and Moose Cree. Kanti's ancestors were Woodland Cree, and so, Shady supposed, it was natural she'd feel the pull of what lay ahead; she always had, despite also loving the beaches of California and the theme parks of Florida. Woodland was in her blood, and yet only recently had she understood why.

Spying a clump of rocks, she sat down upon them, cradling her head in her hands and sighing heavily—a lone figure among nature's giants.

She had wanted to be a teacher, and now look at her—rubbing shoulders with the devil.

He wasn't the devil. He was just a man.

That's what Annie had said, had insisted—a damaged man, who was certainly guilty of devilish things. And yet what Joan Parker had done as Goldie remained a mystery. Had she been involved in the killings? If she had, wouldn't she be in prison still, along with other surviving members of the so-called Family? Did the fact that she wasn't, that she was free and had been doing something as mundane as shopping for groceries in a Walmart in Idaho, offer a crumb of comfort? Perhaps. It could even refute Annie's theory entirely. Only more research would tell. Research that *had* to be done; deep down Shady knew that. Ray and Annie might even be at it now. Googling a character called Goldie…

Shit, Kanti, what do I do? Should I walk away from this, or am I already in too deep?

She knew well enough from dealing with Mandy that once a psychic connection had been made and a picture emerged, it demanded completion.

And she was the one who could walk further than most in another person's shoes, see through their eyes, experience what they felt—every damned emotion that had raged through them, able to tear her apart as it had once torn them.

Kanti, what do I do?

Again, she asked, listened to the silence that surrounded her, the trees whose leaves rustled in the breeze, as if whispering to her, whispering…

Do what you were born to do.

CHAPTER SEVENTEEN

There was no mention of a Goldie online, not one who'd been a member of Manson's Family, at any rate. Shady, Ray and Annie had combed the internet, typing in Joan Parker's real name, Goldie, and variations on both, reading article after article on Manson and those that worshipped the ground he walked on, that swallowed all the lies he fed them.

A damaged man, Annie was right, his mother something of a jailbird herself, an abusive woman who'd allegedly once sold him for a pitcher of beer. But again, Shady found it hard to find sympathy in her soul for him. Maybe if she hadn't met Lisa Marie, she might have been able to, but she had, she'd seen, she'd listened to how her friend had struggled to do the right thing, how she'd battled against what she was a product of. Manson hadn't. He'd been born into darkness and been happy to stay there, claiming at the end it wasn't just nine killings his Family were guilty of but more than thirty, burying their bodies in the desert.

"Jesus, he's despicable," murmured Shady.

Annie, who was intently reading also, peered at Shady over the top of her glasses. "Remember, it's his disciples we're focusing on, not him."

It was Sunday, and they were at Annie's house in Mason,

the museum experiencing a rare day of closure. Both Shady and Ray had been to Annie's house before but only fleetingly, once as they'd waited for her to pack for their road trip with Mandy, and thereafter to pick her up on the few occasions they carpooled. Set back from the town's main street, it was a single-story house, sitting in its own garden, a picket fence surrounding it.

A pretty house, pale violet in color, its interior wasn't home to many trinkets or ornaments; rather, what few shelves there were remained empty. Annie, it was clear to see, was not one to bring her work home with her. This was her haven, her sanctuary, items that made it within carefully chosen, nothing attached to them except good memories, notably a framed photograph of her and her now deceased partner, Donny, which perfectly captured how happy they'd been—the pair of them with their arms around each other and beaming at the camera. Both dressed in brown, which had made Shady smile. Now, however, Annie's home had become a hub for research, and all three were crowded around a small but sturdy oak table in the dining area—delving into an episode of American history that fascinated as many people as it repulsed.

"Speaking of the disciples, it looked like most of them had nicknames," Ray said. "Squeaky, 'cause, well, she used to squeak a lot, apparently, you know, during…"

"We know what you mean, Ray," Annie said, saving him from having to elaborate, even able to offer a smile despite such a grim subject.

"There was also Tex, Gypsy, Lulu, and Snake, but no Goldie, not as far as I can see. You know, we could be barking up the wrong tree here."

"Absolutely," agreed Annie. "We've already established that. Even so, it appears Goldie was part of a similar setup, and so this research gives us an insight into her psychology, at least."

"Or Shady could just visit her again?" suggested Ray. "It's not as if she's dead."

"She's in a coma, Ray," Shady pointed out.

"You can still read her."

"I can't. She won't let me. I can read what's in the mirrors because she poured her heart out to them. But otherwise she's blocking me. She's...frightened, I think."

"Of facing up to what she did?" asked Ray.

"Could be exactly that."

"Interesting, this obsession with mirrors," Annie commented. "That the house she occupies is so full of them. She hoards them. And yet we have one."

Ray seemed to also contemplate this. "It's the one that got away."

"Uh-huh," replied Shady. "Somehow. Why?"

"Oh look, this article's good." Ray became engrossed again in the material he was reading on the laptop he'd brought. "Like you said, Annie, it's focused entirely on Manson's disciples, and yeah, they were drifters, mainly women at first, but he was keen for more men to join, using the women to seduce them. Before things took a more deadly turn, the gang was involved in the usual kinda crimes: store robberies, panhandling and, ugh, creepy crawling."

"Creepy crawling?" asked Shady. "What's that?"

"Where he sent his followers into people's houses at night, and, literally, they'd creep around the house, robbing them."

Shady exhaled, her imagination all too readily picturing people crawling around her own home while she and her parents slept, unaware of the intrusion. She shook her head to rid herself of the mental image, although goosebumps remained on her arms.

Annie spoke next. "As you say, Ray, it was drifters that joined him, the young and the impressionable. There's one girl here aged only fifteen, a runaway, something we know that Joan Parker was too. Her mother had left home before her, leaving her with a father who was perhaps—" Annie appeared to choose her next words carefully "—a little overbearing. And so she ran. The question is: Where to? When Joan was young, a lot of people headed to Haight-Ashbury in San Francisco, heaps and heaps of them, more than the city could cope with. Not just drawn by the music and prospect of free love—drugs were also quite the allure, which were dished out like sweeties. It was a troubled time, a time of transition, and so many people went in search of their tribe."

"Annie," Ray said, "do you think it's so different now? I mean, the times we're living in, there's a lot of unrest, a lot of people that still feel adrift."

"Oh, I agree, Ray. Every decade brings with it troubles of its own, and America, because it's so vast, because it's a melting pot, can be...volatile. There's a lot of injustice still, a lot of bigotry and racism, and poverty. But back then, there was just something in the air, you know?"

"Besides the smell of pot?" Ray replied, smirking.

Annie smiled too. "Besides the smell of pot," she said. "LSD was the drug of the era, and, again, it's something we think Joan Parker did."

Shady pushed her laptop away. "I asked Lisa Marie yesterday if she could find out from hospital records where Goldie was born."

"And?" said Annie, clearly intrigued.

"It was just inside Idaho, a few miles from the Utah border, a small town called Lancing. Doesn't look like there's much to it, even now. It's nowheresville, basically."

"And from there about a thousand miles to California," Annie wagered.

"Something like that," Shady said. "A long way for a young kid to travel."

"A young kid with probably very little money," Ray mused. "She must have hitched."

"Undoubtedly," Annie said.

"All the way to hell," Shady muttered.

* * *

There was a fire in Shady's dream—a tower of it. She'd seen fire like this before, in a vision, and her grandmother dancing around it. This time, there was no grandmother; she was alone, standing close, too close. She could feel the heat of it as it seared her skin, but still she didn't step away. She couldn't. Her feet were rooted to the ground.

What was that in the fire? A face? Taking shape and evolving, ever so slowly. It *was* a face, but the flames, dancing and leaping manically, did their utmost to obscure it.

Who are you? The devil?

If only she could turn, run away, escape. But that seemed

futile, as escape wasn't always what it promised to be.

Oh, it was hot. This fire would surely consume her. She had to try to move. She didn't want to burn, not like so many others had burned before her, women accused of being fey, of being witches. Women who, in the main, were only trying to help… What was wrong with her legs? Why were they refusing to cooperate? She looked down. Had they really taken root, and she'd become a part of this strange and terrifying landscape? If it was a wilderness, there was nothing majestic about it. Instead, it was bleak, apocalyptic.

The face was becoming clearer. Eyes flashing at her, molten black.

I've got to get away!

Damn her body for betraying her. She couldn't even turn her head now, could only look ahead, into the flames, into evil.

Don't fear it.

That was Kanti's voice! Although she was nowhere to be seen, she was in her head—more than that, in her heart.

Stand your ground.

She had no choice but to do so. Is that what this dream meant? Because on some level, Shady knew well enough that this wasn't real, that her brain was jumbling so much together in an attempt to make sense of it, processing what was tantamount to an assault. But Kanti was real. And her advice was the only thing that made sense.

Do what you were born to do.

Kanti had also said that via the whispering trees, and so Shady continued to watch the flames, swallowing the fear that burrowed, wormlike, into the pit of her stomach.

Did the face really belong to the devil? Just who or what was the devil anyway? If a negative force, then he was in so many people, lurking, waiting to strike, to take advantage of the vulnerable. And then there were those, as Annie had said, that sought him out, like Goldie had, the minute she'd left home. Swapped one devil for another.

I don't fear you.

She'd not only face the devil, she'd face him down.

I can look into your eyes and remain untouched.

Just like Lisa Marie had. Lisa Marie, who'd kissed her cheek so recently and whose lips had lingered…

I'm not afraid!

And yet fear wouldn't sit still within her. It stirred and agitated, rose up again.

The flames were not just leaping and dancing, they were parting, scheming with the face that lay at the heart of them, burning white hot, the skin beginning to melt on her own face; she was sure of it, although she couldn't lift her hands to check if it was coming away in sheets yet. She was burning, yet she was frozen, through to the core.

You can't frighten me. I won't give you the power!

Faced with evil, though, it was all too easy to feel power*less*, as it sucked the life out of you, bore down upon your will and shattered it, as easily as a fist could shatter a mirror…

The face was evolving further, becoming more familiar. Eyes still so dark, skin raw and blistering. The mouth was opening, becoming wider, twisting, turning, distorted.

At last something about Shady was able to move—her own mouth, which followed the motion of the other, as though it was her own reflection that she looked at.

But it wasn't. The flames had parted completely now. It was Goldie in the flames, and she was screaming, as Shady was screaming.

The sound was one of sheer agony.

Stop! Stop! Please stop!

Despite Shady's plea, it continued.

You have to stop!

It was far worse than the heat of the flames. Even more relentless.

STOP!

"Shady! Shady, wake up."

Huh? "Mom? Is that you? What…what's happening?"

"Of course it's me, honey. Were you having a nightmare?"

"A nightmare? Um…yeah…yeah, I think so."

"I walked in here, and you were thrashing about, whimpering."

Whimpering? No, Ellen had gotten that wrong, surely? In the dream Shady had been screaming—the agony that had engulfed her, Goldie's agony, still an echo in her body, making her ache, feel nauseous, and so terribly sad.

She swallowed as she stared into a more pleasant face altogether. "Mom, is that why you woke me, 'cause you heard me whimpering?"

"Oh no, honey, I came in because I heard your phone ringing. Look"—she pointed to the nightstand, where Shady's phone was charging—"there must be about a dozen missed calls on there. Someone sure is desperate to get a hold of you."

CHAPTER EIGHTEEN

"Shady, hi, it's good to see you again." In the reception of the Eastern Idaho Regional Medical Center, Lisa Marie stepped forward to embrace Shady. "I'm sorry to have called you so early, but…I just thought you'd want to know."

Joan Parker was awake. She'd recovered consciousness, although for how long was anyone's guess.

"I got into work really early," Lisa Marie continued, "and, well, I just had this feeling, you know, that I should go check on her." A look of confusion briefly stole the light from her. "Call it intuition, if you like, after, you know, what we'd discussed Friday night. By the way, Gina's gone now. I checked on that as well."

"She went to stay with her sister in Montana," Shady said.

"Yeah, I'm not surprised. What happened to her was scary. Hopefully up there she'll find some relief from this…this…curse."

A curse? It was that, all right, in its own way.

"Did you see Joan? Did she see you?" Shady asked.

Lisa Marie shook her head. "No, the nurse on duty told me, not one I'd met before. Wanted to know if I was a friend or a relation. I said I was a friend of Joan's friend. She told me she'd regained consciousness but was still very ill."

On hearing this and remembering the dream that Ellen had woken her from, Shady bit her lip. "D'ya think they'd let me in to see her a second time?"

Lisa Marie smiled as she nodded, a glittering smile, and Shady suddenly understood—the girl Lisa Marie had reinvented herself to be could persuade anyone to do anything.

"Follow me," she said, winking at Shady.

They took the same route as before, Shady's heart beating in her chest at the prospect of encountering Joan Parker again, an ill woman, as the nurse had said, not dead but not wholly alive either, trapped in the in-between. She'd opened her eyes. If Shady was indeed allowed in to see her on the continued pretext of being a concerned friend and neighbor, Joan would be able to see Shady too, not just sense her. As in the dream, they'd come face to face. What would Joan's reaction be? Horror? Anger? If there was even the merest chance of causing any more stress that could endanger her recovery, should Shady just turn around and get the hell out of the medical center?

She couldn't; she'd come too far. Joan's reaction might well be one of horror and anger at the person masquerading as her friend, but, really, was this guise so far from the truth? Despite the white lie, Shady only wanted to help her. This woman was in mental torment. The dream had highlighted that. What in her history had caused it all?

They'd entered the ICU, Lisa Marie speeding up as she approached one of the nurses, perhaps the same one she'd spoken to before. The woman, somewhere in her thirties and tall with dark hair scraped back, immediately smiled on seeing Lisa Marie, the pair of them exchanging a few words before the nurse, glancing briefly at Shady, nodded her head.

Lisa Marie returned to Shady's side. "You can go in, like before, just for a few minutes."

"How did the nurse say she was?"

"Still critical. Do you want me to come in with you this time? I'm happy to."

"Knowing what you know about her?" Shady was only half joking as she asked.

"Despite that," Lisa Marie replied, deadly serious.

"You know what? I'm okay on my own." *I can do this.* That's what she'd told herself in the dream and what she told herself now. *I have to.*

At the door to Joan's room, Shady took a deep breath and pushed it open, expecting to be hit by a tidal wave of black emotion, intended to drive her back and prevent her from probing further into the woman's psyche. She'd braced herself for just that—and to retaliate if need be, not in an attempt to goad Joan but to say, *I know you, something of you, at least, and I'm still here.* For Joan's sake, and for Gina's, who was being drowned by this woman's energy. Montana, Shady suspected, not far enough out of harm's way.

"Miss Parker," Shady began, "I'm sorry to upset you again…"

The words died in Shady's throat. Goldie lay in the bed, nothing more than a scrap of a human being, the monitors she was hooked up to still beeping and blinking furiously. She was looking at Shady, eyes somewhat glazed but having widened slightly. And there was a tear on her cheek. A tear that stole Shady's breath, because it wasn't what she'd expected.

For a moment Shady stood perfectly still, as if she'd indeed taken root, and then she broke the hold that shock had on her and stepped forward, seating herself by the woman's side before taking her birdlike hand in her own and closing her fingers around it. Goldie clung just as hard.

"I know who you used to be," Shady reiterated. "You were a runaway, a drifter. A child who'd seen too much ugliness, who'd soaked it all up. You were ugly too, weren't you, your soul, I mean? At least that's what you thought. You'd come from ugliness, so how could you be anything less? It—" to her surprise, Shady found her own cheeks were wet "—it doesn't have to be that way. It really doesn't. You're in agony. I know that. I can feel how much just from holding on to your hand. It's like…agony is coursing through me, eating me alive, like it's eating you. Goldie isn't a name you've used for years, that others know you by, not now, but it's who you think you are still. Goldie won't let go, will she?"

The woman didn't answer. Perhaps she couldn't. But her eyes remained fixed on Shady, another tear falling. Yet again, Shady only had minutes to see her, minutes ticking by all too quickly, words continuing to tumble from her mouth.

"A car hit you, do you realize that? You're pretty badly hurt, enough to be in the ICU. You've been in a coma all this time, and this is the second time I've visited you. Before, you…you didn't want me here. Goldie didn't, anyway, but maybe for Joan Parker it's different."

Joan's hand seemed to squeeze a little tighter, Shady not

knowing how to interpret this, whether it was Joan embracing her or Goldie issuing a warning.

Her heart began to beat as fast as it had when she'd entered the room, and Shady glanced at the door before leaning closer to Joan, feeling a resurgence of dark emotions, the tears on the older woman's cheeks drying.

Time was running out in more ways than one.

"When you ran, where did you end up? Who was the man that made you feel special? Was it…?" She swallowed, not wanting to utter his name but having to. "Was it Charles Manson, or someone like him? Joan, who did you get yourself involved with? And do you regret it? Is it your involvement with the Family that tortures you still?"

The tips of Joan's fingers began digging into Shady's hand, indeed an act of rebellion. Her eyes had also turned as black as the dream image.

Don't be afraid.

Again, Shady had to tell herself that. Some people were bad to the bone, had slaughtered the good wolf within them, but was Goldie one of them?

"What did you do, Joan? What are you guilty of? You've admitted all of it, but only to yourself. I've been to your house—yes, that's right, I went there, I went inside. There are so many mirrors. You're obsessed with them. And when I looked into those mirrors, I *became* you. I felt what you did. There was hope, initially, when you found him. He gave you something you craved. But he also corrupted you, made you do things."

"Do you love me?"

Shady was stunned. The woman had spoken. It was a cracked, brittle sound, her lips moving, but only slightly.

"What do you mean, do I love you?"

"Would you die for me?"

Shady swallowed. "I don't understand. Are you asking me, or—"

"Would you kill for me?"

Those last words were spat at Shady, filling her head and expanding. Yet, still, Joan's mouth had barely moved. What should she do? How should she react? She wanted to pull her hand away; she could easily do that—couldn't she?

Something in her refused to put it to the test, an element of doubt. Instead, she attempted to bury her fear and bewilderment.

"Joan, are those words he said to you? What was your answer?"

When there was silence, Shady threaded her voice with steel.

"Do you know what my answer would have been? It would have been no, I will *not* die for you. I will *not* kill for you. That isn't what love's about. That's control."

A jolt! The woman had responded, but, once more, not as Shady had expected. It was as if another feeling had surged through Shady, leached from the other woman—hope?

"We visited your home, and we researched you. There's nothing about Joan Parker or Goldie anywhere in the public domain that we could find. You didn't kill for him, did you? You certainly didn't die for him. You ran again, escaped again. Am I right, Joan? Am I?"

Was that a nod of the head? Or Shady merely willing it to be? It was a nod. It had to be.

"You got away! Oh, Joan, well done. I was so scared...so

worried. If it was that Family you were involved in, I wasn't sure I could cope. What they did...the atrocities..."

There was a movement behind her. Even without turning her head, Shady knew what it was—the door opening, the nurse calling time.

But that was okay. That was fine. Wasn't it? There'd been a breakthrough today. Shady might even have found out all she had to. This woman had once been a part of something evil, but she hadn't succumbed, not fully. So, was it merely the guilt that still tortured her? If so, that was something they could work with, they could resolve.

The nurse was here, but Shady had more to say, her voice barely above a whisper, issuing words meant just for the two of them:

"Joan, there's a way back. There's redemption."

"I'm sorry," the nurse said, "but the patient really needs to rest."

"Joan." Shady was desperate now to get a response, an acknowledgement from her. "You've suffered all your life, I think. Perhaps there's no need to suffer anymore."

"Did you hear what I just said?" the nurse continued.

Shady turned to the nurse, saw both concern and a tinge of indignation in her eyes. "Just one more moment, please. It's important."

Before the nurse could reply, she turned back to Joan, her voice still low. "Let go of the anger, the pain. Memories are only memories, they're the past. Don't let them continue to hurt you or"—she thought of the mirror and the impact it could have—"anyone else."

"I really do have to insist."

The nurse was coming closer, maybe even intent on

physically removing Shady.

"Please," Shady whispered to Joan, "show me that you understand."

A hand arriving on Shady's shoulder showed the nurse would accept no more resistance. "I want you to leave."

Damn!

Shady rose. She had no choice, beginning to extricate her hand, severing the connection. No more skin against skin, just fingertips now, pulling apart. And then Joan reached out again, so quickly it reminded Shady of a rattler striking. Her hand was back to skin on skin, to being gripped, such strength in the other woman still, such...hatred.

"Joan, what's the matter? What are you doing?"

Even the nurse looked surprised by what was happening. "Joan, are you okay?" she asked, the slightest hint of a tremor in her voice, an inkling that this was far from natural.

"Mirror!" the older woman hissed.

"Mirror?" Shady repeated. "What do you mean?"

"Mirror?" the nurse also repeated. "Does she want to look in a mirror?"

Shady shook her head. "No," she answered, suddenly understanding. Joan wanted *Shady* to look in the mirror, the one back at the museum—the one Joan Parker had gotten rid of, the *only* one, because she couldn't stand to look into it? Couldn't stand the truth of who she really was.

As the older woman's hand finally fell away, as her eyes at first fluttered and then closed, the nurse left Shady's side to see to her patient, muttering that perhaps it was unwise to allow visits quite so soon, that Shady should have listened when she'd said their time was up.

Although Shady was duly backing away, she kept her eyes on Joan and Joan only.

You succumbed to evil after all, didn't you? Somehow. Someway.

And via the mirror, so would Shady.

CHAPTER NINETEEN

"So, let me get this straight," said Annie, "you want to take the mirror back to Joan Parker's house. Trespass again."

Shady nodded. She, Ray and Annie were back in the basement of Mason Town Museum, positioned around the mirror, although no one had yet taken its dustsheet off. Shady had explained what had happened at the hospital, that Joan had been lucid for a short while and the exchange that had taken place between them.

"I just think it'll be more effective there than here, that's all. Think of the mirrors as a…jigsaw. To see the whole picture, we have to gather the pieces together."

"What about Gina's mirror, though? Isn't that a piece of the jigsaw?" asked Ray.

Shady screwed up her nose in frustration. "I know, I know. Shit, I wish I hadn't buried it. I need to go back there, try again. Building work starts real soon."

"Building work has already started," Ray said, causing Shady's eyes to widen.

"What? How do you know?"

"Because I went back just yesterday. The site's closed off now. The contractors are in."

"You never said you were going back!"

"No, well, I just…I wanted to help, that's all."

Shady smiled at Ray, at what he'd done for her, touched by it, but also upset about what he'd said about the land now cordoned off.

"Shit!" she said again. "We may never piece Joan's story together after all, not entirely."

Annie immediately consoled her. "We work with what we've got. That's the best we can do. It's *all* we can do. It was the case when we were dealing with Mandy, and it's the case now. You can never know everything, and maybe…well, maybe that's for the best."

Although Shady agreed, part of her still felt despondent.

"It's an interesting theory you've got," Annie said, steering the conversation back to the matter at hand, "that in order to see more effectively, the mirror needs to be returned to its source."

"Uh-huh," answered Shady, "and I know we'd be trespassing, but…I think we're pretty safe from the cops there. I think they tend to keep away unless absolutely necessary."

"Don't tempt fate, Shady," Ray said grimly.

"I'm worried, though," continued Annie. "If we do what you propose, what you'll see might be more of an onslaught than a vision, and I mean worse than before."

"It's got to be done, though," Shady said, concealing her own worry about that.

"We'll be with you," Ray assured her. "Won't we, Annie?"

"Oh, of course. Absolutely. But if it gets too much—"

"You'll break the connection." Shady smiled as she said it. "You'll haul me out."

Annie nodded. "Like I said—I keep saying—we do our

best, that's all."

"I just have to understand the mystery that surrounds Joan Parker. Annie, there's like this need in me—"

"You're not responsible for Joan Parker's accident."

As far as Shady was concerned, that was debatable. "There's a need in her too, to make peace with her past. And yet at the same time, every inch of her fights against it."

"Well, if she doesn't thank you for the big reveal," said Ray, "maybe Gina will."

Annie moved toward the mirror and stood in front of it.

"Annie?" said Shady. "What are you thinking?"

"Why not give it another try here?"

"Excuse me?"

Annie turned to her. "We know so much more about Joan Parker now. So, just a hunch, but try it here first before we go back to her house. Look in the mirror again and see what you can. I'm still worried about putting the mirrors together out there, about it all being too much for you."

"But—"

"Hear me out. If Manson's was the cult Joan was involved with, or, to be honest, any of those cults that sprang up during that time, then that's bad enough. But that's a memory she can *stand*."

"Because she's still warped?" Ray asked.

"Maybe," Annie said. "But, in contrast, there's a memory she *can't* stand. Maybe it came much later in her life and has nothing to do with her teenage years. Something happened to her, or she did something, and it's that memory, poured into this mirror, that she fights against."

"So what the hell is it?" Now Ray looked worried too.

Finally, Shady reached out a hand and pulled the dustsheet off the mirror.

As she did, all three gasped.

They all knew the mirror had a crack in it, long and jagged, reaching from top to bottom. This time, however, it was different. Although the glass remained in place, it was completely broken, some shards of glass wispy grey in color.

Others, though, were entirely black.

* * *

What had happened to the mirror sealed the deal. Shady, Ray and Annie were going back to Joan Parker's house and taking the shattered mirror with them. But not that day. Annie refused, said they should take the rest of the afternoon off to "go and have fun."

"Fun?" Shady said, as bemused as Ray by her insistence.

"Absolutely," she replied.

"Um…why?" asked Ray.

"Why should you have fun?"

He colored a bit at that. "Well, yeah."

Annie sighed as she led them up the winding stairs of the basement and back onto the first floor of the museum. "I want you to do something fun this afternoon because…because it provides a contrast, I suppose. This job of ours, our mission, if you like, can become all-consuming. Dominate every thought we have and everything we do. We need to solve this mystery; I'm not disputing that. Like you said, Shady, it's begging for conclusion. It's time. Especially with Joan Parker so ill in the hospital. And so, we have to visit her house, uninvited, as trespassers. Needs must. But first I want you to see your friends, go a bit wild, a bit crazy, laugh. Just make sure you have a decent night's sleep, though—that's imperative. And then tomorrow... tomorrow we give it another shot, try to lay this whole sorry business to rest."

Shady looked at Ray, and Ray looked at Shady before turning back to Annie.

"And this is paid fun, is it?"

Annie smiled. "I won't be docking your wages, don't worry."

"And what about you?" asked Shady. "What will you be doing?"

"I'll be having fun too, in my way."

"Which is?" Ray asked.

"I'll see the day out here, at the museum, and then I'll go back home, cook something a little extra delicious for myself, watch a favorite movie and then read some favorite passages from a book at bedtime." When Annie smiled, it made her seem years younger than she was. "You know, that really is rather blissful to an old broad like me."

Ray stepped forward and hugged Annie, surprising Shady. He was a sweet guy, a great friend, but he wasn't overly given to displays of affection. He'd felt the need to hug Annie, however, and in turn it inspired a need in Shady. When he let her go, she hugged Annie too, Annie looking rather flustered but also pleased.

"My, oh my, what's all this?" she kept saying while smiling widely.

Eventually Shady and Ray left, headed back to Idaho Falls, Ray texting and making a few calls on the way. Sam,

Brett and Teddy were up for meeting at The Golden Crown.

"And guess what?" Ray added.

"What?"

"Lisa Marie is too."

"Great," Shady said, feeling both pleased and a little trepidatious.

"Couple of hours to kill before everyone gets there, though. Fancy a late lunch?"

"Or it could be an early dinner."

"Same difference."

"Yeah, I guess. Where d'you suggest?"

"Dixie's? I could murder their southwest chicken sandwich."

"Dixie's it is."

While in a booth in the retro diner, Ray asked Shady what she had meant when she'd said to Annie that Lisa Marie had overcome obstacles in her life.

"Like, how do you know? She's told you?"

That he had waited this long to ask was commendable; Shady knew exactly how much he'd been wanting to bring the subject up before. But what could she say? The truth, she supposed, remembering Annie's words about how they should always be open and honest with each other, or at least strive to be. Just the basics, though, not wanting to betray Lisa Marie's trust somehow or dent the armor of the new person she'd become.

"Far out," Ray said at the end of it all. And that was *all* he said, somehow sensing Shady's awkwardness, at how torn she felt, and not wanting to make it worse for her. A good guy, special—he was all of that and more. Brad Pitt didn't stand a chance.

At just after five, Shady and Ray, both groaning about their bulging bellies, made their way to The Golden Crown, Brett already there, waving a hand at them as they entered. The three were soon joined by Sam, looking as if she didn't just work in a clothes store but modeled for them too, and then Teddy. Word had spread, and others joined them: Carrie Harris; Jon Ditton, whom Carrie was interested in; and Tonya Wakefield. Lisa Marie turned up an hour after everyone else, heads turning toward her as she swept in.

The hours passed, the drinks flowed, and there was never a gap in the conversation.

"Hey," said Brett, having just returned from smoking something dubious outside, "you know what we should do?"

"What?" Sam said, snuggling into his side.

"Go on vacation, all of us. Rent a house somewhere by the coast. Escape this hole for a while."

"A vacation?" Carrie squealed when she said it. "Are you serious?"

"Sure, why not?" he answered. "It'd be fun. Teddy, you up for it?"

"Always," Teddy said without taking his eyes off Lisa Marie.

"Ray," Brett continued. "You?"

"Game for anything, man," Ray replied. "Shady?"

"Yeah, sure." Shady also looked at Lisa Marie, who was sitting right by her side, shoulder to shoulder. "Are you coming too?"

There was a smile on Lisa Marie's beautiful face, perhaps even a twinkle in her eye. "If you're inviting, then I'd love to." It was a purr of a reply, one that caused Shady to look quickly away, hot and cold waves sweeping over her.

With Brett's talk of a shared vacation having stirred up yet more excitement, Shady grabbed her drink, relaxed back into her seat and just enjoyed the chatter. Truth was, they might all go away together, they might not. All that really mattered was being together tonight, rocking a town that could sometimes fail to match their youth and enthusiasm.

This was her tribe, and she belonged to it. Some were more Ray's friends, others hers, and Lisa Marie was somewhere in the middle, a newcomer who'd quickly integrated. Shady would sure miss her when she moved on, but it was also something she didn't have to think about right now. All she had to do, as Annie had insisted, was have a little fun.

A family. In many ways, that's who these people were. Not blood-related but chosen.

And yes, as she listened to Lisa Marie's laughter, Ray's shy banter with her, Brett still enthusing about a group getaway, and Sam swapping fashion tips with Carrie and Tonya, she had to admit, it felt good to belong. Blessed with loving parents too, she just couldn't imagine being an outcast with no one to call her own.

As she took another swig of low-alcohol beer, a smile formed. Almost.

She couldn't imagine, but with her gift she didn't have to.

Because this time tomorrow, she'd know.

CHAPTER TWENTY

Darkness. Lights, but only in the distance. And a road that stretches on and on. I don't know where it's going. I don't care. I've come from nothing, and if nothing is all that waits for me, then let it be. Anything is better than being stranded with him.

Did Momma travel down these very roads when she left? Not on foot, like I am, but with a man who drove her in his car, who whisked her away from the shit she'd otherwise endured, day in, day out. That we'd endured. Both of us. So why do it? Why leave me alone with him—just thirteen years old. Her only child. Abandon me?

"Shady, are you okay?"

"Yeah, Ray."

"If it gets too much…"

"Annie, I really am fine. Honestly. Again, it's like I'm looking at fragments of her life."

"That'd make sense," Annie replied.

They were in Joan Parker's living room, where they'd brought the mirror back to, the place they assumed it had once lived, positioning it against a far wall, Shady staring into it, both Ray and Annie flanking her. "The shattered mirror could be a representation of that."

"Shattered mirror, shattered life," said Ray.

"But at the same time," Shady said, "this is the whole

story too. It's what we need to know. Right now, it seems I'm back at the beginning when she took off, not long after her mom had gone. She'd disappeared into the night, and so did Joan."

"I wonder what became of her dad?"

Shady corrected Ray. "It was her stepdad. And I don't know. This isn't his story. It's hers. She may never have known either."

"Shall we carry on?" Annie asked.

Shady nodded. Although they hadn't turned on the lights—not wanting to attract attention—it wasn't as dark as their previous visit. They'd brought flashlights with them, and their beams reflected off the mirror as Shady stared into it, although nothing could lift the darkness that the mirror attracted. Nonetheless, Shady *was* okay to carry on.

None of them were sure when Joan had gotten rid of the mirror, only that it had been years and years ago, having been in Glenda Staines' possession for so long. But there'd come a time when she'd had to do just that, burying deeper the secret that haunted her. And Shady's hunch—that bringing the mirror back to its place of residence would somehow further spark the energy attached to it, make it more lucid—was working. She was Shady, but she was also Joan Parker, who became Goldie, the younger version of herself, the child.

It's getting late. I'm tired. My feet are sore; they're blistered and bleeding. Maybe if I curl up in a ditch somewhere, I can get comfortable enough to grab some sleep, start walking again at first light. Surely, someone will stop their car for me then, give me a ride to wherever they're going. They might even ask me if I've eaten, buy me some food from a truck stop. Go one step further and offer to put me up for a night or two so I could get some proper rest. Wouldn't that be nice? To be able to sleep without having to barricade the door in case he came barging in, drunk, swearing he'd lost his way, that he was heading to the bathroom, looking at me the way he did... Peaceful sleep. Not sure I've ever had any. Got no memory of it. I crave peace. Can someone out there give me that? The world can't be full of just bad people. Although, for certain, I ain't met a good one yet. This road is so long. Nothing but prairie on either side. There are mountains in the distance; I can just about make out the shape of 'em, and this road winding snakelike through it all.

Sleep. I'll get some sleep. Things'll be different in the morning. Someone will come along. Someone will save me.

"Christ!"

"What is it, Shady?"

"Oh, Annie, it's just...some people, you know. How could you abandon your own child?" Shady shifted position as her eyes traveled to another fragment of glass, one that reflected a portion of her eye, her hand reaching out to touch the mirror, to heighten the connection. "She was hitchhiking, she slept, and then someone did come by and pick her up. A man. Young. Wearing a plaid shirt. Good-looking too, in a way. She liked him. He liked her."

"Bonnie and Clyde scenario?" asked Ray.

"You know what? Kinda. He was older than her but not *that* old, maybe, like, in his early twenties, and good-looking, like I said, but...yeah, troubled too."

"Like calls to like," murmured Annie.

"Doesn't it, though," Shady said, sharpening her gaze.

I don't know what to think at first. But then he tells me what to think. And I listen. It's just…it's easier to do that. He said it would be, and he's right. I'm tired of thinking, plain tired, and still there's no peaceful sleep. He hasn't got a home, not a proper one; he goes from place to place. I can stay with him, but there are conditions. He likes me, you see. And I like him; I do. When he ain't in a mood, he's fun. He tickles me, makes me laugh, touches me. But when he is in a mood, well, then it ain't so much fun. I keep out of his way if I can, think of running. But that endless road weaving its way through so much land, the dark night, just a few stars in it, and cars passing by, their drivers looking straight ahead rather than at me…I can't face it, not yet. There's something about that long, dark road that frightens me more than he ever could. How alone it can make you feel. Smaller than a bug. And like I say, he's not all bad. He's nice on occasion; he can be sweet. I'm getting to like what he does, the way his hands caress me. I'm learning when to keep quiet too and not set him off, because then the bruises…well, they can last for days.

Shady's sigh was heavy.

"You need a break?" Annie dug out a thermos she'd brought with her, with coffee in it.

"Maybe," Shady answered. "Just for a minute."

It seemed such a strange thing to do, to be sitting in the living room of a woman they knew only psychically, a woman with a history that was both heartbreaking and terrifying, learning more and more about her from an object that had been her only confidante. If being in her house was trespassing, then how could you describe this trespassing on her life story? It was odd, outside of normal, but so much was, as Shady was discovering, a new normal taking over instead.

The door resisted when they'd entered the property, Ray worrying that someone, maybe a neighbor with a key, had come along and locked it. Eventually it had yielded but reluctantly, Ray having to put his full weight behind it to get it open. It was dark inside, just like before, but that darkness had even more of a denseness to it. They'd ventured in, once again listening to the sound of police sirens in the distance, a soundtrack stuck on repeat, and Shady could have sworn it was the house this time that didn't want them there, timber and drywall that had also soaked up Joan's energy, that were full of her. Too bad, because Shady and her colleagues were every bit as determined as the house was. Boldly, they'd continued walking down the hallway, straight to the epicenter—the living room—where Shady had previously tripped out courtesy of someone else's life, wanting further insights because to postpone it anymore, to linger with such memories playing in her head, was worse than facing them head on.

After having described the latest episode of Joan Parker's life, Shady finished her coffee before getting back to it. Handing her cup to Annie, she smiled, albeit wryly.

"Here I go again."

"This guy she picked up," Ray said, "or, rather, who picked her up, is he…you know, *the* guy?"

"Don't think so. He was young…good-looking. A drifter."

"Kinda fits the profile," Ray replied, shrugging.

"That's the thing, though, isn't it?" said Annie. "So many do. At this stage we mustn't assume. He could be anyone."

"But he's a creep?" Ray asked.

"*Such* a creep," Shady confirmed. "Maybe the sex was consensual at first, but…she was a kid, she was thirteen, and he ought to have known better. And he's hitting her too."

"The abuse continues," remarked Annie, sighing. "So sad."

"It is." Solemnly, Ray glanced down at the flashlight in his hand, his red hair several shades darker because of the gloom.

As she positioned herself in front of the mirror again, so many other mirrors surrounding her, a shard near the top caught her gaze—Shady peered into it before losing herself, feeling a frisson of something a fraction of a second before she did. What was it? Excitement?

We did it! We went in there and took everything he got, raced back to the car and sped off! There's so much money. We're rich! We can rent a place where the roaches don't shit on every surface. We can eat what we want. Drink what we want. We can buy clothes too! When I left home, I took almost nothing with me, just the clothes on my back. I try to keep 'em clean, but it's not easy when the places you find to stay ain't clean either. He'll buy me something pretty, he says, floaty and white. And the gas station we robbed, sitting by itself, all alone, surrounded by nothing but scrub, well, there's plenty more of them. We'll seek 'em out and get richer still.

But we need a gun.

That's what most of the money is for.

We need a gun, and I need to learn how to shoot. "That'll be your job," *he says.* "Ya know, to pull the trigger if it comes to it."

My man is true to his word. He gets a place for us to rent, buys me that pretty, floaty dress, and he gets the gun. Bringing it home, he shoves it into my hands, the metal cold and hard, and tells me to caress it like it's a man, to love it like it's one too.

"The gun will make people respect us," he says. "It's what makes us unstoppable. In America, you ain't nobody if you ain't got a gun."

Shady blinked as the scenes playing in her head changed to the desert. There was a vision of a young girl with her arms extended, holding a gun and shooting, the bullet ricocheting off a tin can that had been set up in the distance. She couldn't see the man; he was but a mere shadow. But she could feel the emotions in the girl—and yes, there was excitement, but also trepidation. This girl didn't like the gun; every time she pulled the trigger, it hurt her fingers, bruised her as much as the man bruised her. It was also heavy. Too heavy. And she'd hit the can only because he'd stood behind her and positioned her arms correctly. Left to her own devices, the bullets would fly everywhere.

"Don't waste 'em!" he'll say, he'll scream at me, and then, quick as lightning, his hand will come out to strike the side of my face. I'll scream back, I'll cry, but out here in the desert, there's never no one to hear. Just try harder, that's all I have to do. Please him. We're a team. We can ride the crest of a wave together. But I have to do better! I have to listen more; I have to learn. If I don't...well, those moods of his, they're getting blacker, not just bruises all over me; he nearly broke my arm. Took weeks to mend. And it set us back. Ain't no way you can pull a trigger if your arm's busted. And that's my job. "The only job I've given ya, so do it properly!"

"Christ, I would've turned the gun on him! Why didn't you, Joan? Why?"

"Shady—"

"Oh, it's fine, Annie, it's just…the man she was involved with was such a shit."

"Is it Manson?"

"Ray, I don't know! Stop asking, okay? He's a shit. Right now that's all we need to know."

Ray was immediately contrite. "Sorry."

"No, I'm sorry, but…" Quickly she related what had happened. "Like I said, if it had been me, I'd have gunned him down."

Again, staring into the mirror, she braced herself, that excitement she'd felt before ramping itself up, this time bordering on manic.

"Do like she says and keep your fucking hands where we can see 'em! You don't do what we want, then she'll shoot you dead!"

The man he's screaming at is no pushover. We're in another lonely gas station, miles from anywhere, two of us against one, and still the guy behind the counter refuses to open the cash register and hand us over our money.

"This is your last warning," he continues to scream at him. "We mean it. Do as we say or kiss God's green earth goodbye. Now open it! Open the fucking register."

The guy is a lot older than us, in his sixties, slim arms and legs but with a belly that sticks right out, that shows he's a man of indulgence. He should be scared. I'm scared. But all he does is stand there looking at us, this strange expression on his face, one I can't fathom right away. Does he pity us? If so, we don't want his pity! We don't need it! How dare he feel sorry for us;

he ought to save those feelings for himself.

I've lowered the gun a little, but I aim it high again.

"Just do what he says!" I'm the one yelling now, cursing the wobble in my voice and hands that visibly tremble. Yet when the guy replies, his voice is as smooth as butter.

"You don't have to do this, neither of you. This is no way to live your life. Come on, now, lower the gun, turn around and just…walk away."

"SHUT UP! JUST SHUT UP, OKAY! OPEN THE DAMN REGISTER!"

I've never heard my man sound like this before, and by now, we've robbed many gas stations in many states. We're practiced at it. We're good. But no one's ever resisted. And he doesn't like it, not one bit. He's losing his shit, shaking harder than I am.

"Honey," I say, "perhaps we oughta—"

He spins around to face me instead of the guy, spit covering his face. "And you shut up too! You do what I tell you. That's why I put up with you, why I let you stay."

"Hey, hey, hey!" It's the guy again, not looking quite as calm now. "If it means that much to you, I'll open the register and give you what I got. What the fuck? It's money, that's all." He has his hands up, but he begins to lower them.

"What are you doing?" my man asks, so antsy he's jumping like a bean.

"You want me to open the cash register, right?"

"Don't pull no funny stuff!"

The guy eyes me. "Wasn't intending to."

But he's a liar, that guy. The worst kind. The kind you almost believe.

He doesn't open the cash register; he pulls out a weapon from underneath the counter, the biggest rifle I've ever seen. And he aims it right at me.

"I'll take bets I'm a better shot than you are, darlin'," he says, and, again, there's sympathy in his voice. I try to look for smugness too, but I can't find it. "Now, like I said before, put the gun away, take your excuse for a boyfriend, and get outta here."

"SHOOT THE FUCKER!" More spittle flies from my man's face, his skin not white anymore but crimson with rage. "FUCKING SHOOT HIM!"

My fingers begin to squeeze the trigger, slowly, slowly, bit by bit, but then they stop, as if they've lost all function, as if they just won't work no more. And he hurls himself at me. My man. He grabs the gun, then turns to face the other guy.

That's when I flee. Again. The sound of bullets thunders in my ears as I reach the car and open the driver's door, turn the keys left in the ignition for a quick getaway, and race once more down a long, long highway.

CHAPTER TWENTY-ONE

"Jeez, she was an armed robber," Ray said, his eyes widening.

"You were the one who mentioned Bonnie and Clyde," Shady pointed out.

"So, she escaped him too, the second man in her life. She got away."

"Looks like it."

"Is that the big secret, do you think? Her involvement with him."

Shady glanced at Annie before shaking her head. "I've already seen there's worse to come."

"That's right, dear, you have," Annie replied. "So, in answer to Ray's question, I think we can assume that, no, that wasn't the big secret, only an opening chapter of her life. If we're correct in what we've assumed so far, then she falls into the hands of another monster."

Shady was about to agree when something else caught her attention.

"Hang on...wait. Can you hear that?"

At Shady's words, both Ray and Annie turned their heads and looked around the room.

"Shady, what is it?" asked Annie, her brow furrowed.

"Music."

"Music?" Ray asked. "I can't hear any music."

"Someone's singing…playing a guitar. A man with a soft voice. A nice voice."

"There's no one singing, Shady…Shady?" Annie's voice faded until it was only the man's voice that Shady could hear, low and melodic. It mesmerized her…or had it mesmerized Joan?

Shady's gaze was back on the mirror, but then her eyes closed as she swayed in time to such a haunting rhythm.

Comes a time for living,
A time for dying too.
Think you're living, baby,
But you're crying inside.
Want you to smile.
Want you to live, baby.
Want you to love.
You got the sweetest smile.

No one's ever done that before. Written a song just for me. About my smile and how it moves them, how it captures their heart. Such a beautiful voice. Such a beautiful man. Special. Won't make the same mistake I did before. I've found who I should be with, where fate intended me to be.

His voice is that of an angel. And when he lifts his head so I can look into his eyes—deep pools you could drown in—I know the stars have guided me all the way to heaven.

Laughter. Tenderness too, deep into the night. His hands touch me, stroke me, they softly caress, and his lips murmur the sweetest words into my ears.

"You're beautiful."

"You're special."

"You're mine."

"Would you die for me?"

How quickly I respond. "Yes. Yes, I would!"

"I would die for you. Every one of you."

Right now, though, I don't want to think about the others, although I know they're a part of the deal. I make believe it's just me and him, marvel too at how complete I feel.

He believes in me!

He hands me his guitar and says, "You play a song."

Me! I've never picked up an instrument in my life. "I can't," I say, immediately handing back such a precious object. But he won't take it.

"You can do anything you want."

And I do. I start strumming those chords, and he sings along, making up lyrics, again about me, his beautiful, brave warrior, clapping so hard when I finish.

I put the guitar down at last, and I bend down and kiss his feet.

Holy, that's what this man is. A Father to us all.

"Shady? Whatcha doing?"

If that was Ray speaking to her, his voice quickly faded. She didn't want to listen to Ray; she wanted more of this man, finding him just as enthralling.

We're in the city, but the city's getting crowded. People keep coming, day in, day out. I sit on a bench and watch 'em sometimes, my legs dangling, men and women with such a look in their eyes, weariness but also hope. Sometimes another word comes to mind: desperation. And a strange thought: that looking into their eyes is like looking into a mirror, like looking at me when I first arrived, praying, always praying for just a little bit more.

We're staying in an apartment, but it's getting cramped. These people are finding out about us; they're coming to call. It's him, you see, he draws them like the beacon he is, each one eager to bask in his presence, hanging on to every word he utters, yearning for a nod of approval, for a glance that lingers just a fraction of a second longer than it does on anyone else. I yearn too, but I've had to practice patience. He'll reward me. He always does.

We leave the city and move to the desert, to a much bigger place, rented to us by an old man who seems…amused by us. We don't mind that he's amused. He kinda amuses us too, as crazy as a coot, that's what he is, rarely outta bed. Only thing that matters is we have a big enough place to be together—the Family. And he'll sing. Every night we light a fire, gather around it, and he'll sing of a world far better than this one, in which it's us that reign, not just a family but the chosen. My eyes will close, everybody else's eyes will close, and we'll sway to the music, more potent than any drug on offer.

"Would you die for me?"

We all would. We'll do what we are told.

"You don't have to like it," he says when we're alone, "but know this: I'm grateful for your attention to other men on the ranch. We have to keep everyone happy, right?"

I lower my eyes rather than answer, and gently he cups my chin and lifts my head.

"Ain't fair if it's just us that's happy, now is it?"

"But I'm special? You said so."

"You're special, all right. Like gold."

Like gold. Goldie. That's who I become.

"Rebirth." Had that word just left Shady's mouth?

Perhaps. Joan had been reborn. She was happy at last. All that hate in her, that…ugliness…banished.

Temporarily banished, remember? Shady did. When she'd touched Joan Parker's hand in the supermarket, it was all still there, deep inside her. Hatred, then love and wonder, then back to hate. *What's your secret, Goldie? What are you trying to hide?*

"Ray. Ray," she called.

"Shady, I'm here, right by your side."

"Dance with me."

"What?"

"Dance with me. Just…dance."

Arms went around her and held her as her body continued to writhe. Ray's arms. But…they didn't feel like Ray's. And the smell in her nostrils, it was earthy, patchouli-like and pungent, not like Ray at all, who smelled of soap and water. It tantalized her; she breathed it deep into her lungs, captured it as she wanted to capture this man.

"You're special." Over and over he murmurs this into my ear. Does it make the other girls jealous? We're all one or supposed to be. We shouldn't harbor feelings such as jealousy, but I still wonder. Because I can't deny it, I'm jealous when he's with someone else, I seethe *with jealousy, and I hate it when another man's hands are on me, even though I smile. I smile because I have to. That's what we agreed. Keep everyone happy. The women serve the men. It's the way of nature. And we are nature's children.*

So happy. The days pass in a haze, dreamy days, out in the desert, the sun always shining, all of us fooling around, and he does this for us. He's provided an Eden.

Dreamy days…

217

"Shady? Why are you pushing me away? What is it? What's happening now? Annie, do you know what's happening? Should we stop this? Get her out of here?"

There's no stopping any of it! The stars lit the way, led me into his arms. And I was happy. I was! Life was blissful. It was everything I wanted it to be. So how could it change, and so fast? How could he turn like he has…? Against me.

Before, they weren't lies that left his mouth. I know that. I cling to that. But what he's asking…what he wants us to do now…

And we're hungry. Looking back, I realize we always have been. But for a while it didn't seem to matter—we dined on love, and it was enough. And the smell of us! There's nothing heady about it at all. We stink. This place stinks. And the sun keeps beating down, searing us.

"Would you die for me?"

I would. Just go back to being who you were, full of love and light and promise. Not this person…angry, just like the other one was angry, but the other one wasn't angry all the time. He is. There's a volcano inside that won't stop spewing.

What triggers it? I don't know. Something to do with his songs. Other people don't like them, not like we do. People that could catapult him into the hearts and minds of others, aside from us. Place him where he deserves to be, at the very top, revered not just in our world but the world over. He's been scorned. Worse, ignored. God, his moods are black! People leave, but he's always said they could. Free love. Free choice. So why does it infuriate him, send him crashing around the ranch, smashing things, smashing his guitar, his beloved guitar? It lies on the floor in pieces. Those of us who stay do so because we want to, because we still believe in him. Wholly. He's the pinnacle. An angel that glitters. And we tell him. But the light in his eyes, I can't see it no more.

No money. We're running out. Truth is, you can't live on love forever. And with no money there are no drugs, and with no drugs the scales are dropping from people's eyes. That's what I hear one of my sisters saying, and it makes me so mad, as mad as him. "They can see this is bullshit," she says and then laughs, actually laughs.

We have to get money. Steal it again. Any way we can.

And it's not him that'll do it. It's us.

"Do whatever it takes, you hear?" He looks at me and hands me a gun, just like the other man handed me a gun. "Don't be afraid to use it."

But I hate guns. I loathe them. I go out and purposefully, secretly, leave it behind. We get ourselves money. But it's never enough. And more people are leaving...

"Would you die for me?"

I say I would, so do others.

"Would you kill for me?"

"Shady! Come on, I think that's enough. You're not just dancing. It's like you're in some kind of frenzy. You need to break the connection—"

"No, Ray! Not yet! I...I can't."

It was as she'd thought—not just the mirrors but this entire building was possessed by Joan Parker. The woman had shut herself away with nothing but memories, and someone like Shady was able to come in here and relive them. She had to know what happened next...

"The visions, they're coming so fast," she tried to explain further, surfacing but briefly, already feeling as if she was beneath the waters again.

We're sent out, me and some others, those that are most devoted, that he trusts above everyone, that sit at his right hand, he says, the crutch he leans on, his safety net. This time he wants a lot of money, more than we've ever been able to steal before. And he tells us exactly where he wants us to go. Somewhere exclusive. The homes of those that squander money, that revile those who have none.

"Do what you have to do. There should be no witnesses."

I drive. The others in the car…they're bouncing. So alive. Ironically. Eager…always eager. They're doing the work of the savior.

Finally, the journey is over. We park the car and walk the rest of the way. No attempt at stealth, they whoop and cheer each other on, smiling so hard they look like caricatures. A dog barks in the distance, it howls, and it whines. Some birds swoop down, blacker than the night. And all I can think of is him, back at the home we share, having commanded us. Refusing to get his hands dirty, just like the other one had refused, but wanting ours to be stained bright red. And all in the name of love…

Screaming. Laughter. Begging. Cheering. A riot of colors and a stench like iron.

I brought the gun this time. I drop the gun. The others have knives.

They have power.

The power he's given them.

That he wields over and over.

That has nothing to do with love. Why? Because, just like us, he has no idea what love is.

More screaming—it's gut-wrenching, pleas for mercy that never comes.

I scream too, then turn from all that's unfolding.
And run.

CHAPTER TWENTY-TWO

"She didn't do it! She didn't kill anyone!"

"Shady, what the hell? Look at you, you're covered in sweat!"

"So what? Who cares? Ray, Annie, she didn't kill anyone at the gas station, and the other man she met, the man we think is Manson, she didn't kill for him either. Both times she ran; she got out of there. Maybe the second man wasn't Manson, but it was someone like him. She got involved because she thought she loved him. When she realized she didn't…and what he wanted from her…she ran."

Her head pounding—the images, so vivid just seconds ago, already beginning to ebb— Shady looked from Annie to Ray, at expressions caught between confusion and horror.

"That's good news, isn't it? That she wasn't one of the guilty?"

"Shady." The solemnity in Annie's voice ate away at some of her euphoria. "She was."

"What? I don't understand. I've just told you what happened. She was a victim, an innocent, manipulated, but she wasn't a killer."

How chill the atmosphere grew as Annie continued to

gaze at her, Shady shivering suddenly, a violent jolt tearing right through her.

"Annie, I've just seen what happened."

"I know you have. But, Shady, look at the mirror."

"The mirror?"

"Yes. And you, Ray, look what's happened to it now."

The mirror. The one that had gotten away, that Joan Parker had stared into and made her confession to as though it were a priest. And then what? She'd gotten rid of it because she couldn't bear her reflection in it anymore, the horror that stared back at her, the...*disgust?*

"Shit!" Ray said, having obeyed Annie.

Shady knew she had to look too, but she felt such reluctance. Joan Parker, a runaway kid, had gotten involved with some of the lowest people to crawl this earth, violent people, selfish people, deluded. Her own desperation had made her blind to their true natures, just as it blinded so many. But she hadn't sunk as low. Ever. And Shady had been so happy about that, so relieved. Damaged she might be, and naïve once upon a time, prey for the stalkers to feast on, but she wasn't evil. There was hope for her. And because of that, there was hope in Shady also.

But that hope withered and died as she, too, turned to look at the mirror. The glass was mottled when whole, blackened in places when shattered. Now it was wholly blackened, a phrase coming to mind, one from the Bible: *we see through a glass, darkly.* She knew what that phrase meant, had learned about it in school. From the writings of the Apostle Paul, it meant we do not now see clearly, but by the end of time, we will.

This was end of times. A time for truth. And nothing but

the truth.

Joan Parker was a woman as guilty as sin.

Should she, Shady Groves, go further with this? As when she'd first visited Joan at the hospital, the temptation was to get the hell out of this run-down house in this run-down neighborhood and run too, all the way back to the comfort of her own home and her good, decent family. To clutch the piece of leather that had once belonged to Kanti and draw comfort from it—to believe that if the stars guided you, *truly* guided you, it would always be toward the light, never damnation. But if she did that, if she gave into that desire—and, for certain, a voice in her head continued to encourage her: *Do it! Run! Get outta here!*—would comfort ever be hers again?

Joan Parker might have fled from violence twice, but at one point she'd run headlong toward it. Not shied from an atrocious act but committed it.

Although her legs felt leaden, Shady forced herself closer to the wrecked object. There were other mirrors in the room, the whole house was full of them, but none held the secrets that this one did.

"Shady." Ray's voice was heavy with concern, but it was Annie who stilled him, not Shady.

"We have to know," she said, "not just for Joan's sake, but for Gina's too."

It was connected, all of it. And this was the only way to find out how.

Oh, Joan, what the fuck did you do?

A few inches from the mirror, Shady reached out and grabbed it by the frame, felt its energy to be stronger than ever. It raced through her veins, tensioned every sinew, images flashing through her mind as furiously as they had before.

Darkness. Lights, but far in the distance. And a deserted road that stretches on without end. Just me. Alone. Always alone. I've learned so much. I'm not who I was: a scared little girl, someone who trusted, who wanted to belong, who craved acceptance. Who wanted more than anything to find peace and to be loved. Love, though, is such a false god.

Sometimes, as I drive and drive, as I continue moving from town to town, picking up work in bars and casinos, I can cope with the truth. It's harsh, but it's simple. I don't want or seek love, not anymore. I've been purged of that. I use men, just as I use everyone I encounter, to satisfy my needs, not theirs, although sometimes it's easier to let them think otherwise. I really did think I loved him. For a while he overshadowed all else. I don't want to, but I can so easily recall his voice as he sang to me, the smile that was a mask.

But then his face fades, and in its place is another. Sal Parker. Momma. The same question arises: Where did you go that night? Where did this mean old highway take you?

Obsession is a gradual thing.

I spend years continuing to drift, existing, no longer a part of anything and belonging to no one. If a newspaper catches my eye, his face gazing out from it, those eyes of his blacker than ever, I turn away, not reading the headlines that announce his crimes. I don't own a TV. The past is done, and I want nothing to do with it.

But slowly, surely, I resurrect it.

Is she still alive? Is she laughing? For so long it was only him in my thoughts, and I wonder now if that was something to be grateful for, if that's what I truly seek? Some respite. Her face is back, a redefined memory from which the dust has been blown away. I can see once again, vividly, the excitement in her eyes as she took off that night, and a mouth that twitched only with relief. She was leaving to pursue another life with another man. Was it a man she stayed with? Had children with?

Where is she?

Where the fuck is she?

Obsession. Not just with you from the moment you wake, it's there when you dream. You can't escape it. Unconditional love. The love a mother has for a child. Another big fat fucking lie. Has she forgotten all about me? Or sometimes…just sometimes…does my face haunt her dreams too? And if it does, does it provoke a glimmer of something in her? Guilt? Regret? I'm her child! Born of her body. The same blood, the same flesh. Her responsibility.

Do I look like her? She had blonde hair and blue eyes; my hair is blonde too, but straight, whereas sometimes she would curl hers. And my eyes—they're grey-blue.

Do I smile like her? Is my laughter the same? Do I cry like she does?

I stare in the mirror, in all the mirrors, searching, confiding, obsessing.

Where did you go?

In her twenties when she left, she'd now be in her thirties.

Where'd you end up?

So many highways. But if I was aimless before, I'm not now. For the first time I have a purpose, so I search and search. I stop in so many towns and ask so many questions. "Do you know her? This is what she used to look like and how old she'd be by now. That's it, her name's Sal. Her last name might have changed, but Sal Parker was who she used to be. Me? Oh, I'm a friend of the family. I'm Goldie."

Or, rather, I've fully become her. I'm not Joan Parker. Not now.

I'm done with Joan Parker.

I never thought I'd see my mother again, but there she is, in a small grocery store in a small town. She looks…younger than I expected, like the years haven't touched her. I didn't expect my heart to do this, but it flips. She's in this town—I already found that out but not her address. The man I asked wouldn't give that to me unless I told him my business. And I didn't want to do that. Why ruin the element of surprise? But everyone needs groceries, right? Momma too. I knew she'd visit this store eventually; all I had to do was lie in wait.

My heart skips a beat at the sight of her, and my mouth falls open. My momma…she's beautiful. Not a drunk, lurching about, her breath sour with beer. She is radiant.

And, yes, she's laughing. She's standing with the clerk, passing the time of day, animated, and so, so alive. Vitality oozing from her.

When she leaves the store, I follow in my car. We get all the way out of town before she turns right and heads down a track, a big ranch at the end of it, one surrounded by all the colors of spring.

I sit in my car for so long, on the dirt and gravel shoulder on the other side of the highway, staring at that ranch and at the entrance to it, where a series of letters hang on a horizontal pole: Cades Home Farm. *That's its name.* Home. *That word in particular seems to catch the breeze. She has one. And I don't.*

With the sun blazing down, I start up the engine of my car and get out of there.

Driving down another long road, on and on and on...

There was a sigh of relief, Shady startled to realize that it had come from her. Annie and Ray were right beside her, and she turned toward Annie first.

"She found her mother, but she didn't kill her. She didn't! She found out where she lived, a place called Cades Home Farm. I was expecting her to go in there or something and cause trouble. But she just...drove away. Annie, Ray, listen to me, she drove away!"

Annie was about to answer, Ray as well, the pair of them relieved too, perhaps, when Shady turned her head back to the mirror, whose blackness swirled before her as though it were a living thing, thickening, congealing, churning out yet more insight.

"What the fuck...?"

Thirteen! I was thirteen when she left me. A kid. Just fucking thirteen!

The rage that emanated from the mirror swamped Shady.

"Annie," she said, staggering as she reached out.

Annie grabbed her. "Shady, dear? What is it? What's happening now?"

"Stop it! Can you stop it?"

This is too much! Make it stop! This is bad...real bad. No...I can't see this.

Shady's protests, both silent and otherwise, amounted to nothing.

Thirteen! Why should others have a life and not me? What was it about me at that age that made me so unlovable? So easy to leave. I was thirteen, for fuck's sake! And so are you. You're thirteen and loved. So fucking loved. Why you? Why not me? Why? Why? Why?

"No!" Shady was shouting, was screaming. "No! Please!"

Annie and Ray had tightened their grip, were dragging her away from the mirror, her feet practically off the ground. But what was in there was coming at Shady; it had latched on, and now it wouldn't let go—the darkest energy, the darkest memory of them all.

Goldie was screaming, Shady was screaming, and someone else too—a thirteen-year-old child that Goldie was attacking, one face twisted with fury, the other with agony, as the woman brought the knife down, all the way down, and stabbed her with it.

CHAPTER TWENTY-THREE

The well of tears was seemingly endless, each one hot and fierce and pouring down Shady's face. Joan Parker, who'd become Goldie, was a murderer—worse than that, a *child murderer*. She'd chosen someone the age she'd been when her mother had left, and vented all her anger, hurt and betrayal upon her.

Murder. Could there ever be an excuse for it?

At home, in her bed, Shady snuggled deeper under the comforter, not wanting to think anymore, to question or keep seeing the visions that wanted to cram themselves inside her head even though she was far removed from Joan Parker's house.

Annie and Ray had gotten her out of there, that dark, pinched old place on the edge of town. Not just screaming, she'd been scratching at her own eyes too, yelling for Goldie to stop, to not commit such a cruel act. The victim's only crime? She was thirteen and happy.

In Annie's car, Shady had continued to sob hysterically, hardly able to catch her breath. When still a good distance from Shady's house, Annie had stopped the car and turned around to face her. She was in the back with Ray's arms around her. Annie hadn't said anything, just reached out to place a hand on Shady too—both of them trying to warm her with love. It took a while, but she'd calmed. Enough to be taken all the way home and sneaked past her parents' bedroom and into her own, the tears still coming all through the night.

Her occupation was more than just earning some bucks so she could have a life; it was a vocation. And no one had ever said it would be an easy ride. Annie hadn't. She'd warned her how tough it might get, right from the start. "There'll be times when you'll want to pull back, but if you continue, always remember, there are many, many of us out there, doing the same thing. And for one purpose only: the purpose of good."

Annie had said it to Shady, and she'd said it to Ray, and both had stood and listened, shaking their heads resolutely, absolutely sure they wanted to get involved.

But it was different now.

She'd wavered before, while sitting with her head in her hands in the woods, but only for a moment. Now she was shrinking back from it.

She was the one who saw, who delved too deep into the pasts of others.

But no more, not when people were guilty of crimes such as this.

Demons plagued everyone from time to time, causing anger, self-doubt and jealousy. But most could contain these demons or eventually send them packing. Others, though, like Joan Parker, had taken them by the hand and danced with them.

Still trying to push the visions away, Shady started

praying, not to God but to Kanti, her lips moving rapidly. *Help me, Kanti, let me sleep, just sleep, no dreams at all this time. I want an abyss to fall into, a well that's empty. I'm not born to do this. You said I was, but I'm not. You can't expect me to carry on, you of all people. This gift we share broke you, and it might just break me too. I'm not strong enough, I'm not! Goldie thought the stars were lighting the way to a brighter future; she thought they were guiding her too when she followed them. She was wrong. What if I'm wrong too? How is it possible to see what I've seen and remain sane? To see it again and again, not just in Goldie but in others like her, worse than her. Because there will be worse, there always is. Oh, please help me sleep, to forget. Just for a little while.*

And Kanti must have answered her prayers, because she did sleep, deeply and dreamlessly. She remembered falling into the chasm she'd craved. It was like stepping forward, off a ledge, and descending into warm folds of unconsciousness, receiving it gratefully because, in it, there would be nothing but stillness.

Falling…healing…her heart shattered too, like the mirror, like Goldie's heart, pieces of it only gradually drifting back together. Falling deeper, never to resurface…

"Shady, honey, wake up. Shady, it's urgent, apparently. Come on, now, it's late. You've slept all day. I was getting so worried, but…sweetheart, listen to me, you have to wake up. You can't stay like this."

Shady shifted and stirred, having to climb back up through layers and layers, not that she was happy about it. Where she'd been, nowheresville again but a *true* nowhere this time, was where she wanted to stay, but for one thing: she didn't belong there. *This* was where she belonged.

Where there was light, noise, hustle and bustle. And demons.

"Mom?"

"Yes, honey, I'm here. Shady, are you okay? I know...I know not to interfere too much. You're an adult now, you make your own decisions, I respect that, but...are you okay?"

Shady opened her eyes at last to see Ellen's familiar face just above her own, framed by honey-colored hair and filled with concern and love.

"What is it, Mom?" she said, rising to a sitting position. "What's urgent?"

"Ray's here."

"Ray?"

"And that lovely young lady from the hospital is with him."

"Lisa Marie? Why's she here too?"

"You'll have to ask them that. Should I tell them to give you a few minutes so you can get dressed?"

"Yeah...um...yeah. Actually, Mom, could you send them in here?"

Ellen frowned slightly. "So that you can talk in private?"

"Mom..."

Ellen held her hands up. "I get it. I understand. I do. I'll go fetch them."

At the door, however, she lingered for a moment before turning again to her daughter. "Just...if something's wrong, don't shut me out. I'm here for you, okay? Always."

Tears pricked at Shady's eyes again. She had to choke them back before she could form an answer.

"I know, Mom," she finally said, "and I love you so

much for it."

* * *

"Shady! You're okay. Ah, thank God! I'm sorry, so sorry you had to go through that."

Ray was first into her room, rushing over to her bed, bending down and scooping Shady up in his arms, enveloping her in a bear hug.

"Ray!" she said. "Get off me! I haven't showered yet. I stink!"

"Your armpits smell sweeter than roses," he said, pulling away. "They always do."

Shady found she was not only smiling but laughing, something she wouldn't have thought possible a few hours ago.

Ray shuffled to one side, and it was like the sun coming out as Lisa Marie stepped into full view. So much so that Shady heard herself gasp, her hands reaching out just as Lisa Marie's hands were, clinging to this newfound friend. The sleep had only healed her so much, she realized, Ray's and Lisa Marie's hugs finishing the job. There was so much radiance and warmth in both, so much...giving.

Some people took from you, exhausted you, because all they did was take. Annie had a term for them when they'd discussed it once—*psychic vampires*, people to be wary of. By contrast, Ray and Lisa Marie *recharged* Shady. This boy who'd only been an acquaintance as a kid but was now a cherished friend, and this girl who'd come from nothing but had the biggest heart of all.

"It's all right," Lisa Marie murmured as she held Shady. "It's going to be all right."

Such soft words, quiet, barely heard above the sound of Shady's renewed sobbing, but they sank in. *It's going to be all right.*

Eventually, the two girls parted, and Shady rose from bed, pulling the old Green Day tee shirt she was wearing down a couple more inches. There were some shorts at the bottom of her bed, and she grabbed them and pulled them on.

Sitting on the edge of the bed now, the other two having also found places to sit, she eyed each one. "What's urgent?" she asked, then drew a deep breath.

"We've got news," Ray said, torn between eagerness and solemnity.

"About Joan Parker?"

"Who else?"

Shady exhaled. "Yeah, I guess."

"We've been doing some digging," Lisa Marie explained.

"We have," Ray said. "After dropping you back home last night, the state you were in...well, I couldn't sleep and neither could Annie. So we started on some research."

"All through the night?" Shady had to admit, Ray looked tired, his hair messier than usual, dark circles beneath his eyes such a contrast to his pale skin.

"Yeah, most of it," he said. "Then Lisa Marie called. She'd been trying to get a hold of you but couldn't, so she contacted me. She...um...got involved too." He shot a grateful glance at Lisa Marie. "She helped us out loads, actually. Shady, what we found—"

"You guys, I...I don't know if I want to know. I—" again, she hesitated "—I'm not sure I'm strong enough."

Ray was about to open his mouth, dive back in, but Lisa

Marie beat him to it.

"Shady, I understand, really I do. Ray explained what happened."

"And you don't think I'm nuts?"

"You know I don't."

Shady swallowed. "It was pretty…it was pretty awful. What I saw. What she did."

Lisa Marie nodded, validating what Shady said. "Ray and Annie searched all night for news of the killing of a thirteen-year-old, and then when morning came, I joined them. I have access to some databases—and the internet, of course—but this is a big country. Sad fact is, there are hundreds of murders that take place every week, and with only a vague timeframe to go on, well, that made the task even harder."

"Joan Parker's a free woman," Shady said. "I first encountered her in Walmart, for God's sake. In this country, life means life. If she'd been convicted of murdering a kid, she'd be in prison still, wouldn't she?"

"She would," Ray agreed, a glint of excitement in his eyes that annoyed Shady.

"So, she got away with it. She just… Justice was never done." Making a fist, Shady brought it down hard upon the bed. "Even Manson got caught for what he did, him and his asshole followers. He might not be alive now, but they are, and they're where they belong for the senseless crimes they committed, either in jail or a very dark place."

"Maybe…" Lisa Marie suggested, "Joan's actions weren't entirely without sense."

"Huh? What do you mean? What could you *possibly* mean?"

"Hold up a minute, Shady," Ray interjected. "You gotta listen to the full story."

"Okay." She was still indignant. "Go ahead, I'm all ears."

Lisa Marie retook the reins. "We had a breakthrough. Not too long ago, in fact, just a few hours, a little after lunchtime."

Shady glanced at the clock. It was now pushing six in the evening, a part of her marveling at how long she'd slept. Hour after hour had passed, hours in which she'd been lost, but her friend and colleagues…they had carried on.

In the glare of the light hanging above their heads, Lisa Marie paled a little, but there too in her cornflower eyes were the beginnings of excitement. "We trawled through everything we could. Annie had gone home to sleep—she was exhausted, finished—and Ray and I didn't know how much longer we could go on either, but we pushed through." Her smile was tinged with sadness. "There are only so many acts of murder you can take in. It all gets a little depressing, and, well, I fight hard against that."

Sorry she'd gotten angry, Shady hung her head. "I know. And you do great."

"Okay to go on?" Lisa Marie checked with them.

"Be my guest," Ray replied.

"Like I said, we were about to give up. There was nothing on record about Joan and nothing about a Goldie either. We'd explored every avenue and come to a dead end. But then…well, I had an idea. We know from checking Joan's records before that she was born in Lancing, just near the Utah border."

"Right," Shady said, nodding.

"And we also know that old saying 'The apple doesn't fall

far from its tree.'"

"Yeah." Shady was frowning now, but, inexplicably, her excitement was growing.

"In this case," Lisa Marie continued, "*two* apples."

"What are you trying to say?" She was growing impatient but also knew that some stories, well…they took time to tell.

"Cades Home Farm was where Joan Parker's mother lived. And you saw in your visions that she visited there."

"I did."

"She went back, Shady. Joan Parker went back. Repeatedly. From the highway, she sat in her car, and she watched a little girl grow up."

"What?" Shady's frown deepened. "I never saw all that. Only that she'd visited once and then she took off. It was too painful for her."

"Cades Home Farm is about seventy miles from Lancing. Joan might have traveled far and wide, but ironically, Sal Parker never did. I have no clue if the man she was with was the one she'd run away with, but like I said, she didn't go far. I have no clue either what happened to Joan's stepfather, but Sal never remarried. She lived with a man there and had a child with him. His name was Alan Gearing, and the child was Sarah Gearing."

"Come on, you gotta tell me, how'd you find all this out?"

"Because, playing on this hunch, we did a search on the back issues of the *Lancing Tribune* and narrowed it down. Finally, we found it. It was all there in black and white."

"Found what?"

"How the town was rocked by a terrible attack on the

child of a former resident. A kid, thirteen years old, was stabbed multiple times. And the mother, Sal Parker, was distraught about it. Who could possibly do such a thing to her beautiful, her beloved, her *only* child?"

CHAPTER TWENTY-FOUR

Something in Shady skyrocketed—a rage, as black as Joan's had ever been.

"Only child? She said that? She actually said it? How could she! She's Joan's mother too. You can't just forget about your own child like that!"

"She *was* Joan's mother," Ray corrected. "Sal Parker is dead."

"What? Is she?" Shady held not an ounce of sorrow as she said this. "Well, if she is, then you know what? Good riddance to her. It's like…I don't know…she was the true devil here. Did…did the shock of Sarah's death have something to do with it?"

As Shady said this, Lisa Marie glanced at Ray, and he quickly looked back at her too, his eyebrow lifting slightly.

"Guys? What is it? Is there something more?"

"Shady," Ray informed her, "Sarah Gearing isn't dead."

"What?" Shady said again, recalling the visions she'd seen so recently. Just as quickly, she shook her head, a violent action, trying to dispel them. "But I saw what Joan did! She attacked the girl with a knife, multiple times. No one survives that kind of attack."

"They can," Lisa Marie said. "And she did. She's alive, in her forties and currently living just over the border in Utah. She didn't fall too far from the tree either, at least not where actual distance goes. Cades Home Farm is also still standing. Ray and I looked at it on Google Maps, but it looks pretty decrepit, like the landscape and vegetation is trying to bury it."

Remembering a certain cabin in the woods when she, Ray and Annie had been trying to find out about Mandy, Shady nodded. "Nature has a way of doing that," she said. "Trying to cover up, to erase the actions of men...and *women* that have corrupted it."

"She's alive," Lisa Marie continued, "and she's willing to see us."

Something else flared in Shady now. Disbelief.

"You gotta be kidding me!"

"We're not."

"She's willing to see us? Does she know the reason? Who we are?"

Lisa Marie nodded, so enviably calm. "She knows it all."

"When did this happen? When did you even contact her? I know I've lost a day, but, jeez, what you've all achieved!"

"You paved the way," Ray reminded her. "Put us on the right path."

The right path? Shady shook her head at those words, excitement, fury, disbelief and now something else vying for attention, a feeling bigger than all of them. How could he say such a thing when all she thought she'd done was lead them into desolation and failure? How could he be that gracious? And if there was any truth to his words, was the purpose of this mission so much greater than she'd realized?

Before she could give voice to those thoughts, try to assemble them, Lisa Marie spoke again, doing her utmost to explain to Shady, to get her on board too. "I called Sarah, and I spoke to her. She sounded older than she should...and tired. She never knew the identity of her attacker or what motive there was behind it, if there ever was one, and it's plagued her for a long time. From what we can put together, Joan was in her late twenties when she did what she did. *If* Joan had returned many, many times to the farm—this is only a theory, by the way, but we're pretty sure about it—if she'd returned, she'd done so just to observe, to watch. When I said this to Sarah, she seemed to confirm it. Many times before the attack, she'd spotted a car, a blue Ford, but the road they were on wasn't isolated, it was a highway, and there were other farms dotted around, cars and trucks always passing. She'd spotted this car, but it hadn't registered, you know, not consciously. Not until after."

"When everyone was trying so desperately to look for a reason."

Lisa Marie agreed. "Joan probably dumped that car after the attack, left it somewhere in the desert scrub to rot. Whatever she did with it, it was never found, just as Joan was never found. Both just...disappeared."

"Okay, so Joan watched, and she waited," Shady said, trying to envision this now, remembering also what had been said before, when Shady had tuned into Joan's life—about obsession and how dangerous it was. How Joan was given to it. "She watched, she waited, and she became obsessed. Obsessed with a girl who should have been her, whom her mother had loved, and her fury grew, it peaked.

It *focused*."

"When Sarah was thirteen," Ray said.

Shady's voice was low as the pieces of the puzzle fell further into place. "The same age Joan had been when her mother went off to begin life all over again with a new family, erasing the old completely. Maybe she was even pregnant at the time she left. Certainly, it wouldn't have been too long after." She exhaled. "You said Sal Parker's dead. What happened to her?"

"Car crash," Lisa Marie replied, "according to another newspaper article. It was just a few weeks later. En route to visiting her daughter in the rehabilitation center she was in."

Shady swallowed at hearing that—divine justice? Joan, at least, might think so.

"Sarah told us her father has passed too, although he died some years later. A man broken by his perfect life falling apart."

"There's more," Ray said, causing Shady's jaw to fall open.

"Seriously?"

"Uh-huh," Lisa Marie said. "You see, Sarah's agreed to meet us, but she's also agreed to meet with Joan."

In a bid to process this, Shady jumped to her feet. "I can't leave you alone for five minutes, can I, Ray?" she said, half joking. "Okay, I get it, I get that Joan and Sarah are half sisters, but there was never any relationship between them. Joan tried to kill her, for Christ's sake, pumped with jealousy, unhinged by the injustice of it all. And it *was* unjust…it was so fricking unfair. I get that too. So why would she want to meet a woman who wanted her dead?

243

Because Joan thinks she *is* dead. She's certain of it. In her mind she killed a kid, and not just a random kid, her half sister. Left her lying there, in a pool of blood, after ambushing her at home in broad daylight when her parents were out somewhere. And then she took off. She ran again. She got away with it. Until now."

"She will never be brought to justice, Shady," Lisa Marie said.

"Why not? It's not too late."

"It will be, soon."

Looking at Lisa Marie, Shady steeled herself.

"A couple of days ago, when we were last in the ICU, I asked the nurse there to contact me if Joan should deteriorate."

"And?"

"And that phone call came through early this morning. That's why I tried calling you, to let you know. She's dying, Shady. Joan Parker is finally letting go."

Shady swallowed. "I thought she was getting better. She'd regained consciousness."

Lisa Marie shook her head. "I said that Sarah's tired, that you could hear it in her voice. Well, I think Joan is too. Tired of running and tired of hating." To Shady's surprise, Lisa Marie's voice cracked slightly. "And I can understand that."

Shady closed the gap between them, not meaning to read her as she reached out, only to offer what comfort she could. Despite that, the images came, the flashes of insight.

Lisa Marie, this golden girl, clever, brilliant and kind, had hated once upon a time too. Somewhere in her late teens or very early twenties, the weight of neglect, of parents obsessed only with themselves, had understandably gotten to her. She'd fought hard for a better life and peace of mind, and she'd won, but it had taken a lot of effort. For a time, she'd blamed her parents for everything; her stomach had churned with blame, and her mind had also become something quite fractured. But unlike Joan, perhaps unlike Sarah too, she'd quickly pieced it back together, not heading further down that route but seeking resolution rather than submission. Even so, she knew how heavy the burden of hatred was, and her heart went out to those who carried it—even, it seemed, Joan Parker.

"How long has Joan got?"

Lisa Marie shrugged. "Anybody's guess. It could be days. It could be hours."

"Hours?" Shady was horrified. "It's gotta be a two-hour drive to the Utah border, so a four-hour round trip at least."

"It is," Lisa Marie confirmed. "Which is why if we're going to do this, we have to leave now."

"And Sarah Gearing will be waiting for us?" Shady asked.

"Yes."

"She really wants to do this?"

"Wouldn't you?"

Such simple words, but they stopped Shady in her tracks. *Wouldn't you?* Maybe. Sarah Gearing was still relatively young. If she laid the trauma of her past to rest, she could live again.

"And you're sure this isn't a trap?"

Ray cocked his head to one side. "How d'you mean?"

"That the reason she wants to meet Joan is because she wants revenge."

"Lisa Marie spoke to her, and, well"—he produced a shy

smile, aimed at Lisa Marie—"I kinda trust her instinct."

Now both sets of eyes were on Shady, the atmosphere expectant.

She'd raised a valid point. Sarah Gearing might not be tired of hating her attacker at all but hell-bent on getting even. Joan Parker had hours left, days at most, yet her life could end even sooner if Shady was right. Did she trust Lisa Marie as much as Ray did? She'd known her such a short time, and, yes, she could read her, but she was one of the first people she'd ever been able to read. What if she'd interpreted something incorrectly?

Do I trust you? And your judgment?

Her eyes fixed on the other girl.

Yes, she guessed she did.

"So, it's another road trip we're going on, Ray?" she said at last.

When he grinned like he did now, he burned as bright as Lisa Marie.

"I guess so."

"And is Annie up for it too?"

"Annie said for us three to go ahead. She thinks we'll be able to handle it just fine."

Shady nodded. "Okay, fair enough. I'll jump in the shower, and then, yeah, there's no time to waste. Better hit the highway."

CHAPTER TWENTY-FIVE

"We've moved the patient to another room. Somewhere...brighter," said the nurse, the same one who'd previously tried to oust Shady from Joan Parker's room. This time she was smiling, albeit sadly. Shady, Lisa Marie, and now Ray and Sarah Gearing were the only people who'd come and shown any interest in a woman who was dying, and so she had no issue with them, no argument at all. Not anymore. If they wanted time with her, they could have it, because time was truly running out now—there was no more the doctors and nurses could do for the woman lying in a bright hospital room. She was dying. She'd chosen to. Every breath she took closer to the last.

"You ready?" Lisa Marie asked Sarah, and Sarah nodded.

"Let's go," she replied.

Sarah didn't want to go in alone. They'd already established that. Although willing, she needed the others with her.

As soon as Shady had set eyes on Sarah Gearing, she knew she'd been right to trust Lisa Marie. Throughout the entire journey to her home, the highway stretching on forever, just as it had once for Joan Parker, she kept imagining what the woman would look like. Joan was small; was Sarah as petite? Did she share the same color eyes, that same haunted look? What she hadn't expected when they'd arrived at her house in the freezing-cold evening was a woman in a wheelchair. Sarah Gearing hadn't died after Joan's frenzied attack, but she'd been left unable to walk.

She had greeted them, then ushered them into the house and into a living room.

Sarah lived alone, her house adapted to suit her needs. And Lisa Marie was right; she was tired, not because she'd waited into the evening for them. It was far more ingrained than that.

"There were times when I wished she had killed me," she'd confessed, having offered them some homemade biscuits and coffee—something to fuel them for the long drive back to Idaho Falls that was now pressing. "For so long I wished that. It was such a long haul back to recovery, but pretty soon we knew my legs were useless. I was just thirteen, and not being able to walk, run, ride the horses we had at the ranch, climb the trees in the woods, I just...I couldn't imagine it."

There were a thousand questions Shady wanted to ask, but she held back, let the woman speak, unburden herself further.

"I was good at sports as a kid, you know?" she said, a soft tinkle of laughter on her lips. "Basketball, track and field, volleyball, the usual. And Mom and Pa, they'd come and cheer me on, never missed an event if I was in it. They were always so proud of me."

The woman she was talking about—Sal Parker—was hard to reconcile with the woman Shady knew via her firstborn daughter, and something in her eyes must have alerted Sarah to this. She leaned forward, soft curls framing a face that had hardened slightly.

"I want you to know this, I want you to realize, I loved my mother. She was good to me. She was perfect, in fact. An angel. When she died on her way to see me while I was recovering—and know this too, she never missed a day, not one—well, I thought my heart couldn't break any further. But it could. It just kept breaking and breaking. I loved Pa too, but Mom and me? We had such a bond. I can't think badly about her. Even now. I won't."

Shady took a deep breath. "How much do you know about her from before she met your pa?"

"Only what this young lady here has told me."

Which she'd learned via Ray and, of course, through Shady.

"Do you know about me too?"

"You've got psychic abilities? That right?"

"Kind of. Does that sound crazy to you?"

Sarah shook her head. "I know all about crazy," she said. "I've brushed shoulders with it many times, not just with the woman I now know is my half sister, but since."

When her voice cracked and tears fell, Shady looked at both Lisa Marie and Ray for silent advice on what to do. Lisa Marie inclined her head toward Sarah and nodded, giving the go-ahead for Shady to reach out and comfort her. *Learn* about her.

Oh, Sarah Gearing knew hate, all right. After the attack and her mother's death, this was a girl who'd reached rock bottom and stayed there for many, many years. Formative years. And how had she chosen to express such painful feelings, maybe even shameful ones? All the things she wished on her attacker, the agony that she would, in turn, return upon her…?

A seismic tremor engulfed Shady. Sarah reacted only slightly to it, quickly relaxing into Shady's arms again and letting the tears continue to fall.

She'd held a mirror, that's how—a hand mirror, one with a long, pale stem. She'd sat in a room, not at the ranch but somewhere different, a room where flowers wilted and which daylight avoided, shunning everyone, her father as good as dead, just a shadow of his former self, and she'd let her own demons run free as she counted all the ways to exact retribution. Her life had been destroyed, and she'd be a destroyer too. Merciless.

It was Gina's mirror she'd looked into.

Shady was certain of it.

Shit!

Gina had picked up the mirror in a thrift store. Not Joan Parker's after all, though God knew the emotions attached had run along the same lines, had become indistinguishable, pain at the root of both. Yet Sarah had gotten rid of her mirror not because she couldn't bear to see her reflection anymore, or what she was capable of, but because somehow she'd dragged herself back from the brink of despair, summoned the courage and strength to set herself on another road to recovery—that of her mental health.

She'd been lucky, eventually.

And she knew it.

For full recovery, though, the final scenes had to play out.

When Shady finally released Sarah, Sarah reached out and laid a hand on Shady's arm, maintaining their connection for just a few moments more.

"However you all came by this knowledge, whether through fate, psychic ability, instinct, sheer intelligence, or a mixture of the four, I'm so grateful you got in contact, that you took a chance and let me know. We have to get going, I understand that, but on the journey to Idaho Falls, I want you to fill me in on everything about the sister I never knew I had. And I mean every last detail. Don't try and be kind, don't spare me. This is a time for truth, for total honesty. I had everything, and from the sound of it, she had nothing." She looked down, her gaze lingering on her legs, but only briefly, before gesturing all around her to a room that was light, airy and welcoming, where the scent of flowers was as heady as the home baking. "I *still* have everything," she said, wiping away the last of her tears.

Finishing their coffee and biscuits, they'd then all got back into Shady's Dodge, Sarah's Travelite wheelchair in the trunk. And throughout the entire journey, Shady'd done as Sarah had asked, no detail spared.

When they'd arrived at the Eastern Idaho Regional Medical Center and helped Sarah to transfer from the car back into her wheelchair, Shady had looked carefully, albeit surreptitiously, into her eyes. Now that she knew everything, would some of that hatred, that bitterness she once harbored, return? If anything, her eyes were brighter and her smile softer.

And now it was time to enter Joan Parker's room—for family to reunite.

* * *

There's such a long road ahead of me still. Will it never end? And there are no lights; they're gone. It's all so dark, but it's not an empty darkness. If only it was. There are shadows that linger within it, and some are all too familiar. They wait and they watch, such patient things. I know what they want. For me to become a shadow too and join them.

Perhaps it's time. I've always been in the darkness, and it's there I'll stay.

"Joan, it's me, it's Shady. Joan, I know what you're thinking. I know what you've done. The secret that even you couldn't bear to think about. And you're wrong. You don't belong in the darkness. You deserve some light now. That's the only thing it's time for."

In the hospital room, Joan lay perfectly still, her chest rising but only lightly, her mouth open as air continued to find its way into her lungs before being expelled again. She was still, and all those around her bed were still too, but Joan's thoughts fought back, the rage she was given to, that had been well established within her, close to the surface.

Who are you? What are you? You're worse than those that hide from me! As unnatural. And you don't know what I've done—how could you? I've never spoken a word about it, not to anyone or anything. I've suffered, I've caused suffering, and I will suffer further. It's monsters like him that wait for me in the shadows. To whom I'll belong once more.

"You don't belong to him, Joan."

It was as though the demon inside the older woman was spitting and thrashing. *I do.*

"You don't. And you never did. Evil does not have a hold on you."

I'm a murderer!

"No, Joan. You're not."

Shady inclined her head. Had the demon quieted?

She seized her chance. "Sarah, will you come forward?"

From the moment Sarah had entered the room, her eyes had never left the figure on the bed. They'd become so wide and filled with such a mixture of emotions. Yes, there was fear. But fear didn't stand alone. There was sadness too, and a sense of wasted opportunity. Regret about what could have been. Not if Joan had been a different woman—if Sal Parker had been.

A tear lay upon Sarah's cheek as she wheeled herself forward. Ray helped maneuver her into place before stepping back to stand beside Lisa Marie, who had not one tear but several racing down her face.

For only the second time in their lives, the two women were mere inches apart.

Shady cleared her throat. "Joan, this is Sarah Gearing, the girl you attacked, your half sister."

Silence. Nothing more. No response from Joan or the demon inside her.

Sarah looked up at Shady questioningly, Shady having to hide the frown that threatened to form.

"Joan," she tried again, "can you hear me?"

"Shady," Ray said, "the heart monitor's making a different noise."

She looked up at it. Yes, it was, but it wasn't flatlining, not yet.

Don't you dare, Joan. You face up to this before you go! You realize!

Shady hunkered down and grasped Joan's hand.

"Joan, there's life in you still. Your heart continues to beat. And your sister is here. She's traveled from another state to see you. She's here. She's alive. And she doesn't hate

253

you. She did, once upon a time, but not any longer. There's no hate left in her at all."

Why was there no response? Joan wasn't dead. And hearing was the last sense to go.

"Joan, please! I know you're listening!"

The veins on Joan's hand reminded Shady of the cracked glass in the cane-and-wicker mirror—a mirror that might've never been in Joan's possession either. Shady had a sudden insight, an instinct. The oval mirror had been Sarah's too, hanging in her bedroom the day of the attack. It had seen; it had witnessed everything, and after the deed, Joan had stood there and looked into it. Maybe just for moments, nothing more than that, but in that brief span of time, it had captured everything about her. Her blood-spattered essence. And Joan knew that it had, knew too that she'd admit to many things but not this, never this…doing what he'd done so long ago and making the innocent pay. The mirror had eventually found its way to a thrift store, just as all the furniture in Cades Home Farm had, Sarah's father unable to live there without his wife and child. He'd sold everything, but those who came after could never find peace either.

"Joan," Shady begged. Had all this been for nothing? The effort everybody had gone to. Did Joan cling to her guilt because it was as familiar as hatred, even if she'd never faced up to it, had tried to hide from it?

"Joan, come on. Don't die like this. Don't believe that only hell's waiting."

Another hand reached out.

It was Sarah, taking hold of both Joan's and Shady's hands.

Shady was the one looking questioningly at her now, but Sarah's blue eyes were back on her sister, her mouth opening to utter just three words:

"Joan, I'm sorry."

If anyone wasn't breathing in the room, it was Shady. She couldn't, as if her heart was being squeezed in anticipation.

Come on, Joan, please. If you go to the darkness, it'll be the same as it was for you here. You won't belong. Can you suffer that again?

Still the seconds ticked by, the monitor attached to Joan becoming quite erratic.

Lisa Marie had turned away, her shoulders heaving as she continued to weep silently, Ray holding her, doing his level best to soothe her.

Shady withdrew her hand from Joan's and Sarah's and stood, ready to admit defeat.

We tried. Like Annie says, sometimes it's all we can do.

About to step away, something made her turn back toward Joan's bedside.

The woman had opened her eyes and was staring straight back at her sister. And for eyes so dark, there was a spark of light in them.

"Sorry…too," she said before closing them again, before flatlining.

An ugly life was over. The ride had ended.

And in her mind's eye, Shady saw all the mirrors that had once belonged to Joan and Sarah—every single one—explode.

CHAPTER TWENTY-SIX

It was snowing now, big, fat, beautiful flakes careering down from the skies, Idaho Falls set to rival record-breaking Boise, perhaps, if it continued. But in spite of the snow, Lisa Marie was still leaving. The project she'd been working on at the Eastern Idaho Regional Medical Center had come to a natural conclusion, and she was, surprisingly, heading back to California—to hook up with her folks, whom she hadn't seen in such a long while.

"It's time," she said to Shady as they sat in The Golden Crown together, grabbing a last drink. "Can't keep running."

Shady couldn't argue with that. The weather was bad, though, no sign of a letup, not according to forecasters. When Shady voiced that concern, Lisa Marie shrugged it off.

"It won't be snowing in San Francisco. Likely, it'll be rainy and foggy instead."

Damn it. She couldn't find an argument against that either.

"I'm gonna miss you," she confessed, glad that it was a quiet night at the bar, no sign of their other friends, just the two of them at a table, a small gap between them.

"We can keep in touch," Lisa Marie assured her. "And I

may head back this way at some point, you never know. I'm going home, Shady, but that doesn't mean I'm going to stay there. My folks, I'll try with them, you know. I think…I think I understand them more now. Why they acted the way they did, and still do. They're unhappy. More than that, they're like poison together. I'm wondering if I could speak to each one alone and make them see that. That just because life's shit, it doesn't have to continue being that way."

"You're actually gonna try to split your parents up?" Shady asked, and Lisa Marie laughed.

"I know, it usually works the other way around, right?"

"Usually," Shady agreed, drinking her Coke.

"But some situations…they're a long way from normal. Again, that's something I understand better now."

Lisa Marie picked up her Coke too, her eyes staring at the condensation on the glass.

A period of quiet gave Shady time to reflect.

She'd envisioned the mirrors exploding—all of them. Whether or not she was right, she didn't know. There was to be no more trespassing on Joan's property, which would no doubt be seized by the bank soon. She suspected she was right, however; they'd either exploded or turned to dust, at least symbolically, and that was good enough. Because when Joan had finally taken her last breath, with her half sister holding her hand, something had shifted, dissolved—not just hatred but sorrow too. Finally, both had worn themselves out.

But was Joan's apology enough to save her from the shadows? Was she now in the light, feeling a part of something at last?

Shady liked to think so.

And could there ever be an excuse for deliberately harming another? A short while ago, she'd have said no, but now she realized just how many shades of grey existed. Sarah was a victim, Joan was a victim, hell, even Sal Parker could have been a victim—Shady knew nothing about her life before she'd abandoned her first daughter, only that she'd been unhappy too, deeply, hence why she'd taken off. A chance for a better life had come along, and she'd grabbed it. Again, Shady would have said that was such a terrible thing to do, unforgiveable. Just look at the consequences of her actions. But would she be right to say that? Because if you didn't forgive, if you couldn't find it within yourself to understand not just one set of circumstances but a whole mélange, then you'd hold a grudge forever. And the only person that would hurt in the end would be yourself.

Unhappy people sometimes did unhappy things. Humans were flawed. They got onto a dark highway and just kept on going. But not Joan, not at the end; she'd stopped, finally, and allowed her soul to soar. And Sarah? She'd gotten off that highway pretty damned quick when she realized where it was headed, recognized it for what it was: a road to oblivion. And who wanted to get stuck on that?

"How's Gina?"

Lisa Marie was talking again.

"Doing great," Shady replied, smiling. "After staying at her sister's, she's back at home and slumbering peacefully, apparently. No more nightmares. She says she feels…lighter."

"That's great, such a relief. You been back to the place where you buried Sarah's mirror?"

"I have, actually, yesterday. They've started building there. One of the best hotels Idaho Falls will ever see, according to the billboards. I might even book myself a room there if I ever get rich!"

"Just to check?"

"No. For some time out."

"They sure owe you a night's stay for the favor you've done them."

"Too bad they'll never know. Even a free meal in their restaurant would have been nice. I'd be happy with that."

"You're amazing, you know that?"

Lisa Marie grew serious, her blue eyes intent as they fixed on Shady's.

"Oh, well, you know..." Shady tried to joke. "I aim to please."

Lisa Marie's expression remained the same, never wavering. In the background some tinny tune was playing on the radio, something from the early noughties, familiar too, although Shady couldn't for the life of her recall the name of it. She couldn't think of anything else except this girl in front of her, who'd not only said she was amazing—a step up from *nice*, that was for sure—but was also now thanking her.

"The best hotel in Idaho Falls might not be able to thank you, but at least I can. I'm going back home, like I said. I'm running *to* chaos rather than from it. No offense to my folks when I say this, but I'm facing my demons head-on. And, Shady, that's momentous for me. That's...something I never thought I'd do. And it's all because of you. Heck, the likelihood is they'll play along, then revert back right after. If so, I'll pack my bags again and head off. Put both land and sea between us this time, head to Europe like I've dreamed of. Venice, maybe, Rome or Paris. But, yeah, I'll have tried. That's what counts. And that'll bring me…further peace."

"That *is* what counts, Lisa Marie. And I know it won't be easy for you. But you're doing the right thing. I'm proud to know you, to have you as my friend."

"No one's ever said that to me before."

"Well, I am, really proud. You're kinda amazing too."

"I suppose I'd better be gracious and accept the compliment. After all, you know me better than anyone."

Shady blushed. "Yeah. Sorry about that."

"Don't be."

Before Shady could utter a reply, Lisa Marie had moved closer, one hand reaching out to cup Shady's chin, to bring her forward. Their lips met, and there was another explosion, this time in Shady's heart. She'd never kissed a woman before—in truth, had never felt the desire to—but this kiss, so soft, so gentle, and all too brief, was like no other kiss she'd experienced, on many levels. Having blushed before, Shady was now sure she was suffused with red, her cheeks burning like the fire that had been lit deep inside.

"I…um…I don't normally—"

"I know you don't. Neither do I. But, Shady, you have a place in my heart."

"And you in mine," Shady whispered.

Lisa Marie shuffled backward on the seat before climbing to her feet. "Couldn't put that off any longer," she said, her lightness back, "and guess I can't put off other stuff either."

Shady stood too. "You'll be safe on the roads?"

"Sure, the highways should be pretty clear. I'll be fine. Walk me to my car?"

"Of course."

Both trudged side by side through the snow, the cold not able to touch Shady at all. She felt warm inside, glowing.

Before climbing into her car, Lisa Marie placed another kiss, a mere peck this time, on Shady's cheek. "Take care, okay?"

"I promise."

"And thank you again—"

"Lisa Marie, I also want to thank you. If I hadn't met you, realized just how much people could overcome, then maybe I wouldn't have stuck by Joan. I'd have abandoned her too."

"If I was your guiding light, you were mine."

Once more, Lisa Marie stole Shady's breath.

In the driver's seat, Lisa Marie placed the key in the ignition, the engine roaring into life. She turned to wave at Shady before checking her mirrors and pulling onto the street.

"Good luck!" shouted Shady, doing her utmost to keep pace with the car, for a few feet, anyway, before having to admit defeat. "Good luck!"

Lisa Marie continued to drive down the road, eventually disappearing from sight. Still on the sidewalk, Shady reached her hand into her jeans pocket for the leather scrap.

The softness of it reminded her of Lisa Marie's lips.

But the stars reminded her of Kanti, of her own heritage.

And all that she was born to be

As much as I love writing, building a relationship with readers is even more exciting! I occasionally send newsletters with details on new releases, special offers and other bits of news relating to the Psychic Surveys series as well as all my other books. If you'd like to subscribe,
sign up here!
www.shanistruthers.com